Anna Bell is a full-time writer and writes the weekly column 'The Secret Dreamworld of An Aspiring Author' on the website Novelicious. She loves nothing more than going for walks with her husband and Labrador.

don't tell the boss

anna bell

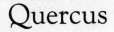
Quercus

First published in Great Britain in 2014 by

Quercus Editions Ltd
55 Baker Street
7th Floor, South Block
London W1U 8EW

A CIP catalogue record for this book is available
from the British Library

PB ISBN 978 1 84866 366 4
EBOOK ISBN 978 1 84866 367 1

10 9 8 7 6 5 4 3 2 1

Printed and bound in Great Britain by Clays Ltd, St Ives plc

Typeset by Ellipsis Digital Limited, Glasgow

For Mum and John

Thank you for always encouraging
me to follow my dreams

chapter one

princess-on-a-shoestring top tips:
Keep Calm and Carry On

Buttonholes breaking, visible panty-lines, the groom's ever increasing underarm sweat patches - whatever drama happens on your big day put it in perspective and think of the bigger picture. I've never been to a wedding where I've thought 'ooh that flower's half-cocked' and, even if I did at the time, it wasn't a lasting memory. You've got to ask yourself whether the wonky buttonhole/VPL/sweat patches are going to stop you or the groom saying your vows. Unless the smell of the sweat makes you faint, then I'm guessing the answer is no. In short - don't worry about the small stuff. As long as you get your names right and you say 'I do', then that's all that's important on your wedding day.

Tags: wedding, sweat, top tips

I can't believe it's almost twenty past eleven. Where the hell is she? I know that brides are supposed to be late, and I know I can't really talk as my wedding didn't exactly start on time, but still, I'm beginning to feel a tad claustrophobic. This table was not designed to have people hiding under it. To be honest, it's so small I don't think it was designed for much of anything.

Now, I don't usually go around hiding under tables, but I have a very vital role as music maestro at this wedding. I've got to put the music on for the bride to walk down the aisle to. Lara and Ben are tying the knot in a registry office, and one of the bride's stipulations was that she didn't want the ceremony to appear amateur or awkward. I was under strict instructions that the music should start seamlessly, without anyone obviously having pressed play. So my job is to fade it up when she walks in and fade it down once she reaches the front. I reckon even I can manage that.

The only problem is that I didn't pick my hiding place very well. This table is ridiculously tiny and my legs are starting to tremble. Perhaps I should have hidden behind the heavy silk draped curtains. At least then I wouldn't have dead legs. And, also, I might have been able to catch a sneaky glimpse of the bride as she came in. From where I am now, I'm going to be lucky if I manage to see her shoes underneath the tablecloth.

But don't worry; at least I know what I'm looking for. I've already seen the bride's shoes, and her dress. In fact, I've seen all the elements of this wedding before. You see; I planned it.

'Where is she, Penny?' hisses Ben.

I'm clearly not the only one wondering where the bride is. From behind the tablecloth, I see the groom, who has crouched down to fiddle with his shoelace.

'Don't worry, brides are supposed to be late,' I whisper in as calming a voice as I can muster.

'I bloody hope she's coming.'

'She is. Of course she is.'

A woman like Lara, who has talked of nothing but this day practically twenty-four/seven for the last few weeks, wouldn't not turn up. In fact, she's been ringing me all week worried that *Ben* wouldn't show up. She thought he and his best man would get so drunk the night before that he wouldn't make it up the aisle. That was why I was despatched from wedding HQ at Lara's mum's house at eight a.m. to go and wake him up, and make sure he arrived on time.

Lara was right to be worried. When I got to Ben's this morning, he looked like he was auditioning for the role of

3

a Neanderthal. After a shower, shave and some industrial-strength mouthwash, he started to look like a hopeful cause though, and with each hour that has passed he's looked less like a vampire and more like a fully functioning human being.

I don't know if that's really in the job description of a wedding planner, although I'm sure you've already guessed from my rookie mistake of hiding under a table that I'm not an actual card-carrying one. I'm just a girl who works in HR who agreed to plan this as a one-off. I'm a tad obsessed with weddings; it started when I was planning my own to my now-husband Mark. To feed my need for wedding fixes now that I don't have my own to think about, I write a budget-bride blog. One of my blog readers begged me to organise her wedding and I jumped at the chance.

'Would everyone be upstanding for the arrival of the bride,' says the registrar. That's my cue! I can hear the guests rising from their seats, and Ben has finally stopped pacing like a caged tiger and he's come to a standstill just in front of the table.

If I can just unlock the iPod, and press play, the sound of 'Halo' by Beyoncé should be playing any second now. Any second NOW, I scream in my head. The iPod seems to be playing, but no sound is coming out. I tested this when we got in the room and it worked just fine. After all, Mark has taught me well about the seven ps; Prior Preparation and Planning Prevents Piss-Poor Performance. How could it have gone wrong already?

The registrar is clearing her throat noisily, presumably for my benefit, but it's just adding to my nerves. My fingers are now so wet with sweat that they're sliding over the touchscreen of the iPod. And then, to my relief, with just a hint of a crackle through the speakers the song suddenly bursts through. Now I'll be able to relax as the bride glides up the aisle and soon everyone will be gasping at how beautiful she looks. It's a shame I can't see their faces, but I can imagine them.

Wait, is that laughter I can hear? Why are they laughing?

Oh. My. God. That's not 'Halo' playing, it's 'Single Ladies'. I jab violently at the iPod, but I still can't get any grip on the touchscreen.

Maybe Lara could style it out. You know, walk up the aisle doing the Beyoncé shimmy thing. I mean it's probably more fitting than 'Halo' anyway; there are rings involved in today's proceedings. It would be like we were in our very own musical where the pop songs have been shoe-horned into a story that doesn't make a lot of sense. All we need to happen is for Ben to theatrically put the ring on Lara's finger when she reaches him.

Thoughts of Lara doing the trademark Beyoncé shaking

with her voluptuous G-cup chest and rather plunging neckline suddenly pop into my head. That would not be good. On second thoughts, perhaps it isn't such a good idea for Lara to style it out.

'Um, Penny,' says the registrar from very close to me. The side of the tablecloth is lifted and I see Deborah's beady eyes looking at me.

'I'm trying to fix it,' I say through gritted teeth as I attempt to sit upright, banging my head. Ouch, I bite down hard on my lip so I don't swear. I think people have probably sussed by now I'm under the table, I don't think I need to draw any more attention to myself.

Finally, I click on 'Halo' and the beats from 'Single Ladies' are replaced with some proper gliding music. I can hear everyone murmuring, and the hum of camera flashes tell me the bride is finally walking up the aisle. Whilst everyone is enjoying this beautiful moment, I'm freaking out that I'm never going to be able to turn the volume down in a swift fading action.

The registrar clears her throat again, in what I can only describe as a phlegmy smoker way. I take a deep breath as this is the pre-agreed signal for me to turn down the music. Here it goes. Much to my relief, the music goes quiet. I'm usually not a fan of silence, but right now it sounds like the best thing I've ever heard.

DON'T TELL THE BOSS

'Thank you, everyone, you may take your seats,' says the registrar. 'We are here to celebrate the love of Lara and Robert as they embark on their journey to join themselves in marriage.'

Uh, hang on, Robert? Who the hell is Robert? I can hear a ripple of laughter echoing round the room.

'Who's Robert? Lara, anything you want to tell me?' asks Ben.

'Of course not.'

I can't see Lara, but I can hear her voice and, boy, she does not sound impressed. First the music issue and now the name issue. This is turning out to be both amateur and awkward, the two As forbidden by Lara. I wonder if she'll still pay me.

'Oh, dear, it's not Robert, is it?' says the registrar.

'No, try Ben,' says Lara, sarcastically.

'Ben, got it. Sorry. Right, as I was saying, we are here to celebrate the love of Lara and BEN,' says the registrar, practically shouting it out.

Blimey, hopefully if I don't mess up the rest of my musical duties, then people will remember this faux pas rather than mine.

I soon tune out the voice of the registrar as she starts the marriage ceremony. All I have to do now is wait until it is all over and then play Jason Mraz as the happy couple walk back down the aisle. After that, I've got to oversee the photographs, deposit the bride, groom and the guests in the restaurant, and after that my duties as supreme-wedding-planning-goddess will be over. Then I have to get back to my actual day job.

It's sad to think that this is the last time I'll plan a wedding. It's been so much fun. More so than my own, because it wasn't planned around a lie. I wanted to have a massive princess wedding and I lost £10,000 on internet bingo trying to win enough money to make my dream come true. And, stupidly, instead of confessing to Mark, I planned the wedding in the style of *Don't Tell the Bride*. Poor old Mark was in the dark about everything; not the best way to start a marriage.

Although hiding my gambling habit might have been the biggest mistake I've ever made, the upside was that I organised an amazing wedding for the princely sum of £5,500. It opened up a whole new world of what was possible on a budget and led to the inspiration for my blog, Princess-on-a-Shoestring.

The great thing is that I've stopped gambling, and my blog fills the empty hole it left in my life. I know it's a cliché to set up a blog and, if I'm honest, I never expected anyone to actually read it. But you know what, they have. In the first six months of it being fully operational, Princess-on-a-Shoestring has had over 40,000 hits.

My husband thinks it's about time I got over my wedding obsession. Who can blame him? It led me to gamble and almost ruined our marriage before it even began. But he's pleased that I haven't gone back to losing money. Instead, I'm actually earning it. Not a lot, but the advertising on the site has raked in almost a hundred pounds, and I'm hoping that eventually (after many, many years) it will cancel out what I lost when I was a dirty little gambler.

When Lara first asked me to plan her wedding I laughed, thinking she was joking, but it seemed she was deadly serious. After a bit of research, I realised that there aren't any budget wedding planners. It's something to do with the fact that wedding planners have minimum fees which are pretty much equal to the entire wedding budget for cash-challenged brides. So I agreed to do Lara's wedding for a flat fee of £500. Not the best business model in the world, but it's only a one-off. I promised Mark that it would be. He was worried that I'd become addicted to planning weddings and then it would take over what little free time I had at home and he'd never see me. I couldn't argue with that; after all, we don't want other people's weddings ruining our marriage.

So far, it's been an easy £500. Not only have I managed to help Lara stick to her budget, but we worked out that I helped save her £1,500 by negotiating discounts and getting my friend Betty to let out and adapt Lara's mum's wedding dress for a lot less than a professional seamstress would have charged.

The room has erupted into clapping. Is that it? I glance down at my watch and see that it's 11.25 a.m. Fifteen minutes, that's all it took? Wow. And to think my wedding lasted an hour and a half. We'll just gloss over the fact that we had a bit of a delay waiting for Mark to turn up, and then there was me fainting . . .

That reminds me, I've got to put the music on. I unlock the iPod, select Jason Mraz and press pause. This time I'm going to be ready. The hack comes from the registrar and I press play and, thankfully, it works a treat. It's possible I'm imagining it, but I'm sure I hear a big sigh of relief coming from Lara.

'Penny, you can come out now,' says the registrar after a couple of minutes.

'Thank goodness for that,' I say as I attempt to crawl out from under the table. All my muscles feel numb and I'm walking like Bambi on ice as I try and stop my legs from going into spasm.

'Well, how did it go?' I ask.

'Apart from your little music cock-up?'

'Apart from that,' I say hanging my head in shame.

'And my little name problem. It was fine. Lara and Robert seem like they'll be a very happy couple.'

'Lara and Ben,' I say correcting her.

'Bugger, I did it again. I hope I actually got it right during the vows or it won't quite be legal,' she laughs as she tidies her papers. 'Right, I've got to go and meet the next couple, will you excuse me?'

'Of course, nice to meet you,' I say. I pick up the iPod and speakers and make my way out of the room.

There in the lobby are Lara and BEN, and they look so happy. They're posing for photos and Lara looks like a million dollars. I may have already seen the hair and make-up trial and the dress, but it hadn't prepared me for the look when it's all combined: she looks radiant.

For a minute I wish it was me standing there, being admired by all and sundry on the happiest day of my life. I wonder if Mark would go for us renewing our vows, or whether he'll think it's too soon. I could wear a lovely little tailored suit, something classy, and we could have it in the grounds of the museum where we had our reception.

'Excuse me, are you the wedding planner?'

I instantly snap out of my daydream and turn to the tall auburn-haired woman now standing next to me.

'Yes, that's me,' I say as I feel my cheeks start to turn a little crimson, remembering the music disaster. 'Ah, I'm so pleased to meet you,' she says as she links arms with me and walks me over to the corner of the lobby. I feel like I should be on hand for Lara to help with the photographs but whoever this woman is, she's quite forceful with her leading.

'I work with Lara and she has told me all about you,' she says, releasing me from her grip.

'She has?' I ask tentatively.

'Oh, yes, she has. She told me all about how you planned the lovely wedding on a ...' she leans forward before whispering, '... on a *budget*.'

She says the word like it's a profanity. It sounds even funnier coming from her posh, dulcet public-school-girl tones and it makes me want to giggle.

'That's right,' I say. I'm wondering where this is going.

'I want you to do the same for me.'

'Oh, I'm flattered, but I'm not actually a wedding planner,' I say.

'But you should be.'

Is she joking? The sound of 'Single Ladies' is ringing loudly in my ears.

'Were you here for the whole ceremony? You know, when the bride came in?'

'Yes, I've been here since eleven,' says the woman.

'And you heard the music?'

'You mean when you played "Single Ladies"? I thought that was brilliant. Such a great little joke to lighten the mood.

It unwound the groom no end. That's exactly what I want.'

Oh great, she wants to hire me to plan her wedding because of the comedy value I can add. I'm like a magician or balloon modeller you can buy in. It has nothing to do with the fact that I planned an awesome wedding or anything.

'I want a wedding planner who can help me have a special day even if I must have, you know, a wedding on a budget,' she says.

The word budget is not coming naturally to this woman. She keeps looking over her shoulder as if she's checking that no one is listening to our conversation.

'Well as I said, I'm not actually a wedding planner. I'm really flattered though, thank you.'

'Whatever Lara's paying, I'll double it.'

'It's not about the money,' I say.

But, you know what? A thousand pounds would come in quite handy. It would only take ten weddings with that fee and I would have made back what I gambled away on Internet bingo. I know Mark made me promise that it would be a one-off, but surely he'd be pleased with the extra cash? I mean it wasn't that hard planning Lara and Ben's wedding, and it didn't really take up too much time. I have a quite a lot of knowledge in the area. I also have to write blog posts for Princess-on-a-Shoestring and this way I could combine the two. And I do get loads of special offers and hints of discounts from local suppliers who want editorial on the website, so I could possibly do this wedding, just this once.

What am I thinking? I can't. Mark made me promise and I've learnt that our relationship is not worth risking.

'Well, if it's not about the money, what is it about? What can I do to get you to be my wedding planner? I'm at my wits' end. My fiancé has insisted that we plan our wedding with ten thousand pounds and I can't for the life of me work out where to start. I mean, what could I possibly get with that amount? I thought my dress would cost that much.'

A shiver runs down my spine as I feel like I've been there, done that, worn the T-shirt.

'I mean, seriously, Penny, please, I'm begging you.'

I can't say no to someone that's begging me, can I? I mean, maybe I could get Mark to understand. And, before you ask, yes, I do have to tell him. I nearly lost him when I started keeping secrets and I've promised to be one hundred per cent honest with him. Which I am, ninety-nine per cent of the time, except when I buy shoes.

'When's the wedding?' I ask, hoping that it isn't going to come back and bite me on the arse.

'Hopefully this summer. Oh, Penny, I'm thrilled you're taking me on as a client. Thrilled.'

'Hang on a minute, I haven't said yes yet. Look, I need to

talk to my husband first and then perhaps we could meet up and discuss it?'

'Sounds great. How soon can we meet?'

'Um, well technically I'm still working at this wedding, so why don't we start with you giving me your name and number.'

'OK, my name's Henri. Henri with an i and then the surname is Scott.'

As I store the number from Henri in my phone, I look over at Lara and Ben, who seem to have finished photos and are now greeting guests. I'd better get my skates on. I've got to get them out of the registry office and to the reception, and soon as I'm due back at work at one-thirty.

'Thanks, Henri. I'll be in touch.'

'Super-dooper,' she says before tottering back off to the other guests with her sky-scraper heels. I can't believe I didn't notice them before. If I'm not mistaken, they're Miu Miu; this season Miu Miu. I can suddenly see why the word budget doesn't come naturally to her.

I'm just putting my phone back into my pocket when it beeps at me.

Hey honey, hope the wedding went well. Just wanted to say good luck with the meeting today, I'm sure you'll knock 'em dead.

Oh, why is it whenever I'm up to something Mark contacts me? It's like his Spidey senses tingle and he just knows. And the meeting! With all the pre-wedding palaver with a groom who couldn't say more than 'eh' at eight this morning, I'd forgotten about the meeting. It's with my new all-powerful boss. He's meeting the whole team one to one to get to know us. I look at my watch; I'd better get a move on. I don't want to be late. Something tells me that this new boss isn't going to be good news.

chapter two

princess-on-a-shoestring cost cutters:
Something Borrowed

You've got to have something borrowed as part of your wedding outfit, it's like wedding-day law, so why not extend it to the whole wedding? What can you beg, borrow and steal from your loved ones on the big day? Veils are great things to borrow and it's supposed to be good luck to wear one belonging to a happily married woman (just choose wisely). But there are heaps of other things like tiaras and jewellery that friends and family can loan to keep the cost down. On a more practical level, do you have guests who could offer you things to spruce up your reception: a Polaroid camera or props for the evening, such as inflatables or fancy dress?

Tags: wedding, borrow, cheapskate.

What a lovely wedding reception. If I hadn't had the loveliest wedding in the world last year, I would have wanted one just like that. The Greek restaurant came up trumps. It felt like we'd all been transported to Greece, rather than the reality – Guildford on a rainy April day.

The top floor of the restaurant had been transformed. The tables were arranged into a square, with seats for the thirty guests laid round it. There were fairy lights twinkling over the indoor plants, and candles flickering on the table. The smell of lamb kleftiko filled the air and Lara and Ben told me it transported them right back to when they first met in Greece when they were working as holiday reps. Apparently the only thing missing was the overripe stench of sick and the pungent smell of Ouzo that apparently their apartments stunk of. But as a top wedding planner, I told them that was something they could easily recreate in their honeymoon suite later that night. I even left them a parting gift of a bottle of the Greek liqueur that I bought from the restaurant.

I only wish I hadn't had to leave when the reception was just getting started, but my job was done and I was, after all, only the wedding planner. I wasn't Lara's friend to start with and I didn't deserve to be one of the thirty guests. So instead, I'm back here at work on an ordinary, drizzly Friday afternoon.

'Penny, I'm ready for you now.'

I look up and see Giles Bishop, my new boss, standing over my desk. I glance hesitantly up at my screen to make sure I've clicked off the Miu Miu shoe website. Not that I've been looking up how much Henri's shoes had cost or anything.

Luckily for me, all that's on my computer screen is my clogged-to-the-brim inbox, so that it actually looks like I'm supremely busy and he's interrupted me hard at work, rather than daydreaming about weddings and expensive shoes.

'Fabulous,' I say in a horribly fake voice that I reserve for strangers on the telephone and anyone in a position of power at work. It's an awful infliction that I blame on my mother.

'Do I need to bring anything?' I say, like an eager beaver picking up a pen and the notepad that I always take to meetings, though in fact I only ever seem to use it to make lists of possible blog ideas.

'No, as you are,' says Giles walking towards his office.

I work in a large multi-national engineering company and most of us minions sit in an open-plan office. My desk is opposite Shelly's, and next to Marie's. I think I've got the best position in the whole place as I have a wall behind me. Which means I can do the odd sneaky bit of browsing and no one can see me do it. Except the all-seeing IT department who, I imagine, keep a beady eye on what everyone's up to, or people, like Giles, that walk up to my desk stealthily without me realising.

The door to Giles's office is just behind Shelly's desk. Since he arrived two weeks ago, his office door has remained firmly shut. His management style is world's away from our previous boss Nigel-come-in-my-door-is-always-open-Pearce.

I sit down in a chair that is as new as Giles. Nigel used to have comfy swivel chairs that made you instantly relaxed. The one I'm sitting on now is made of white plastic and looks like it was on special offer at IKEA, though I bet it cost a fortune. The room's a bit chilly and I shiver. Maybe it's all the stark white surfaces that make it seem cold. I've never seen an office so devoid of all home comforts. I glance around the room hoping to find at least one feature to prove he is a human being and not a soulless zombie.

Now, if this was my office, there would be comfy cushions, photos of Mark, an under-desk foot heater. All the important items. In fact, I'd get maintenance to paint it a warming yellow, and maybe on the floor I'd put that bright-orange rug that I bought in Morocco. It's currently languishing in a cupboard in the spare room because Mark thinks it's hideous.

'So, Penny,'

I look up at Giles and am almost surprised to see him behind the desk, my daydream was that vivid.

'Yes.'

'Well, as you know I'm holding these little meetings with the department to "get to know everyone".'

I cannot believe he just did air quotes with his fingers, Giles is just as embarrassing as my dad.

'Yes,' I say nodding sagely, trying to give him the impression I am wise beyond my years.

'Great stuff. So I understand you've been working here for four years now.'

'That's right,' I say.

'And from your appraisals I can see you've got an excellent record with us. Nigel wrote some glowing reports about you.'

I'm chuffed at this. I know Nigel was a bit soft on us, but I like to think I am pretty good at my job.

'Now, then, as I'm sure you're aware, I'm going to be making some changes.'

I personally would have thought that the word *changes* warranted their own air quotes. I know exactly what changes he has in mind. You see, Giles hasn't replaced Nigel directly as HR manager. He's one of the senior directors in the company and is apparently 'filling in' Nigel's position. But I know he's here for more than that.

21

I was in Sweden last month for our annual meeting with all the different global HR departments and I was chatting to Kim, a girl I knew from the US office. When I mentioned that Giles Bishop was going to be my new boss, she started avoiding eye contact and looking down at the floor. After plying her with biscuits, I managed to coax out of her what the shifty behaviour was about. It turns out he'd 'filled in' in their department too and had restructured and stripped not just the HR team, but a fair few of the others in the office too. Her parting advice was to befriend him. But just how do you befriend a soulless zombie?

'So, are you happy here, Penny? You've been here four years, no promotion.'

Gee, thanks, Giles, for bringing that up. I'm fully aware that I'm stuck in this position. The only step up in this department is Nigel's job, which I'm not qualified for. I could always try and move to one of our global offices, but then Mark would have to change jobs and since his company paid for all his accountancy training, he'd have to pay them back if he leaves within three years. And anyway, I don't want to move companies yet because Mark and I are trying to have a baby (stage six in our life plan) and my company has excellent maternity pay and benefits.

'No, no promotion,' I say.

'Yes, it's the same with Shelly too. You must have started around the same time.'

'We did, she started just before me.'

'And she's in the same boat too. No promotion either.'

'No.'

'Well, during my time here I'm going to be looking at how the department works.'

Here we go. Here's the talk of redundancy.

'Where do you see your career going, Penny?'

How the hell do I answer that? I don't want him to think I'm time-wasting here until I become a baby factory and go on maternity leave, year-on-year, until I've had all the babies I want. But, at the same time, he must know that I have nowhere to go.

'Well, I'd like to have more responsibilities of course, and to be in a more managerial position at some point.'

That's it, be vague, Penny. It's not that I'm not ambitious. I'd love my career to keep progressing, but realistically I don't want to work my arse off for the next few years and then give it all up to have kids. Or, worse, have to keep up with ridiculous hours and ferrying my children to endless childcare situations.

'That's good. That's good. And I'm sure that we've been helping you out, putting you on courses for CIPD?'

'Yes,' I say.

'Excellent. Well, I've only just arrived, and I still need to get the lay of the land, but I'd imagine that we're going to be getting rid of Nigel's old position.'

Here we go, before I know it he'll be telling me that we don't need an HR department at all.

'Oh, really?' I say, the words catching awkwardly in my throat.

'Yes. I think these days with all the communication tools we have to hand, there really isn't a need to have local HR managers. Having looked through Nigel's notes, I think that perhaps we could create the new position of HR supervisor, it would have a little less responsibility than Nigel's role, but it would still be a bit of a step up from the assistant's post.'

My heart is starting to race in a good way. That sounds like a perfect promotion for me. Is Giles going to promote me, right here, right now? And there was me thinking he was the axe-wielder. Maybe I've had Giles all wrong. In my mind, the money from my raise is already pouring into my bank account.

'I think that it would be perfect for either you or Shelly.'

Me or Shelly? Uh-oh, that doesn't sound good. I hope they don't interview us for the same job. Shelly and I have never been particularly close outside of the office, but we do have a really good working relationship. For instance, she always has Frazzles lurking in her drawer and she always gives me a packet if I'm having an afternoon crisp craving when I can't be bothered to walk to the vending machine.

'Right,' I say, trying to hide the disappointment in my voice. I'd already imagined handing out my new business cards and more importantly, spending my increased salary. Those Miu Miu shoes that Henri was wearing were only £750, out of my league normally, but if I had just a bit (or a lot) of a raise I could afford them.

'It's obviously early days at the moment. But I thought you might like to bear it in mind,' he says, raising one of his eyebrows like he's starring in a black-and-white suspense movie.

'OK, I will do.'

I'm trying to keep a smile plastered on my face but, as much as I don't want to spend the next couple of months throwing paperclips across the desk at Shelly and fighting over the job, I wouldn't want her to be my boss either.

She's one of those really sweet people most of the time, but if you piss her off she holds a grudge. One of our colleagues once borrowed her stapler whilst she was at lunch and didn't return it until the next day. Not only did she practically launch a steward's inquiry to find the missing stapler, but once she knew who'd taken it, she didn't speak to him for three months afterwards.

'Great. Well, thanks for coming to see me, Penny,' says Giles, smiling.

He really is a mystery. For someone who works in such a sterile office with his door shut, he seems to be able to chat like a normal human being, when he wants to. Then I'm struck by what Kim from the American office had said: befriend him.

I hesitate before I get up out of the chair. I'm guessing Giles is expecting me to leave as he's placed his little glasses on the bridge of his nose and he's gone back to looking at his computer.

'So, someone was saying that you used to work here before? In Farnborough, I mean,' I say.

Giles looks up at me as if he'd forgotten that I am still here.

'That's right. Before I transferred to head office about fifteen years ago.'

'Oh, so is it nice to be back?'

'Well I had to come back this summer for my daughter's wedding, so this temporary posting is killing two birds with one stone.'

Weddings; now there's a topic I can talk about.

'How exciting that your daughter's getting married.'

Giles has now slipped off his glasses again and he's rubbing his eyes. I'm not sure if that's in irritation or not.

'Yes, I suppose.'

'That's lovely,' I say, smiling and nodding. This is just like being friends, right? 'Where's she getting married?' I ask.

'I'm not sure. In London I guess, or somewhere expensive at least, if I know my daughter.'

That couldn't have been further from my £5,500 wedding at a museum.

'Sounds delightful,' I say still in über-posh work mode.

He puts his glasses back on: Business Giles has returned.

'So, Penny, over the next few months I want you to impress me. OK?'

'OK.' Blimey, that's just what I need, having to be both conscientious and impressive at work. But if someone is going to get that promotion, then it had better be me.

'And tell Shelly to come in.'

I walk back out of Giles's office with the new knowledge that I have a frenemy. I sit down and wonder how I'm going to act with her.

'So?' says Shelly scrunching her eyes up at me in curiosity.

'Giles wants you to go in,' I say casually, trying to avoid eye contact. She'll find out soon enough what's coming.

'But what's he like?' she asks.

'Surprisingly nice.' Or surprisingly human is what I want to say.

I watch her walk in; she's almost dragging her feet along

the floor. When she comes out of that office my working life will be different. Either we're going to be competing with each other, or one of us will be the other's boss. Work will never be the same again.

I know I'm being melodramatic but I'm feeling down in the dumps. Maybe it's post wedding-planning blues. I wonder how Lara and Ben are getting on?

'How did it really go?'

I look up and see Marie leaning over her desk. She's not in the running for the promotion as she's only been here about six months, and she's fresh out of university.

'Not good,' is all I say. I don't want to put Marie in the middle of it. I go back to my emails and hope that I can get through the rest of this crappy Friday.

'Hey, honey,' says Mark as he walks into the kitchen.

'Hey, you, I didn't hear you come in.' Or else I would have tried harder to look like I was actually cooking. I've been standing looking at the salmon fillets waiting for them to magically get themselves out of the packet and into the George Foreman grill. They may be clever little blighters when they're alive and swimming upstream, but not when they're wrapped in cellophane packets.

'So, how did it go?'

'It was amazing.'

'That's great news, Pen,' says Mark walking over and slipping his arms around me before pulling me in for a kiss. 'I'm so pleased. You were worrying about nothing, then?'

'Well, not nothing. There were a few little hiccups. I played the wrong music when Lara walked in and then the registrar got Ben's name wrong.'

Mark sighs, and I realise from the look on his face that he wasn't asking about the wedding.

'You meant the meeting with Giles,' I say, wincing.

'I did. As much as I do want to hear how the wedding went, I mainly want to know if you're being made redundant.'

That seems fair enough, when he puts it like that.

'Well, there's no talk of redundancies, but there is talk of a promotion,' I say as I finally start to cook the salmon. 'They're getting rid of Nigel's post and they're going to replace the role with an HR supervisor.'

'That would be perfect for you.'

'I know, but apparently it will be between me and Shelly.'

'Do you know when it's going to happen?'

I shake my head. 'Not for a few months. Giles told me that I have to impress him.'

'Impress him?'

'Yep. I think it's going to get competitive with Shelly,' I say, sighing dramatically.

Mark opens the fridge and pulls out a bottle of white wine.

'There's no competition, Pen, you're going to get it hands down. That promotion is yours, baby,' he says, pouring a large glass and handing it to me.

I take it gratefully; it's exactly what I need.

'So, go on then. Tell me about the wedding, I can see you're bursting at the seams to.'

As Mark sits down at the table, removing his tie, I tell him everything, from the disastrous groom in the early morning to the Beyoncé balls-up.

'And that's when Henri came up to me,' I say cautiously, wondering if I've mentioned it to him too soon. I've just put his dinner in front of him and I'm hoping that the food will make him so happy that he doesn't bat an eyelid about my next wedding-planning adventure. 'She's one of Lara's work colleagues and she wants me to plan her wedding for her.'

I stare at my plate of food as if steamed green beans are the most interesting thing I've ever seen in my life. Mark rests his knife and fork on the edge of the plate.

'I thought that Lara and Ben's was going to be the only wedding you planned?'

'And that's exactly what I told Henri, because I promised you.'

'Yet something tells me that you're going to do it anyway. You've got that look in your eyes.'

What look in my eyes? Damn the lack of ability to hide my emotions on my face.

'Well, I won't do it if you don't want me to, but it's just that she said she'd pay me £1,000.'

Mark picks up his cutlery and starts eating again. Clearly this is a good sign.

'She's offering £1,000. For a bit of planning? Just like you did with Lara and Ben?'

'Uh-huh.'

'But wouldn't it bring up all the old memories of gambling?'

'If anything, it takes my mind off it.'

'I'm not convinced, Pen. I just don't think all this wedding stuff is healthy.'

'I know, but it's not like I fantasise about getting married any more,' I say, thinking that it is definitely too soon to bring up renewing our vows. 'It just gives me a buzz. And instead of making me feel like crap like the gambling did, it makes me feel happy, like I'm helping people.'

Mark sighs.

'You know if you did do it, you'd have to fill in a tax return for your extra earnings?'

'I know,' I say groaning, although really I'm thinking that you don't get a dog and bark yourself. I mean, I married an accountant. . .

'And you've got time to plan it?' asks Mark.

'Yeah,' I say. This is far too easy. I at least expected to have to expose a little flesh, maybe promise to wear something other than my flannel pyjamas to bed. But this actually sounds like he's agreeing to it.

'Are you sure? What with impressing your new boss at work and the fact you're mentoring at the gambling group.'

Impressing the boss is one thing, it's not like this wedding planning is going to get in the way of my day job, but I'd forgotten about being a mentor. Me, Penny Robinson, becoming a fully fledged mentor. I'm one year clean of online gambling and I managed to give it up with a little help (or rather a lot of help) from the gamblers' support group.

Are you proud of me? I'm bloody proud of myself. And now, Mary, the group leader, thinks I'm ready to mentor one of the new members of the group. Sadly, there's been a huge increase in people wanting to join, so the group has now split into two.

I think about whether I'll have time to plan this wedding, but then again, how much time does it take to be a mentor? I mean I only called on Josh, my mentor, once really outside of our weekly meetings.

'I think I'll be fine.'

'And your blog. Are you still going to be writing that? You always seem to be hunched over the laptop.'

It's true that, considering I only post three or four times a week, it does seem to take up a surprising amount of time.

'I'll just blog about the ideas I come up with for Henri's wedding, so it wouldn't take up that much extra time.'

'What about trying for a baby?'

'We're not having *that* much sex. I'm sure it won't interrupt our few moments of passion.'

'I didn't mean it like that. You said last month that we've got to try and remain relaxed and unstressed while we're trying to conceive.'

I did say that. Gosh, Mark really is a good husband and listens to everything I ramble on about.

'And what about when you get pregnant? That pregnancy book we read said you'd be tired early on and probably sick. Do you really want to plan someone else's wedding feeling like shit?'

I know Mark is right, but not everyone gets morning sickness and some people have much busier lives than mine and cope with pregnancy, right?

'I just think it's the wrong time for you, what with everything you've got on your plate.'

'But . . .'

33

I struggle for words; Mark is making my life sound busier than the prime minister's. But I work in a hectic HR department and, to be honest, I'm used to project management and juggling lots of different pieces of work at once. I can handle this and, if I did get pregnant, then the wedding would be out the way well before the baby was born.

'It doesn't need to take up that much time. I mean, I'd only help Henri with the big things, and I'd set her ground rules so that it didn't interfere with my other commitments.'

I don't know whether I've won Mark over or not, his brow wrinkling is giving me no clues.

'So, can I do it?' I ask eagerly.

'I'm never going to stop you doing anything in your life, Penny. You know I think that you should give up your obsession with weddings, but you lit up like a flipping Christmas tree when you talked about Lara's wedding. I don't want to stop you being that happy.'

I lean over the table and give Mark a big, fat kiss. Which is gross as we've both got stinky salmon breath.

I'm the luckiest woman in the world for having such a patient and understanding husband. I must remember to text Henri in the morning to sort out our first meeting.

Wow, the next few months are going to be fun; new wedding to plan, new responsibility at the support group what with being a mentor, possibly a promotion at work and – who knows – maybe even a mini Robinson. But it's all perfectly manageable, I just need to be organised and business-like and I'll get through it.

chapter three

princess-on-a-shoestring real wedding:
Abroad at Home

Want to get married abroad but can't afford it? Real bride and groom Lara and Ben recaptured their Greek holiday romance by holding the reception in a local Greek restaurant. It may have been raining cats and dogs outside, but inside guests felt like they were in a taverna in the sun.

Lara and Ben themed their food and drinks, serving vine leaves and other mezze classics as the canapés and then lamb kleftiko for the main course. And what Greek experience would be complete without plate smashing? To copy Lara and Ben, theme your wedding with a few props, food and drink from your country of choice and, *voilà*, you've got a wedding abroad

at home. To read the full write-up of Lara and Ben's wedding,
click here!

Tags: wedding abroad, Lara and Ben.

$\rightsquigarrow$ ——— $\rightsquigarrow$

'I just loved your piece about Lara's wedding on Princess-on-a-Shoestring. You captured the atmosphere beautifully and the photos of the restaurant were simply gorgeous!' says Henri, sitting down at the table. She carefully places her hot chocolate with cream and marshmallows on the table and stirs sugar into it.

My eyes goggle at the extra sugar, but at least it's good to know that this bride isn't afraid of piling on any extra pounds. I wouldn't want to take her on as a client if I suspected she was high maintenance.

'Thanks, Henri. I've had loads of lovely comments on the post. And other people asking me if I can organise their wedding, it's crazy.'

'It's not crazy, Penny. So many people need help with their weddings. I mean, it's a minefield. There are people wanting to take your money for absolutely everything under the sun and you constantly feel like you're being ripped off.'

'I guess so.'

'And the great thing about you is that you do everything on a . . . a small scale. And I genuinely trust, from what Lara's been telling me, that you get things down to the lowest price and that you're not only out to get rich quick.'

I sit a little uneasily in my chair. I'm not going to lie, the £1,000 fee was a pretty big sway factor in me agreeing to do this wedding. But she's right, it's not like I get secret kick-backs from companies I use, and I wouldn't want to rip anyone off.

'That's true. So, tell me, how was Lara and Ben's evening reception?'

'Lively. Those Greeks can sure host a party. All that plate smashing, and us dancing on tables. Lara's usually so quiet, she's like a different woman after a few drinks. I think some of the guests got a shock.'

I smile – none of this is a surprise to me as I've heard some of Lara's rep stories from before she met Ben. I'm just hoping that the dancing on the tables at the wedding involved her keeping her dress *on*. After all, her family were present.

'And now I can't wait to plan my wedding. Where do we start?'

'Firstly, we need to sort out the ground rules, so you know what to expect from me,' I say, impressing myself at how professional I sound. 'We'll probably have one face to face meeting per month to catch up on progress. I'll email you a report detailing what I've done each week, and what's still outstanding. I'll also come with you, where possible, for appointments with venues and suppliers.'

'That all seems fine,' says Henri nodding.

'I think the important thing to remember is that I'm not a full-time wedding planner, so I'm not available twenty-four/seven.'

'Crikey, I wouldn't expect you to be.'

'Great. You can always reach me if there's an emergency, but other than that all communication will take place outside of office hours. I'll be there on the wedding day to ensure smooth running of the ceremony and transition to the reception and then it's up to you!'

'Super, Penny, just super.'

I breathe a sigh of relief that Henri seems to be on the same page. If only Giles could see me now – I'm a manager in the making.

'So, have you given any thought to the type of things you want for your wedding?' I ask, my pen eagerly poised over my notepad.

'Not really,' she says, shrugging.

Not really? What kind of a woman is she? Every woman has a secret fantasy about their wedding. At least, every woman I've ever met has.

'Not at all? Not even a teeny, tiny bit?' I ask.

'Well, nothing out of the ordinary. I just want a huge

dress, a venue that makes my guests gasp and a good old knees-up.'

'That's a start,' I say, furiously scribbling it down.

'I'm pretty easy-going,' says Henri, shrugging her shoulders.

'That's the best way to be when you're a bride. So, if you weren't on a budget what would you have wanted?'

Henri visibly shudders when I use the 'b' word. It's then that I notice the massive rock on her finger. I'm talking a rock so big that it looks like a sugar lump has got stuck to her hand. How on earth did I miss that before? Sod the wedding on a budget, she could sell that and have a wedding fit for a queen; no shoestrings or bootlaces required.

'Um, well it might have been nice to have hired a big country estate, you know antique furniture, silver service and all that.'

'Excellent,' I say.

'And I'd have loved a band or a wedding singer.'

'OK.'

'And, you know, maybe a vintage Rolls to get me to the church.'

'Right.'

'And I love those cakes made of cheese. The ones with the grapes running down the side that look like flowers.'

'OK . . .' I say. Boy, for someone that hadn't really had any thoughts on her wedding, she sure has a lot of ideas off the top of her head.

'But I know that I am going to have to deal with the fact that we are on a,' she takes a breath, 'a budget.'

I'm half-expecting Henri to pronounce the word in a mock-French tone like 'beau-jay', in that whole Hyacinth Bouquet-Bucket way. It also sounds like those aren't her words, I wonder if her husband-to-be has been giving her a little pep talk.

I wonder what her fiancé will be like. Henri's your classic public school-educated woman. Well spoken, impeccably dressed – she's dressed today in a Sloaney type of outfit. Yet she's still an enigma. I can't bring myself to ask why she's planning her wedding on a budget it seems at odds with everything else about her.

'Yes, well obviously we're going to have to work to your budget. But you know, £10,000 isn't a bad figure. I got married on a budget of £5,500. So it can be done.'

'Really?'

'Yes, in fact, I think that you could do it without my help and then you'd save yourself an extra £1,000.'

'Oh, no, Penny. I couldn't do it,' says Henri. She yawns, as if it's exhausting even contemplating planning a wedding.

Henri reminds me a lot of my friend or, more accurately, Mark's best friend's wife, Jane. She had this super-expensive,

I'm talking £50,000 at least, wedding, and she employed a wedding planner who took care of every little detail and yet, somehow, she still got incredibly stressed out by the whole thing. Jane's currently pregnant, so I'm waiting for my invitation to the baby shower, which no doubt is a tradition she'll embrace. It'll probably be held somewhere like Claridge's or The Ritz and the gift list will be registered at Harrods.

'OK, well if you're sure. I'm confident that if we use some of the contacts I know, then I could probably get you some good discounts.'

'Super,' says Henri. She's got a massive dollop of whipped cream on the top of her lip and I have to do that awkward mimicking motion to try and alert her discreetly.

'Oh, thanks, sweetie.'

'So, you said your fiancé is coming along. What time will he be here?'

Henri glances at her watch. 'He should arrive any minute now.'

'Great. I think it's really important to get the groom on board early on in the planning,' I say, giggling to myself at the memory that my own groom knew none of the details of our wedding. But I've been reading up about becoming a wedding planner and that's what they recommend. Well, I practically read up on it; I read a chick-lit novel which was based around a character who was one. Same thing, right?

'I absolutely agree,' says Henri, nodding as if I've just quoted the Bible.

The opening of the coffee shop door is heralded by the ringing of a tinny bell sound. I look up to see an older man walk in. He's wearing a fedora and a rain coat and he looks like he's just stepped out of *Mad Men*. He's no Don Draper, though, sadly. I wonder if this could be Henri's fiancé. He might be a little old for her, but who am I to judge?

Henri's oblivious to the man's entrance as her back is to him. I watch him as he walks towards us and, just as I'm about to stand up and introduce myself, he passes by.

'There is one thing about the wedding,' says Henri.

'What's that?' I ask tentatively. There's something about her tone that makes me suspect that I don't want to know the answer.

'We've got a family dog, Archie, and I'd like him to be at the wedding. In fact, I'd like him to be the ring-bearer.'

Visions of a handbag-sized Chihuahua come to mind.

'I'm sure that won't be a problem,' I say, hoping that it won't be. Most venues are dog-friendly, aren't they? Perhaps I should worry about that when we've actually found a venue.

The bells rattle noisily over the door again and I look up to see another man hurrying in out of the rain. I watch him

43

as he pulls off his dripping raincoat, and suddenly I look away, pretending I haven't seen him.

The man who has just walked in is Nick. Nick-the-businessman as I call him in my head, one of my peers from my gambling group. In his hey-day of gambling, Nick lost £10,000 in one night. He had an addiction to buying and selling stock. It started with the odd investment, but soon he was getting up in the middle of the night to be awake when the Asian markets opened. I don't think he ever told us how much he lost in total, but I'm pleased to say that he's a reformed character now.

I'm trying to avert my eyes so we don't have that awkward eye-meeting moment where he recognises me. It's sort of an unwritten rule we have in the group that if you're with company, you don't acknowledge each other. Or, as I learnt the hard way, it lands you in all sorts of hot water when you try and explain to people how you know the other person.

It's a shame though; I haven't seen Nick for ages because he now goes to the splinter support group on a Thursday night. It would have been lovely to have caught up with him.

I'm suddenly vaguely aware that there's someone standing over the table and I have this awful feeling that it's Nick. I look up at him and I try and do the 'not now' eyes at him, but he's not looking at me. He's looking very intently at Henri.

'Darling,' she purrs, 'you're here!'

I watch in horror as Henri rubs Nick's arm and he pulls out the spare chair.

'Darling, this is Penny, the wedding planner.'

Nick sits down and turns to me and then he noticeably freezes. It looks like his eyes are going to pop straight out of his head. He starts making noises like he's choking, which he tries to disguise in a cough.

'Darling, are you all right?' asks Henri. She leans in close, like she's a puzzled child investigating him.

'I'm fine,' squeaks Nick. He clears his throat and tries again. 'Fine,' he says again in an overly compensating deep voice. 'Penny, how lovely to meet you.'

I was wondering whether Nick was going to confess to knowing me. I know we're not supposed to 'out' each other publicly, but in this instance I wouldn't have minded.

'Lovely to meet you too. Sorry I didn't catch your name,' I say to him, not wishing to be caught out before we've even started.

'Er . . . Nick,' he says. He's obviously not used to this do-we-know-each-other-or-not sketch.

'I'm sorry, Penny, I should have introduced you two. Nicholas Eves, this is Penny Robinson.'

It's a bit weird to learn Nick's full name. Up until that point, he's just been Nick: Nick from the group. Although we know bits and pieces, we know very little personal information. It's like looking at a black-and-white painting of someone's life, all the little details: where they work, who they live with, what their favourite food is, are all a mystery. But here now, seeing Henri sitting next to him, stroking his hand, Nick's painting is suddenly coming into colour.

I'd always assumed Nick was already married; he's got that dependable two-point-four children, family man look about him. Funny how wrong you can be.

'Penny was just asking me questions about what type of wedding we want.'

'Oh, right,' says Nick. 'Yes, the wedding! Have you been wedding planning for long, Penny?'

'No, in fact, this is my second wedding.'

And quite possibly the last. I don't think my heart is up to all this shock and excitement.

'Right. Henri, dear, do you think we should get a wedding planner with more experience?'

'Nicholas! Don't be so rude. You should have seen the beautiful wedding that she planned Lara and Ben, and they had more limited funds. I'm sorry, Penny, I don't know what's got into him,' says Henri, as if she's talking about a naughty toddler rather than her fiancé.

'It's fine.' Don't worry, Henri, I know exactly what has got into him.

'No, it's not. Nick, apologise.'

'I'm sorry, Penny,' he says, sighing.

I'm now connecting the dots between Henri's budget wedding and Nick's gambling habit. It's not just Nick who suddenly doesn't want me to plan this wedding, I've got a sick feeling in my stomach about it too. It's making me think back to my own wedding when I kept my gambling habit a secret from Mark. I hope that Nick's been more honest with Henri. I don't want to be stuck in the middle of that situation again.

'That's fine, Nick. But I don't want to force you into this. If you'd feel comfortable getting a planner with more experience, I would completely understand.'

'Come on, Nick. It was your idea to organise it on a budget. And we need help if we're getting married this year. If you hadn't dragged your feet all these years,' she says, laughing.

I smile awkwardly. I can guess why he's been slow to pop the question.

'Henri's right. I'm sure you'll do a fine job, Penny.'

'Great,' I say lying. 'So, why don't we have a quick chat about what kind of a day you both envision having. Do you see yourselves getting married in a church or having a civil ceremony?'

'Church,' replies Nick.

'Civil ceremony,' replies Henri.

What a fabulous start. Henri and Nick give each other curious looks and then they look back at me.

'Right, I guess you two can have a chat about that and let me know when you've chosen. How about types of venue, are we thinking a classic hotel-type day or somewhere a bit more off-beat?'

'Hotel,' says Henri.

'Off-beat,' says Nick.

'OK,' I say, taking a deep breath. 'Let's get back to basics. When were you thinking?'

'August,' says Henri.

'December,' says Nick.

Oh, dear goodness. I'm almost afraid to ask them anything else.

'Have you not talked to each other about what you want?' I say gently, trying not to come across like a shrink.

Henri sighs heavily. 'We've tried to, but it always comes back to us arguing over what we want versus what we'll be able to afford.'

On reflection, maybe my 'don't tell the groom'-themed wedding was inspired genius. I had no one but myself to be angry at or frustrated with what I was choosing.

'OK. Well, look, we don't have to sort out the nitty-gritty today. I think it would be best if you took one of my budget forms away with you, so it gives me an idea of the kind of proportions you want to spend on each aspect of the wedding. It covers things like food, entertainment and the venue. Then we can have a look at it together and we'll be able to see what things are more important to you. Don't worry if you go over your budget, I just want to get an idea of your priorities.

'And I also think that you really should talk about whether you want to get married in a church or have a civil ceremony location. That will help us when we start looking for venues. It would be especially useful if you've got a particular place in mind in terms of where you want to get married. We don't want to start finding a reception venue that's hours away from the church.'

Henri's nodding her head enthusiastically and Nick looks like he's wondered just what he's got himself into.

I take the wedding budget form out of my folder and hand it to them.

'You might want to browse through a couple of these wedding magazines too, as they could give you a few ideas. Now, these are generally aimed at more high-end weddings, ones that would cost two to three times what you have to spend. But don't be put off. I'm sure if there's an idea you like, if we think creatively we can probably find a budget way to do it.'

'What about us leaving the venue in a helicopter? I always fancied that,' says Nick, looking hopefully at me.

I shoot Nick a warning glance. I'm masquerading as a wedding planner, not a miracle worker.

'Perhaps I can live without a helicopter.'

'Probably wise,' I reply. 'Well then, you've got plenty to talk about. Why don't I leave you to it? Now, as we're probably not going to have much time to plan the wedding if, Henri, you're thinking of August, we should meet again in a couple of weeks.'

'That sounds super,' says Henri.

'Great then.'

I start putting on my coat, ready to leave.

'Perhaps we should go too, Henri,' says Nick.

'Really, don't you think we should stay here to talk about the wedding?' says Henri.

'No, let's go home and I can curl up with a scotch and you can tell me about the wedding we're going to have.'

'Sounds perfect,' says Henri.

'Do you need to run to the bathroom before you go?'

Nick is sounding just a bit like someone's mother. I'm desperately trying to get up and away from this conversation but my bag's tangled in my chair.

'I think I'll be fine,' says Henri.

'Really? With your bladder?'

I'd die if Mark ever said that to me in public. I'm trying to keep my eyes fixed on the table, but I can see out of the corner of my eye that Henri's turned a little bit pink.

'No,' she says, 'I'm fine.'

Nick is looking not at Henri but at me, with pleading eyes. I realise that that little exchange was supposed to get Henri out of the way so that Nick could speak to me alone.

'Now, then,' I say, picking up my bag. 'Remember, you can both call me if you have any questions or worries about anything,' I say raising my eyebrows in a conspiratorial manner to Nick. 'Nick, it's probably a good idea for us to swap numbers, you know, in case there are any emergencies or decisions that affect the groom rather than the bride.'

'Excellent idea, Penny,' says Nick, nodding.

I thought he'd like that, much better than creating fictitious bladder conditions. He takes his phone out quicker than a gunfighter whipping his gun out at the O.K. Corral. We swap numbers and I swear he gives me a wink, but it is so quick and stealthy that I can't be sure.

'I'll see you in a couple of weeks, folks.'

I leave the coffee shop and breathe a sigh of relief to leave them behind. They've got some tricky conversations ahead. I should count myself lucky that I didn't have to go through that with Mark. The only part that he helped plan was the guest list, and that caused enough arguments.

As I reach my car, my phone beeps and I wonder if it's Nick texting already, but it's Henri.

Thanks for the lovely meeting. I'm super-excited that you've taken us on. You'll have to forgive Nick, that's his business brain coming through. He's a teddy bear, really, and he's just as excited as I am that you're on board. Already looking forward to our next meeting! ☺

I read the text and smile. I wish I shared Henri's excitement, but since the revelation of the identity of the groom, I'm starting to feel uneasy about the whole thing.

chapter four

princess-on-a-shoestring friend of foe:
The Wedding Abroad.

I love the idea of getting married abroad: those magical photos on the beach, the sea lapping at your feet. The pluses are numerous: you can almost guarantee the weather you want, the photos will look amazing, and often they can be more intimate which allows you time to really celebrate with your guests. A lot of people think that it's the cheapest option, which it might be for you, but what about your guests who will have to fork out for their flights and accommodation? Not to mention using their precious annual leave and having to have a holiday where you want to get married!

If you're thinking about going down this route, then talk to your friends and family first and sound them out. If you do go ahead, don't be disappointed if some people can't come - and do try and have a party for those that get left at home! What do you think - are weddings abroad friend or foe? Are you planning one - or have you attended as a guest?

Tags: wedding abroad, destination wedding.

Since Giles told us the wonderful news that Shelly and I were going head to head for the potential new job, the atmosphere at work has become a little odd. Funny that. I don't think an outsider would notice a change. You certainly can't detect anything in the way we speak to each other. I don't think even Marie, who sits with us, has noticed the tension that is bubbling under the surface. But I'm aware of the new behaviour.

For example, the eleven a.m. snack break that we always take. Usually Shelly and I would share something like a Kit Kat or a Twix. Not now though. This morning, at approximately 10.42, Shelly opened and ate a Drifter. A Drifter! Our favourite of sharing treats. It was like she was flaunting it right in front of my very eyes. And I had to watch, pretending I wasn't bothered at all, when really inside I was drooling. Then, at eleven, I had to eat the whole of my Breakaway bar by myself. So disappointing.

And, yesterday morning, when it was her turn for the

tea run, she asked Giles if he wanted a hot drink, despite the fact, he's not usually included. She full-on knocked on the closed door and asked him if he wanted anything. And when he said he'd have a coffee, she didn't just go and get him one of the crappy machine ones that taste like tar and burn your hand through the painfully thin plastic cups. No, yesterday, Shelly set the precedent of buying Giles actual coffee from the proper coffee machine from the canteen that actually uses real coffee beans and costs four times as much. Of course, the rest of us all got the crappy machine stuff. I'm surprised she didn't get him a muffin to go with it. Talk about apple for teacher.

Then there's me; I've started to forgo my little web searches during the day. I'm not too worried that Giles will catch me in the act, instead I'm having to keep the one eye I'd usually have on the ASOS website trained on Shelly and what she's up to. It hasn't escaped my attention that if you take the h-e-l out of Shelly, you're left with *sly*.

Oh, hello. Giles's door has opened. I've got a slight advantage over Shelly, as her back is to the door. I sit up a little straighter and furrow my brow over my emails to make it look like the one I'm writing is very taxing. It's actually a very simple enquiry that I get on an almost daily basis. It requires an answer that a monkey could give, but right now my forehead looks so furrowed that it looks like I'm trying to work out what bonus I'd need to get to buy the entire spring collection of Louboutin's.

'Ah, Penny, I'm just off to see Bob in Finance, can I have a word with you on my way back?' asks Giles.

I look at my watch, it's twenty past twelve, I was planning on lunching in ten minutes, but I guess I can forgo my mooch to the canteen and back. Although I had bought the latest copy of *Heat* magazine at the petrol station this morning and was looking forward to a lunchtime read. But, as Mark says, I really should put my best foot forward at work to get this promotion. I'm sure giving up reading 'what's hot and what's not' is exactly what he meant.

'Great, I'll be here waiting,' I say smiling away, like butter wouldn't melt in my mouth. I glance over at Shelly. She's staring at her computer screen, but I can see her nostrils flaring in rage.

'I wonder what that's about,' I say as I watch him disappear over to the 'dark side' of the office, aka the Finance Department.

'I'm sure it's nothing to worry about,' says Shelly, unblinking.

I'm not worried, I want to say to Shelly. It's true, for once in my work life, I'm not worried. Not this week anyway. I haven't been this conscientious since, well, I first started. But now, doubt is starting to creep into my mind. Maybe

Giles has changed his mind since our meeting. Maybe he's realised that he doesn't need an HR department in the UK office after all. Or maybe Shelly's jealous that Giles called me in and not her. Is she playing mind games with me?

I'm distracted from my fears by my mobile buzzing. I smile as I see it's a text from Mark.

Haven't seen you much this week. Fancy going out for a curry tonight?

I mentally run through the evening I had planned: writing a blog post and going over Henri's budget sheets. But Mark's right, we haven't spent a lot of time together lately. I guess I could always get up early tomorrow before work and write the blog post. I reply before going back to worrying about what Giles wants to talk to me about.

By the time that I see his lofty head appear over the open-plan office, I'm fraught with nerves. Shelly has got a smug-looking smirk on her face which makes me think that she can sense my developing anxiety. It's not escaped my attention that she didn't go to lunch either, and instead she's been eating soup from her flask.

I'm about to get out of my chair to meet Giles at his office door when my phone beeps. I pick it up, thinking I'll respond when I get out of the meeting.

Wedding emergency! Call me ASAP!

I know I told her that she could call me in a dire panic, but what kind of wedding emergency can Henri possibly be having? She hasn't even set a flipping date. Unless the emergency is that she's decided to get married this lunchtime and she's on her way to Gretna Green, in which case there's nothing I can anyway. And now is definitely not a good time.

I speed-text my reply as Giles is getting worryingly close and I don't want to appear like I'm texting instead of being hard at work. Although it is after one and I should be looking at 'torso of the week' and tucking into my tuna baguette right now. I hope Giles will realise how dedicated I am, working through lunch, when he hears my stomach growl.

Just in meeting, will call after.

I look up and Giles catches my eye and gives me a finger point. It looks a little ominous, but I think it's too much to expect Giles to manage a friendly wave.

I get up reluctantly and smile at Shelly as I go. He did, after all, single me out, which means I feel a little like the chosen one. The stupid thing is that back when nice Nigel was our boss, we both would have been in and out of his office all day long. I wouldn't have batted an eyelid if Shelly had gone in at nine a.m. and come out at five. There were no cloak and daggers or handbags at dawn then.

I walk into the office and Giles closes the door behind us. The whole thing feels like a clandestine operation and I wonder if I'm going to be trained up for some secret mission. Maybe I'm not being fired after all. Maybe I'm going stealthily into the organisation. Like Undercover Boss. Maybe they'll make me dye my hair and put on some dodgy facial hair. This is probably fairly unlikely as I'm not big or important in the company. Unless it's something like undercover underling and I have to go and snoop around the management. That would be awesome.

'So, Penny, I've been to see Bob in Finance to check some budgets.'

Please don't say that you've realised you don't have enough money to employ me and Shelly. Or that you're cancelling this year's Christmas party. I know we over-spent last year but, really, having the waiters dressed in full Storm Trooper costumes (the *Star Wars* rather than the Nazi kind) went down amazingly well, or so I'm told. It was just unfortunate that I went as Princess Leia and I ordered the wrong costume off the website. I was going for the tent-like white costume, and ended up with the gold bikini. Mark and I never did leave our bedroom. My husband, who hates fancy-dress parties, has suddenly taken an interest in them and he apparently can't wait for the next one.

I just nod, as if I know exactly what budget Giles is talking about.

'Well, I was looking in particular at the team-building trips. Now, I know that last year you didn't do the trip to Wales, because of the, well, the personnel issues.'

Oh yes, the personnel issues that saw one of our top managers getting his secretary pregnant on the trip the year before last. Sorry, the married manager getting his secretary pregnant. It was quite the scandal and they continued to be the subject of office gossip throughout their relationship. When his wife kicked him out, he ended up moving into his secretary's one-bedroom flat with her and, three months later, they both quit their jobs. They're now running a bed and breakfast in Ayrshire. It's got five-star reviews on Tripadvisor, not that I'm nosy and have done the virtual tour or anything.

'That's right,' I say, nodding.

'Well, it's just that the other global offices do these events and Gunther is very keen on them.'

I have no idea who Gunther is, other than being the guy from the coffee house in *Friends* who now has no hair in real life because of the over-bleaching. Giles has clearly noticed the vague, confused look etched on my face.

'Gunther, you know, Jacobson.'

Oh, that Gunther, I want to say. The founder and CEO of our company.

'Right,' I say, smiling as if me and Gunther go way back when, in reality, I've never met him.

'So, I think we should bring them back. You know, a few representatives from each section, good for morale.'

Yes, good for the morale of those left behind who spend the three days sniggering at their poor, unfortunate colleagues who are freezing their balls off in their soggy tracksuits in North Wales. Morale for those on the trip usually hovers just above losing the will to live. That is until I break out my secret supply of Snickers bars that I produce when I get the feeling that the HR Department is about to be lynched for making them go on the trip. Then, for that minute of eating, morale is at a decent level.

'Are you sure we have the budget to do it? I know that Nigel was looking into redistributing the funding into more training courses and—'

'No, Gunther was quite clear. He wants all the offices to do this.'

Great. And there was me thinking I'd never have to see my work colleagues in tracksuits ever again.

I'm not entirely sure where Giles is going with this, and why he's called me in if he didn't want my opinion.

'I think it would be helpful if we went somewhere new this year. You know, get rid of those memories from before.'

'Great idea.'

Preferably somewhere that has locks on the doors between the girls' and boys' bedrooms, just like in between the servants' apartments in *Downton Abbey*.

I can just see us at a spa or a yoga retreat. I'm sure that everyone would be up for it. No white-water rafting, no pot-holing, just nice warmth. I mean, we could always do those naff trust exercises where we fall backwards and stuff – simply in the warm. 'Now, when I was in the Sacramento office, we did an away weekend with some former US Marine Corps guys. It was great. Perhaps you could find something similar.'

The thought of me in a seaweed wrap disappears and suddenly I've got the sound of someone shouting at me in my mind. I'm about to shout, out of reflex, 'Sir, yes, Sir,' when there's a knock at the door of Giles's office.

'Come in,' says Giles, sighing. He clearly doesn't like in-terruptions. Note to self: only knock when I absolutely have to.

I turn round to see Shelly opening the door. I know

she's probably dying to know what's going on, but really, interrupting?

'I'm sorry to disturb your meeting,' says Shelly, giving me a nice smile that only another woman would know was bitchy. 'It's just that, Penny, your phone's been ringing, a lot. I thought that perhaps it was important, and when I picked it up, the text message on it said there was an emergency.'

I look up at Shelly. This is a new low. Interrupting our meeting to give me my personal phone. But then again, no one ever really rings me at work. Perhaps there has been an emergency, maybe it's my mum or dad. Panic washes over me and my hands shake a little as I hold my hand out to retrieve it.

'Thanks, Shelly,' I say through gritted teeth. I can't tell if this is a nice thing she's doing or not. If this was in the days of old and we were in Nigel's office, I wouldn't have given it a second thought. Upon taking the phone from Shelly, I notice that my six missed calls, and goodness knows how many texts, are all from Henri.

In the shock of finding out that I might have to go and buy a new pair of Hunter wellies, I'd completely forgotten about Henri's emergency.

'Do you need a minute, Penny?' says Giles, raising his eyebrows in exclamation.

'No, no. I'm fine to carry on,' I say, swiftly putting my phone on silent and shoving it into my flimsy cardigan pocket.

'Good. Shelly, you can shut the door on your way out,' says Giles.

I stifle a little chuckle as Shelly goes out with her tail between her legs.

I try and turn my attention back to what Giles is saying, but my mind is racing with what could have happened to Henri. I'm sure that she can't actually be having an emergency. I mean, unless the wedding is off, there's no reason to be phoning me now.

'I would like you to organise it, Penny.'

'I'm sorry,' I say, still distracted.

'The trip. I want you to organise it.'

'The whole thing?' I say, just checking that I've heard this right. The trip was always Nigel's domain and, given how much I dreaded it, I was always content with that. Aside from the Snickers bars and doing the session head-counts, I had no responsibilities.

'Yes, the whole thing. I'm sure you'll be all right, Penny. You do organise the graduate fairs, don't you? And, as a supervisor, you'll need to be able to do this kind of stuff in your sleep.'

Blimey, as much as I think I'd be capable of organising this type of event, I'd like to do more interesting things in my sleep. Take last night, for example, I had a wonderful dream where Robert Pattinson and Ryan Gosling duelled over me. There was certainly no one running around in tracksuits, freezing their arses off.

'Of course, Giles. I'd be happy to organise this.'

Suck on that Shelly. Gosh, this whole competing thing is turning me into a super-bitch.

'Great. So you'll have to begin with finding out whether there are companies here in the UK that do this.'

'I take it a staff trip to the US is out?' I say, wistfully thinking of those American soldiers with their tight uniforms and baseball caps. Somewhere hot like the Californian desert. Then, of course, while we were there we could take nice advantage of the exchange rate and go to one of the super-malls and—

'Definitely out. Wales is the only other country you'll get to. Maybe Scotland if you're lucky.'

Practically exotic. No passport needed though and no cheap dollar.

'OK,' I say, sighing. 'And it has to be army?'

'Yes, that kind of thing. If it's anything like the American one, you'll be kitted out to look the part.'

Dressing up? In camouflage gear? A couple of little plaits in my hair, a little camo-paint. Maybe that could be fun after all. Shelly is going to be green with envy.

'Sounds great,' I say, actually meaning it.

'It will be, Penny, it will be. And while you're doing that, Shelly can sort out the revisions to the appraisal process.'

What? Any glee I had over the fact that I was going to plan this and Shelly was going to be stuck at her desk has slipped away in an instant. Revisions to the appraisal process sounds strategic and managerial to me. That surely involves benchmarking and best-practice analysis. Stuff that goes down well when you're trying to demonstrate to those on high that you're ready for the next step up.

'Are you sure you don't want me to help with that? I did help with the revisions to the interviewing process.'

'Yes, I see that in my notes,' says Giles, looking absent-mindedly around his office. 'I just thought this would be a good division of labour.'

I catch something out of the corner of my eye and I see my phone is lighting up through the pocket of my baggy cardigan. I just hope that Giles can't see it over this side of the desk. Damn Henri and her emergency. I've desperately got to keep my head in the game for this promotion.

'Of course. I'd love to organise the Wales trip,' I say in defeat.

'Right then, I'll email you the budget from Bob and then, if you keep me updated on your progress, say every two weeks, that will be great.'

'OK,' I say. 'When did you envisage it happening?'

'I'm thinking early July. Just before everyone goes off on their summer holidays. And that way the weather will be nice and warm in Wales.'

Clearly Giles has never been to North Wales in the summer. Thermal underwear and full waterproofs are usually on the packing list, and the word hypothermia appears in the safety lecture at the start of the adventures.

'Nice and warm,' I say grinning with my fake smile.

'Great. See you then, Penny.'

The glasses are back on and I realise I'm being discharged. I stand up. I'm slowly getting used to this bizarre management style where he's almost human one minute and like an alien the next.

'Thanks, Giles, for this responsibility,' I say. I have obviously been watching too much US TV.

I walk back over to my desk.

'So, good meeting?' asks Shelly.

'Yes, thank you. Giles has given me the Wales weekend to organise.'

I can almost see the cogs turning in her mind. She looks like she's smirking but, at the same time, she's pissed off that I was given the opportunity and not her.

'That should be fun. Hope you've got your down jacket handy.'

'And the thermals.'

'At least you've got your mitt-warmers now,' says Shelly, smiling.

'I do!' I'd forgotten about them; they were my Secret Santa present last year. As we're starting to laugh, I suddenly feel a little sad about the change between Shelly and me. We used to laugh like this all the time. I'm about to tell her that she's going to get her own great project when I suddenly start to tingle in places that aren't quite appropriate at work. I realise that, when I sat down, my cardigan has found its way between my legs and my phone's now vibrating somewhere a phone shouldn't.

'I'm just going to sneak away and grab a sandwich,' I say to Shelly.

'Good idea,' she says.

I hurry down the staircase of the office and pick up the phone.

'Hello,' I say to Henri, wondering how many limbs she's missing which, in my book, is one of the few things that constitutes an emergency.

'Penny? Thank God. If I'd got your answerphone again I would have gone crazy. If I knew where you worked. I probably would have marched to your office.'

'What's wrong? You said there was an emergency.'

'I did. Guess what? My sister has booked flights over from

Australia for the summer, so we've got to have the wedding in July. This is it, Penny – two months and counting! Will you be able to do it?'

Two months? The feeling of déjà vu floods over me. I had to plan my own wedding in just over three months and it was hard-going. Now I've got to do it all over again in two months? Well, at least this will get it over with quickly and then the wedding planning will be finished. Maybe Mark was right, maybe I'd be better off giving my job my full attention and not have to worry about other people's weddings. Then I could impress the socks off Giles.

'Two months is fine, Henri. Just fine. And yes, we will be able to do it in time.'

Yes, two months would be ideal. I'll just get this wedding out of the way and then I'll be able to concentrate fully on my actual job and the promotion.

chapter five

Princess-on-a-Shoestring Top Tips:
planning a wedding in a hurry

There could be all sorts of reasons for needing to plan a wedding in a matter of weeks, and the good news is it can be done. I organised my own wedding in twelve weeks. My top tip in this area is: be flexible. Forget your preconceived notions; you might just have to go with what you can get. Maybe the venue you really wanted isn't available and you might have to consider other options like choosing a mid-week day for the reception. You might not have enough time to get a traditional wedding dress, but there are ways round this: sample sales, the high street, second-hand (eBay/charity shops). Shotgun weddings are not for the fussy, uncompromising bride.

Tags: fast, planning, hurry, shotgun, baby.

I walk into the community centre, puffing my chest out proudly. I used to be nervous coming to my gamblers' support group, but now I'm so excited to get there and see everyone. I say my hellos as I walk in, but my eyes are scanning for Beth, the girl I'm mentoring.

We were paired about a month ago. She's very sweet, and very young. So young. She's still in her first year of sixth-form college. She developed a gambling habit the summer after her GCSEs when she got a smart phone for her sixteenth birthday. She started gambling illegally after she'd 'borrowed' her mother's credit card. She racked up over £5,000 worth of debt on the card before her mum cottoned on.

I spot Beth sitting in the corner. I take a deep breath before heading over, as I haven't exactly bonded very well with her. To be honest, I think I was given her to mentor as I'm the youngest in the group and Mary, the leader of the group, hoped I'd be able to find some common ground. I'm twelve years older than her, and that feels like an insurmountable gap. If I thought I was down with the kids, I was seriously wrong. I used to think I hadn't grown up since I was a teenager, but this has conclusively proven that I have.

'Hi, Beth,' I say as I go over to her. She's sitting in the corner, looking like she's surgically attached to her phone.

'Hey,' she grunts without looking up.

'What are you up to on there?' I ask, trying to peek over at her screen as I sit down.

'I'm not gambling, if that's what you're asking,' she snaps and turns her body away from me.

'Relax, Beth,' I say, trying to channel my inner-mother voice. 'You told me last week that you'd stopped and I believe you.'

Actually, I don't believe her; she's blatantly lying through her teeth. I've noticed that she looks down at the floor if she's not telling the truth. I had an inkling about this and I tested it a couple of weeks ago when she came to my house for tea and cake. She ate one of the cupcakes I'd made and she said it tasted delicious. They were all burnt, and they were chewy in the middle, and later I saw half of one in the bin. The trouble is, I can't do anything but try and be supportive. I can't make her go cold turkey unless she wants to. I had naively assumed that, once she came to the group, she'd give up gambling like I had.

What I can't work out is how she's still doing it because her mother is monitoring her credit card like a hawk, and Beth's still over a year away from having her own.

'Sorry,' says Beth. 'It's just been a shit day at college.'

I'm about to correct her for using the word shit, and then

I remember that I'm not her mum, and I'm supposed to be her cool mentor.

'Yeah, my day has been pretty fucking awful too.'

I know it's not big or clever to use the 'f' word, but not only am I trying to create empathy with our awful days, but I'm trying to impress her with my swearing. It seems to have worked as her eyes light up at the fact that I, a supposedly serious adult, used the 'f' word. Maybe I could be a teen whisperer, after all. Now that I'm on a roll, should I try and go for the big guns?

'Have you decided yet if you're going to apply to uni?'

'Dunno,' says Beth, shrugging.

Mary had suggested that I try to get Beth to focus on her future as a way to distract her from the gambling. But, so far, every time I've bought it up, Beth has shrivelled up like a shrunken violet.

'Perhaps we could chat about it sometime? I tell you some of my university stories, show you some of my photos?'

Emphasis on the word some, there are a lot of stories that whilst might sound impressive to teenage ears, are not entirely appropriate for me to be telling someone so young and impressionable. She is, after all, I think, a fairly unworldly wise sixteen-year-old.

'Maybe some other time,' says Beth.

Before I can try and persuade her to reconsider, Mary calls for us all to sit down as the meeting starts.

An hour and a half later, and we've come to the end of our formal session. Beth ran out before I could even suggest setting a date for our next meet-up. I think perhaps I came across too guidance counsellor and it scared her off. I've been trying to get her to slot in a coffee date once a week, and so far I've failed miserably. Maybe I'll try texting her later in the week, as I suspect that teens only communicate normally with a limited number of characters.

I'm about to go as well because everyone else is deep in conversation with their mentors and I'm knackered. All this working a full day without little browsing breaks is exhausting. And, plus, when I get home I've got to write up a couple of blogs for Princess-on-a-Shoestring. I'm dying to talk about DIY manicures and nail art after I experimented at the weekend. As I get up to leave, I see Nick hovering in the doorway.

'Nick,' I call over to him. He looks nervous and agitated standing there, as if he doesn't want to come into the room.

'Ah, hi, Penny, I'm so glad you're still here. I was rushing from work and I thought you might have gone already.'

'You're lucky, you just caught me.'

'Great, do you want to grab a drink somewhere, have a quick chat?'

'Sure, that would be great.'

To be honest, I've been surprised that Nick hasn't called me before now to discuss me planning his wedding. He looked so shell-shocked when I saw him in the cafe that I thought either he'd talk Henri out of me planning their wedding, or he'd have called me for a chat. But at least we're catching up before I meet Henri for our first official planning meeting for their rapidly approaching nuptials.

I wave at Mary and the others as I head out of the session and I follow Nick out of the community centre. We both instinctively walk over to the nearby pub. As I find a table in the corner, Nick goes off to buy drinks. He comes back a few minutes later with a round of Cokes.

'So, Penny the wedding planner,' he says, placing the drinks down. 'What are the odds of that happening?'

'I know. Small world, right?'

'So how long have you been doing it?'

'Well, I'm only a temporary wedding planner,' I say sipping my drink. 'I didn't mean to plan any, but I have this blog and from that Lara asked, and then Henri was very insistent.'

'Yes, I know just how insistent Henri can be. That's why we're planning the wedding so quickly.'

'I always assumed you were married. I don't know why,' I say, shrugging.

'To be honest, Henri and I practically are. We've been

together a long time and we would have been married a couple of years ago if it hadn't been for my little problem.'

I love the way that whenever one of us in the group is referring to our awful gambling habits, we use euphemisms like 'little problem' as if it was a lost wallet, rather than amassing a whole lot of debt and potentially ruining our and our families' lives.

'I wouldn't marry Henri until I was sure that I was going to be able to give her the life she deserved rather than an unpredictable one that could have seen me lose the house or something awful.'

'And now you're sure?'

'Yes, it's been eighteen months since I gambled. Eighteen months since I told Henri the real truth for the procrastination of the engagement.'

'Thank goodness Henri knows. I thought for a minute that it was going to be like me and my whole "don't tell the groom" fiasco.'

Nick smiles and laughs a little, presumably at the memory of how I almost spectacularly ruined my wedding. I've got to the stage where I can laugh about it all, but only just.

'Yes, Henri knows everything. She did leave me for a few weeks when she first found out, but she came back in the end, on the strict understanding that I was never to play the stock market again. One whiff of me getting a stock tip and she'll be out the door.'

'Well that's great then, if she knows. There'll be no sneaking around and everything's out in the open—'

'No, it's not quite.'

My heart sinks. I can't handle any more secrets. I've had to keep more than my life's share of them. I hoped that if I gave Nick the green light to tell Henri about me, then everything would be out in the open.

'It's just that, Henri is mortified about my past debt and gambling. She's told no one about it and I've been forbidden to tell anyone either. So she can't know that you know.'

'But surely if she realises how I know you, and that we're part of the same programme it will—'

'No, she can't know. It would kill her. It's bad enough that because we're still paying off my debt that we've only got a really small budget for the wedding, she'd feel humiliated if she knew that you knew she was marrying a gambler.'

'Even if I was one myself?'

'Yes. Henri's a complex woman, but she's fiercely proud and cares far too much about what people might think. Her parents especially.'

I'm glad I'm learning about that particular personality trait now: I think it's just made my job as wedding planner about ten times harder.

'OK, I swear that I won't tell Henri I know.'

'Thanks, Penny. I really appreciate it. I am really pleased

you're on board, despite my initial reaction. When Henri gave me the ultimatum last month about the wedding, I was just so worried that she wouldn't be able to cope with the budget.'

'Ultimatum?'

I think I've missed something.

'Didn't Henri tell you? She told me that either I married her by the end of the year or else she was leaving.'

'Wow.'

'I couldn't let her go, so I told her that I'd only managed to save ten thousand pounds.'

'That's still amazing seeing as you lost a lot.'

'Penny, at one point I had a stock portfolio worth over £100,000.'

I practically spit the sip of Coke I've just taken back into the glass.

'£100,000?'

'Uh-huh. I couldn't tell anyone in the group as I know it's more money than most people would ever be able to save in a lifetime. But back in the day I had a lot of money.'

'So Henri's rock on her finger is real?'

'As real as they come. I'm not even going to tell you how much that cost. Henri did offer to sell it to pay for the wedding, but I wouldn't let her. She's barely had anything nice for the last eighteen months, I couldn't take that away from her too.'

I think back to the new season Miu Miu shoes, but I don't say anything. Perhaps shoe-shopping secrets should stay amongst the girls.

'That's fair enough. But, don't worry, £10,000 is totally doable for a wedding.'

'I hope so. I really do.'

'It will be fine,' I say as reassuringly as I can. I can see that this is eating Nick up. 'So, before I meet Henri at the weekend, is there anything else I should know?'

'Just that her parents are sticklers for the finest things in life, so if you could manage to plan a wedding that looked like it cost a fortune, that would be ideal. But Henri said that's what you specialise in. Weddings fit for a princess on a budget. And Henri is definitely a princess.'

I know I should be worried that Henri is being described as a princess, but really I'm just in awe of how much Nick's face lights up whenever he talks about her. I hope that when Mark talks about me, he has the same sparkle and look of love in his eyes.

Thinking of Mark makes my heart pang and makes me want to get back home to him. It's our one-year wedding anniversary next weekend and I can't quite believe how quickly it has gone by.

'Your wedding will be just lovely, Nick,' I say with my mind firmly on mine rather than his. I'm lost in the memory of the waltzing around the floor with Mark during our first dance. At the end of the day, despite it sounding like the gorgonzola of clichés, your wedding is the happiest day of your life, no matter how it happens. I'm not saying we've not been happy since, as this year has been calm and lovely compared to last year. But I just had the best wedding day and would love to do it all over again.

'I hope so. Henri deserves the best after what's she's had to put up with.'

I lean over to stroke Nick's hand as he looks like he's going to cry. I know that look, I've lived that look. It's the look of someone carrying the knowledge that they've caused their partner so much pain and hurt. And the worst thing with gambling is that you have nothing to show for it at the end.

'It will be perfect. Weddings always are.'

By the time I make it back to my own cosy little terrace, and to my husband, I'm feeling the love big-time.

'Hey, honey,' I say as I come in to the kitchen and throw my arms around him like I'm a limpet.

'Hey yourself,' he says, kissing me.

'I love you so much, you know that?' I say, sighing.

'I know. I love you too. Tough group session?'

'Sort of,' I answer. When Mark found out about my gambling, he made me promise that there would be no more secrets, and

I've managed to be true to my word. I've even shown him most of my unauthorised shoe purchases. Yet I feel uneasy telling him about Nick. Our gamblers' group is built on a special foundation of trust and anonymity and I feel that if I told Mark about who he was in connection to Henri, I'd be betraying Nick. It already feels wrong that Henri's in the dark and it would be worse if Mark knew the secret too.

It's not like I'm really lying to Mark, I'm just withholding information about a stranger he's unlikely to meet. Also, he does understand about the confidentiality aspect involved in the group. Not to mention the fact that not only would Henri would be mortified that I knew, she'd also not be too impressed if I start blabbing it about.

'Well, I'm cooking tonight, so put your feet up. Tell me about your day. How was work?'

I sigh even louder. Thinking about work is even more depressing than thinking about the gambling group.

'It was OK,' I say, realising that I've turned into Beth the teenager, maybe she's rubbing off on me. 'I've been having a look into army bootcamp away trips, and there are a few. They all seem like they're in budget, unfortunately.'

'That sounds great.'

'Yeah, I guess so. It's just that they all seem a little bit hardcore. I'm worried that the people who go on the trip are going to hate every minute of it.'

'I doesn't matter what they think though, does it? It matters about how well you plan it. You're trying to impress Giles, not everyone else in the office.'

I guess Mark's right, but it's important to me that people like me. Mark's got one of those analytical brains that thinks about everything in a business or career mode. But I'm more of a people person, which is a good thing seeing as I work in HR.

'I suppose so,' I say. 'I watched some of the videos on YouTube, and it looks like they make you run around with big rucksacks on your back, crawling through pitch-black tunnels and wading through rivers and stuff. And you're not wearing wetsuits or anything.'

I can only see the back of Mark as he's chopping vegetables, but I can tell from his shaking shoulders that he's laughing. 'Don't laugh, it's not funny,' I say sulkily.

'I'm not laughing,' he says in a squeaky voice.

'I can see you are!'

Mark turns round and lets out the giant laugh that's he's clearly been holding in.

'I'm sorry, it's just that I've got visions of you looking like a giant snail with a rucksack on your back, trying to wade through water.'

'Thanks, Mark. Way to be supportive.'

I turn my back to him and start flicking idly through

Mark's copy of the *Financial Times* which has been left on the kitchen table. If only it was something I was interested in reading. Why couldn't Mark have low-brow reading tastes like his wife? Mark knows I hate the *FT* and that I won't really be reading it.

He walks over and hugs me from behind.

'It was just a funny little image, that's all. It's not going to be as bad as you imagine it will be. Just concentrate on organising the hell out of it. Make it all one big military operation and you'll be fine.'

Mark's nuzzling my neck and he's making it impossible to stay cross at him.

'It's not going to work,' I say, trying to keep the sulk in my voice. Only he's now nibbling my ear and planting kisses down the back of my neck, just where I like them. And his hands are starting to run down my sides and, uh-oh, I'm in trouble.

'How about we go upstairs and try some baby-making?'

'What about dinner?' I say, knowing full well that I couldn't give a stuff about it, especially when Mark is running his fingers up and down my thighs. And, besides, we are supposed to be trying for a baby and we haven't for a couple of weeks.

'It'll keep.'

Mark stands up and pulls me up towards him. He kisses

me with such intensity that my knees almost buckle from swooning. This baby-making isn't so bad after all. So it's taking us a little longer than we hoped it would; we've been trying for nearly seven months. But we might as well make the most of this sexy time while we still can. After all, from what I hear from my best friend Lou, when you have a newborn, the closest you get to getting down and dirty is clearing up pooey nappies and sick.

I follow Mark up to the bedroom, too weak-willed to be mad at him for long.

chapter six

princess-on-a-shoestring cost cutters:
Statement Flowers

Want flowers but not the huge florist bills? Go for statement flowers that are eye-catching and that people will remember. Consider the only flowers at the wedding being yours and your bridesmaids. Pick vivid or bright colours that make them memorable and then your guests will instantly remember them - and not even realise there aren't any other blooms in sight. Or, if you do want floral centrepieces, why not go for single stems - like a sunflower, bright and big!

Tags: flowers, bargain.

It's Saturday today, the day you're supposed to do the following things: lie in, treat yourself to a greasy fry-up, and generally mooch around the house in a hungover state. I can't honestly remember the last time I did that. Instead, I was up at stupid o'clock this morning, off to the museum where I volunteer at a Saturday club, and now I'm en route to meet with Henri.

Henri's dog-sitting the beloved family dog, Archie, at her mum's house, so I'm meeting her there. With only a two-week window in July when her sister is over from Oz (which is two months away), we've got to get cracking on finding a venue. I'm just hoping that Henri and Nick have sat down and worked out their little differences with regards to what they're looking for in a wedding day. But, having seen how infatuated Nick was with Henri when he was talking, I get the impression that it won't really matter what he actually wants as he'd bend over backwards to please her.

'In point two miles turn right,' says the automated Sat Nav voice. Her voice grates on me. When she talks to Mark, I get a little bit jealous of her seductive tones, but after playing about with downloadable voices and driving around with Yoda from *Star Wars*, I realised she was the lesser of many evils. 'Turn right, you must,' got old very quickly, let me tell you.

I hope I'm going the right way; all I had from Henri was the house number and postcode. I didn't really think to ask for the whole address or to look where it said it was on the Sat Nav. I just plonked it in and drove off from the museum, worried that I had left it a bit late as I'd stayed for tea and biscuits with the other volunteers.

I go round a big bend and I'm wondering where the Sat Nav is expecting me to turn right into, when I spot a tiny turning. It's a narrow road with cars on the street and only just enough room for my little car to squeeze down. I'm scrunching my eyes up in concentration, fearful that I'm going to meet a car along the way.

After holding my breath for what seemed like far too long, I end up by a cricket green and, before long, I arrive at my destination just opposite a duck pond. As I parallel park, I take in my surroundings and realise that I'm in White Hartnell, a quintessentially quaint British village.

I look at the row of little houses that face the green, and as I'm trying to work out which is the one I want, I spot Henri walking down the path of one of the houses.

'You made it,' says Henri, opening the little gate at the end of the garden.

The garden has neatly pruned rose bushes and a tree covered in blossoming pink flowers. The house itself looks like it is early twentieth century and it has a lovely homely cottage feel to it.

'I was beginning to wonder if I'd gone the right way,' I say, looking around me. 'This place is gorgeous.'

'I know, isn't it? My mum bought it after the divorce from my dad. It was a bit of a wreck inside, but she's managed to do a lot to it. I thought as it was such a nice day, we'd have tea in the garden while we talk.'

'That sounds lovely.'

I follow Henri along the side of the house and to the back garden. It's even more beautiful than the front. Her mum clearly has green fingers, or she pays someone who has, because everything is immaculate. The grass looks like it's been trimmed with scissors and a ruler, the beds are full to the brim with flowers the whole spectrum of the rainbow, and there's not a weed in sight. It's just how I'd love my garden to be. My garden is currently a rectangular patch of grass with small patio. No hint of anything in bloom unless it's a weed, and even that's an effort for Mark to maintain. The only garden I look after is my lady garden, and believe me that's more than enough work to keep tidy.

Henri disappears into the house and I take a seat on one of the over-stuffed and inviting sun loungers. I close my eyes and feel the surprisingly hot sun warm my face. But, before long, it starts to rain. I can feel it all over my leg. That's weird, why is it only raining on my leg? I open my eyes and practically leap out of the lounger in shock. There, in front of me, is Beethoven, as in the dog out of the movie – not the long-dead composer.

'Ah, get off! Get off!' I shout. The dog has clearly taken my surprise at seeing him as an instruction to clamber up onto the lounger and no matter what I say to him, the dog just thinks I'm being loving and licks me more. That's lovely. Dog spit removing my tinted moisturiser. Fabulous.

'Archie, get down,' calls out Henri.

To my amazement, Archie leaps down immediately and places himself at Henri's feet. She unpacks a tray of tea and cake onto the little bistro table.

'Milk, sugar?' as she pours the tea from a teapot into rose-patterned china.

'Just milk, thanks.'

'Sorry about Archie,' she says, pointing to him as if I would have forgotten who he is. 'I think my mum lets him sleep on the sun loungers and he thought you were lying on his bed.'

I stand up immediately, not wishing to repeat that extra-special cuddle. But after Archie settles himself down by Henri's lounger, I decide it's safe for me to sit down again.

'So I hadn't realised that Archie was such a . . . big dog,' I say diplomatically. I could have easily said slobbery monster, but 'big' sounded the most polite option.

'Oh, he's like a gentle giant, aren't you, Archie-woo.'

'And you want Archie to be your ring-bearer?'

'Yes. That won't be a problem, will it?'

'Would it be a deal-breaker if it was?'

'Well, it really would mean a lot to me if Archie was involved.'

Henri has these puppy-dog eyes that sort of make it impossible to not let her have her own way.

'How about we find a venue first, and then worry about Archie further down the line?'

'OK,' says Henri, stroking Archie's ears.

I know that the dog will be at the wedding. Perhaps I'll get her to negotiate with the venue herself; if both she and Archie give them puppy-dog eyes, I think it would be hard for anyone not to agree.

'So Nick was saying that you'd had some ideas for venues,' I say, taking a sip of tea.

'When did you speak to Nick?' asks Henri.

Even though she's now placed her oversize sunglasses down over her eyes, I know she's staring hard at me. Bugger. When do I say I spoke to Nick?

'I, er.' Shit, Penny, think. 'In the week.'

'What about? He never told me that he'd spoken to you.'

With the tone in Henri's voice, I'm fearing this is fast becoming some sort of international incident.

'Well he wouldn't have,' I say.

Henri's actually propped her glasses on top of her head now, and I can see her eyes are screwed-up in scrutiny.

'Why wouldn't he?'

'Because he wanted to talk to me about organising you a surprise for the wedding. I wasn't supposed to say anything.'

'A surprise?'

Henri's tone has totally changed. The frosty hue has melted and now there's a high-pitched. child-like sound to her voice.

'Yes, and I can't tell you any more.'

Henri claps her hands in glee, and I make a mental note to text Nick and get him to plan Henri a surprise. I'm sure he'll be thrilled.

'So, what are you thinking with regards to the venue?' I say, trying to steer the topic to safer ground.

'I'd still really love a big country hotel. There's one just down the road from here and we could get married in the village church.'

I try and swallow, but there's a huge lump in my throat. There's only one country hotel in the vicinity of this village and I know, without a shadow of a doubt, that Henri wouldn't be able to afford it on her beau-jay.

'I think the Walston might be a little bit on the pricey side. But at least you know what you want. So a countryside wedding is important to you, then?'

'Yes, I think so. I love those outdoor photos with the bride and groom surrounded by beautiful lawns.'

'And you want to get married in a church?'

'Yes, better for the photographs, don't you think?'

I nod as they do make for lovely pictures, but I'm not convinced the church would appreciate that as a reason for picking them.

'Have you thought about picking a more unusual venue? Sometimes a quirky building can be cheaper than a more traditional venue?'

'Oh no, my dad wouldn't like that. It's got to look like a wedding.'

'I had my wedding in a museum, and in fact it was like being in a hotel. It was an old officers' mess—'

'I'm sure it was lovely, Penny, but I think simple and traditional is best. Country hotel, National Trust property, old manor house. You know a lot of old manor houses are being let out for weddings so that the owners can afford the up-keep. Even the one in *Downton Abbey* does weddings, doesn't it? That's near here, maybe that could be an option?'

My eyes almost pop out of my sockets, Highclere Castle? Is she joking? Most people that have their weddings there appear on the pages of *Hello!* magazine. It's where Katie Price and Peter Andre had their wedding reception with that glass carriage, for heaven's sake. I dread to think how far £10,000 would get, but I'm not entirely sure it would be enough for the deposit.

'Just a traditional wedding,' says Henri, nodding as if it's the most simple request in the world.

Traditional wedding in July, for under £10,000 all in. That isn't going to be hard at all.

'What about getting married on a day other than a Saturday?'

'Penny, it has to be a Saturday. My parents would throw a fit if it wasn't. I mean, who gets married in the week?'

Um, lots of people these days, especially ones who want to take advantage of cheaper rates, but Saturday it is then, judging by the look on her face.

'It's just it might be a little late to find a venue with just two months to go, especially one in our price range.'

'I know, that's why I've got you to help me!'

Silly me! Of course, I'm Penny the miracle worker. I'll just wave my magic wand and, *voilà*, I'm sure I'll sort it out.

I sigh. I feel like I'm not getting anywhere.

'Any thoughts on guest numbers?'

'Ninety-eight.'

'That's precise,' I say, smiling.

'It was well over a hundred, but Nick was very strict and he told me it had to be sub one hundred.'

'And is that day guests?' I say, hoping desperately that

that's the combined total and that only half of them would be invited to the wedding breakfast.

'Both, we're not have any separation between day and evening. People can come to all or nothing.'

'Wonderful,' I say through gritted teeth. I'm doing sums in my head, and even if we found a caterer as cheap as the one I used, at forty pounds per head, we're looking at £4,000 on food alone.

That leaves us £5,000 for a venue and I'm not even going to think about Henri's dress. Today she's dressed in an Yves Saint Laurent maxi-dress and her feet are in Chanel wedges. I'm wondering if we could do a Becky Bloomwood-esque clothes sale and pay for the wedding out of her shoe collection.

'To be honest, as long as it looks like a proper white wedding, Penny, I'll be happy.'

I'm biting my lip as I nod in agreement. I'm wondering how I'm going to pull this all together and whether I've bitten off more than I can chew.

'I just think that perhaps you need to be a little bit flexible if we're going to get what you're after on your budget. It would be a different story if we had years to plan, but it's just two months, it's quite tight.'

'But that's why I've got you.'

'Yes,' I say taking a deep breath, 'but unless we scoured

the breadth of the country and you weren't fussy where we ended up, it might be a bit tricky. I'm thinking that we'd have to be open to other options, like maybe a village hall.'

I look over at Henri, who is wrinkling her nose up. It makes me smile as this was my trademark move when my best friend Lou was suggesting budget wedding options to me.

'Traditional,' is all Henri mutters.

'OK, well let's leave the venue for now' Much more fun to save that for later, when it gets even closer to the deadline. 'How about we talk about things I know we could do a bit cheaper. Have you given any thought to flowers?'

'Oh yes, I want lovely floral table centres. I want exotic ones. Orchids, lilies, birds of paradise.'

'Well, if you use in-season flowers then it can be slightly cheaper.'

'Of course. But you know, a wedding really deserves something quite spectacular, doesn't it?'

Oh boy. The sunglasses are back on the top of her head and she's giving me the puppy-dog eyes again. This is a far cry from the woman who had no thoughts about her wedding.

'What about photographs? I've recently met this brilliant photographer who's just starting out. He's cheaper as he works out of his flat, and he comes by himself without an assistant. He doesn't do any fancy books or expensive prints, he gives you your photos on a disk.'

'On a disk?'

'Yes,' I say slowly, 'You then get the ones you want printed or make a book from one of the online photo companies. It will save you about a thousand pounds.'

'A thousand pounds?' says Henri tipping her head to the left like a dog. 'That sounds marvellous.'

Phew. One budget area sorted then.

'Of course, I'd have to see his work first. To check I was happy.'

'Absolutely. I'll send you the link to his Facebook page so that you can have a look at the weddings he's done recently.'

'Great. Well I think that we deserve cake now, after all that hard work. I really feel like we're getting somewhere.'

She does? At least one of us does.

'Yes, I think that's quite enough for you to be getting on with. I think that perhaps if you have a look at the types of venues we can get, then we'll be really progressing'

'Are you sure you don't want to get the Internet up now? So we can rule things in or out?'

'No, I think it's best you have a look and get back to me with some options.'

'OK,' I say, tucking into a hearty bit of cake. I know this is only the second wedding I've planned, but Lara and Ben's was so different to this. They gave me a budget, told me they weren't fussy and when I heard about where they'd met, the Greek restaurant popped into my mind and it all fell into place. I'm not entirely sure that's going to happen with Henri.

This is my second time meeting with her and she's still a mystery to me. Finding mutual ground is difficult as we don't have much in common, bar her husband Nick and a shoe collection that I want to steal. She's got that posh vibe going on but, unlike Jane, Henri's got a down-to-earth quality. I just wish I could get a better sense of the real Henri as that might make it easier to think of a genius idea for her wedding.

I sit listening to her as she starts to talk about her dream wedding dress, and I try not to have palpitations after she mentions the words train and Swarovski crystals. For now I'll let Henri dream and I'll cross that bridge when we come to it.

'Right, Henri, I'd better make a move. I've got a hair appointment before I go out with Mark for our wedding anniversary.'

'Oh, how exciting. Where are you off to?'

'Chez Vivant. It's where we got engaged.'

'Chez Vivant! Wonderful! Penny, have a lovely time. And, when you're there, see how much their weddings are. That would be an amazing place to have the reception.'

I smile and nod to Henri. I know she doesn't like the word budget, but I'm also thinking she doesn't actually know what it means. I'm guessing that tonight's meal for two of us, with nice wine, will come to over two hundred pounds. I shudder to think what the hire and food cost for an event would be.

'So being married for a whole year, huh, Penny? I'm guessing it will be babies soon,' says Henri.

I'm taken aback at first. I always am whenever anyone asks me when we're starting a family. It's like one giant kick in the teeth that reminds me that Mark and I are having no luck trying. It seems to be that whenever anyone clocks my wedding ring they think it's perfectly acceptable to ask. It's so intrusive. It's not like Mark and I are officially having trouble, we haven't been trying for long enough to get tested, but other people don't know that. For all they know, I'm barren and Mark's shooting blanks. And let's not get started on what if we didn't want children. But, instead I smile and say: 'That's the plan.' As if you can actually plan those kind of things.

'I'm sure that'll be our plan too, eventually.'

'Well, thanks for inviting me here, Henri, it's such a lovely garden,' I say, trying to change the subject.

'I know. Too bad it isn't big enough for a marquee, eh? It could have made a lovely venue.'

I look round the garden to see if there was any way one could fit, but despite it being a long, thin garden, there are too many water features, flowerbeds and blossom trees in the way.

'Yes, such a shame. Anyway, I'll put my thinking cap on and let you know in the week if inspiration hits me.'

'Great. Thanks, Penny, and have a lovely time tonight,' says Henri. I walk out of the gate and wave and Henri disappears round the back of the house again.

I can't resist popping down to the pond to see the ducks before I go. There's something that stirs in my childhood memories about feeding them. I'm just marvelling at a gander when I hear an almighty shout and, as I stand up to look at what the noise is about, something smacks me squarely in the face.

The next thing I know, I've fallen on my bum.

'Are you OK?' calls out a man dressed in white. He's running towards me and, for a moment, I wonder if I've died and he's an angel. It really wasn't that hard a bang on the head, was it? I mean, I can't die now I haven't got to stage six (having babies) yet, and I've been working so hard at the office, what a waste. I could have been spending my final days surfing the net, and instead I've been having terse conversations with scary sergeant majors.

'I'm so sorry, we've got a new teammate who can't resist a good six. Are you OK?'

The man bends down and holds out his hand.

'Do you think you can stand? We should get you into the clubhouse. Michelle will make you some sugary tea.'

I can't actually speak, which can only mean one thing: I'm in shock. It appears I'm not dead, but I've been hit in the head by a cricket ball.

'We should probably get you some ice for your eye, too. It looks like you're going to have quite the shiner.'

'What?' I say, finally finding my voice. 'No. No, I can't have a black eye. I'm going to Chez Vivant tonight. A black eye just won't do.' I burst into tears. I know I'm being a drama queen, but come on, I just got hit in the head by a flipping cricket ball. I've been telling Mark for years that it's dangerous being a sports spectator but he's never listened to me.

'Chez Vivant. Fancy! I'm sure that a little bit of foundation will cover it right up,' says the man. I might have believed him if I couldn't see him grimacing and crossing his fingers behind his back.

As we get onto the main green, I see that a cricket match is underway. People are sitting round the edges watching, or at least they were, they're now looking at me being led across the grass. The man who came to my rescue deposits me in a chair on the patio outside what is presumably the clubhouse. It's a cute building, a white wooden structure with an extraordinary number of windows considering its proximity to such a violent sporting event.

'Hello, I hear you've had a bit of a bump,' says a woman bringing me a Styrofoam cup of steaming hot tea. She bends down and has a look, 'Oh, quite a lump forming there. I'll go get the ice.'

I can't stop crying now, as I try and come to terms with the fact that my black eye is going to match my black dress.

'There you go,' she says, handing it over. 'Are you all right? Do you want me to call anyone? I don't think you should drive, you might have concussion.'

Concussion? Oh, great.

'I'm fine. My friend's mum lives on the green. I'll go and see her in a minute.'

'That's a good idea. You're a bit unlucky. First test match of the season and already we've got a casualty!'

'Ha, that's typical of my luck. So, are you here to provide first aid to the injured?'

'We don't usually have that many, but with that new guy Johnson, maybe we will. My husband is the team captain. I'm here to do the sandwiches and the tea.'

'That's kind of you,' I say. I wonder if I'd be so supportive if Mark played sports.

'It's nice to be part of what he's up to. Plus there's usually a gaggle of us WAGs that come along.'

'Sounds nice. It's a really lovely cricket ground,' I say.

'Yes, we're really lucky. We got Lottery funding for our new clubhouse and we finished it last year.'

'It's great.'

'Yes, it really is. We've got a new bar in there and everything.'

'A bar? And toilets?'

'Uh-huh,' says the woman, looking at me a little bit strangely.

'Tell me, do you ever have marquees on your lawn, you know if someone wanted to have a wedding?'

'Sometimes, for the village locals, we do. If the cricket ground isn't being used for a match, that is.'

'If my friend's mother lived over there,' I say pointing, 'do you think that would count as a local?'

'Probably, you'd have to speak to the caretaker.'

'And is he in today?'

'He's over there on the boundary, he'll be in in about ten minutes or so when they call tea. I'll introduce you.'

'Perfect,' I say. Maybe getting hit on the head with a cricket ball has knocked a genius idea into my head for Henri's wedding.

chapter seven

princess on a shoestring:
Ask Penny!

Dear Penny,

I'm starting to lose the will to live with my soon-to-be mother-in-law. She keeps banging on about Save the Date cards. My fiancé's brother is getting married too and he sent out really fancy ones. And we can't afford to spend more than twenty pounds. Any tips?

Desperate Bride

Dear Desperate Bride

How about fridge magnets? Big Internet printers do business card fridge magnets for almost peanuts. You can add a photo of yourselves too for that extra personal touch. Always select slow shipping and it will probably cost you under fifteen pounds for fifty! I'm sure the M-i-L-to-be will be impressed she'll have something to stick on her fridge for all to see.

Penny x x

It's bad enough walking into work on a Monday morning normally, let alone when you're walking in with a shiny black eye. Despite being incredibly clumsy and always falling over, I've never had a black eye before, and I was very naive to the problems they cause.

We walked into Chez Vivant on Saturday night, and to say I had a lot of make-up would be an understatement. I had practically taken a cement trowel to my face. I made Nikki Minaj seem like she goes for the natural look. And, despite my two-inch thick foundation, my eye got blacker and blacker as the night went on. Instead of shutting us in a curtained booth for privacy, like we were when we got engaged, we were placed in the middle of the dining room. I'd have thought the maître d' would have wanted to keep us 'ruffians' out of the sight of his up-market clientele. But, instead, it seemed that it was better to give them something to gawp at.

I could probably have just about coped with the funny

looks that I've been given, but that's been nothing compared to looks that Mark's been receiving when we've been out together in public. People have been giving him the evil eye and I've had to tell them that it wasn't him that gave me the enormous bruise. The problem is that I've developed a nervous giggle when I tell them that I got hit in the head by a cricket ball and it makes my story seem so far-fetched they still give Mark the evil eye. He's now refusing to leave the house with me until the swelling goes down.

'Penny.'

I freeze on the stairs at hearing Giles's voice. I turn round and pray that he is too polite to notice that it looks like I met Lennox Lewis at the weekend.

'Morning, Giles,' I say, putting on my best pleased-to-be-at-work voice.

'Crikey, Penny. What happened to you?' No such luck then.

'I, um, well I had an unfortunate encounter with a cricket ball.'

'Oh, do you play?'

'No, just a spectator.'

He nods and the flicker of humanity disappears and the work-mode-robot-Giles appears again.

'Any luck with bootcamp?'

'Yes, I've found a great place that seems to tick all the criteria.'

By this I mean it has people who will shout at us, it involves losing any hint of personal pride about appearance and it sounds like hell. I'm pretty sure that was the brief from up high.

'It's a slight variation on your trip in the States,' I say continuing. 'It's an escape-and-evasion package where we have to complete team-building challenges whilst trying not to get caught by chasers.'

'Excellent. That sounds excellent. I'd like to come on the trip myself.'

Before I can stop it, a mental image of Giles in a shell-suit circa 1990 appears in my mind. It makes me shudder.

'Oh, that would be great.' I'm surprised my nose isn't growing in Pinocchio fashion.

'Yes, Gunther is taking a special interest in this, Penny. A really special interest. No pressure.'

I swallow hard. No, no pressure at all. It could be worse though. Gunther could have decided to come on the team-building trip rather than Giles. 'Have you got an idea of the dates?'

'Yes, Wednesday 3rd to Thursday 4th July.'

'Great, that is perfect timing. That will work very nicely indeed.'

I'm surprised at this point that he isn't rubbing his hands together and cackling as it sounds like he's got some evil plan.

'Good,' I say, trying to share his enthusiasm.

'So, have you thought how you might pick who gets to go on the trip?'

I think I should do a raffle. Those whose lucky numbers come up get to stay behind and those that lose have to come to wet-Wales.

'I thought I'd invite each department head to nominate three individuals based on who they think would benefit the most. You know, those who would make good leadership candidates.'

'Great. Seems like you've thought of everything.'

'Hopefully,' I say. We've arrived at my desk and I remain standing awkwardly next to my chair. Shelly looks up and is looking between me and Giles as if she is trying to work out what we're talking about. I see the two steaming hot cups of Costa coffee on her desk. I'm guessing the extra one isn't for me.

Giles flashes a quick smile at me before turning and walking away. 'Morning, Shelly, Marie,' he says as he passes.

I see Shelly look down at the coffee on her desk and back at Giles. I'm wondering whether she's going to run after him and give him the drink.

'Do you fancy a coffee, Pen?' says Shelly, passing the cup between our desks. Marie looks over, she's obviously as confused as I am. We both thought it was destined for Giles. Marie gives me a quick conspiratorial wink. She isn't being left out – she's a tea-only girl.

'Thanks, Shelly. That's really nice of you.'

I take it from her and have a quick sip. My head is nearly blown off by the strength of it. Clearly it wasn't originally destined for me, I'm more of a latte drinker and this tastes distinctly like a black coffee with an extra shot of espresso. Why didn't she give it to Giles when she had the chance? Surely that would have earned her some brownie points.

I know where Shelly lives and there isn't a Costa near her. The only time we've ever gone out of our way for treats for the office is the week that the new branch of Krispy Kreme opened.

'Well you look like you could do with it. Did you . . .'

I raise my eyebrows at Shelly as I try and get her to spit out what she's trying to say.

'Did you, um you know, have a rough weekend?' she says, hurriedly.

Oh, the black eye. That's what she's looking at. Or, more accurately, that's why she's looking down at her desk and avoiding eye contact.

'I had a great weekend. I just went to watch a cricket match and a rogue ball hit me.'

I can tell that Shelly, like most people I've told, is trying to work out if I'm telling the truth or not.

'That's a bit unlucky.'

'Sure was. Well, thanks for the coffee, Shel. So, are you doing the appraisal stuff today?'

'Yeah, I've got a meeting with the design department to go through some test processes.'

My nostrils do an involuntary flare of jealousy. Shelly gets to hob-nob round the office with different departments in the conference rooms, where it's nice and warm and dry. And I get to hang out with them in the mud when everyone will be just about ready to kill me. It's not exactly a level playing field.

'Well, have fun.'

'Thanks.'

Shelly turns back to her computer and I switch mine on to see what joys the weekend has bought, but my mobile rings before my login loads.

It's Mary from my gambling group. What does she want?

'Hello, Mary,' I say as I answer it. Mary has never phoned me during office hours. In fact, she's only phoned me once before when we were organising our Christmas do.

'Hi, Penny. Have I caught you before work?'

'I've just got in actually. Hang on a second.'

I'm wondering what could have happened to warrant a phone call before nine a.m. on Monday. I'm very aware that Shelly has her head cocked to the side as if she might be listening. I stand up, walk away from my desk and find myself in the safety of the stairwell. No one knows about my dirty little secret at work, and that's the way I want it to stay. I know from personal experience when dealing with other colleagues who have had personal problems that you just don't look at them in the same way after.

'Sorry about that, I needed to go outside. Is everything all right?'

'It's Beth.'

Mary sighs the kind of sigh which makes me think this isn't going to be something I want to hear.

'What about her?'

'Her mother called me to say that she went to a casino on Saturday night.'

'A casino? She's not old enough to go inside, surely?'

'There was something about a fake ID.'

'Right,' I do a sigh to match Mary's. What is Beth playing at?

'Her mum's worried that if she's doing that, she could still be gambling online. How's she doing with giving up?'

I bite my lip and start to feel a little guilty that I've been neglecting Beth over the last few weeks. I meant to drop round and see her, to see how she was getting on but what with everything that's been going on, I haven't had time. Aside from when she came over to mine for tea and cake about a month ago, I've only seen her briefly at the Tuesday meetings.

'Actually, I haven't really got through to her properly yet and I get the impression she's still . . .' I desperately don't want to say the 'g' word at work. 'Still, you know, although I don't know how.'

'I was hoping that wasn't the case. Do you want me to help you with her? I mean, are you not connecting? I hoped with you being the youngest mentor, that you'd be the most likely to get through to her.'

Mary's making me feel awful. I should have been making more of an effort.

'We're connecting fine. She's just evasive when it comes to meeting up. But I'll try harder. I'll drop round on my way home from work tonight. See if we can have a little chat.'

'Would you, Penny? That would be a great help. Her mum's so upset, and getting her into the group was her last hope.'

'I'll get it sorted, Mary.'

'Thanks, Penny. And maybe you could try and do that

looking to the future stuff. Talk about your university days or courses she might want to do?'

'Yes, I'll try.'

'Great, well I'll not keep you as you're at work. Thanks, Penny. I'll see you tomorrow.'

'Will do, Mary. I'll let you know how I get on. Wish me luck.'

'Good luck!'

I hang up and stare at my phone. Trust me to get stuck with the teenager. I can't believe she went to a casino. There's a tiny bit of me that's impressed that she even managed to get in as she looks young for her age. But really, what's she playing at?

When I went to the group I realised I had a problem and I wanted to do everything I possibly could to get rid of the habit. But Beth didn't come to the group voluntarily. Her mum wanted her to and therein lies the problem.

I think that Beth's mum hoped that if she just got her through the doors, that we'd cast a magic spell and she'd kick the habit, only the rest of us know that it isn't that easy. It takes all your self-control not to go online and dabble. You've got to want to give up. I've been clean for well over a year, but even now I still get tempted sometimes. Whenever I feel the urge, I write a post or reply to a comment on my Princess-on-a-Shoestring blog instead. I get a buzz knowing that people value my site, and it's a high that isn't followed by the kind of low I used to get when I lost gambling. What Beth needs is a distraction, something else to put her energies into.

I slowly walk back to my desk, wondering what I'm going to do about Beth. How am I supposed to get through to a teenager? I used to think I was still practically a teenager myself, but the limited time I've spent with Beth has made me realise that there might as well be a hundred years between us rather than the ten or, cough, twelve years there actually is.

'Everything all right?' asks Shelly.

I sit back down at my desk and look over at her. She's actually got a concerned look on her face and it's not her rubbing in that I'm taking a personal call at work. It must be the black eye. Maybe there are some perks to it after all.

'I mean, if you want some personal time, you know, to sort stuff out, I'll cover for you if anyone asks.'

I look up at her in surprise. Of course, over the years Shelly and I have done a lot of that kind of thing. But not since we've been in direct competition for the promotion.

'I'm fine. But thank you, I appreciate it. It's just a friend with a problem. Nothing that can't wait until after work.'

Or at least I hope it can wait until after work. I haven't

got time today to think about it any more, I've got a load of graduate application forms to sift.

'Well, just let me know if you need to sort anything out for this, "friend".'

Shelly has just done air quotes around the word friend. I stare at her open-mouthed and really I want to scream, it *is* a friend with the problem – not me. But what's the use? No one believes me about the black eye. It seems that when a story forms about how I got my shiner, it's impossible to get them to change their mind.

I get on with my work instead. After fire-fighting the weekend emails, I pick up the pile of applications. The first sift is just to eliminate those without the required number of UCAS points and the right type of degree. And then, on the second round, I'll start to look at the more nitty-gritty reasons as to why they think we should employ them, essentially looking for key buzz words. From there, Marie will double-check my selections, and then I give the shortlisted candidates to the managers of the relevant departments to look through. Sounds simple, yet with the economy being in such a dire state for graduates, the last few years has seen the applications shoot up by about 400 per cent. What used to be a couple of days' work for me, now takes me about a week.

I've only made it through two applications when my

phone rings. I sigh and wonder if it's Mary again. Or if Beth has phoned me to admit her problems. But, on picking up the phone, I see that it's Henri. I roll my wrist over to see the time: 9.17 a.m. What's wrong with everyone today? Despite me laying down the ground rules, it seems that my definition of an emergency differs dramatically from Henri's. From my experience of these 999 emergency drill calls, I know it's easier to pick up the phone on the first call rather than the fifth or sixth. Henri is usually much calmer and I won't have annoyed all my work colleagues in the process.

'Hello,' I whisper into the phone.

'Penny. Sorry, is this a bad time?'

'Um, yes, I'm at work.'

'Ah, me too. Look, I'll be quick. I was just thinking, do you think we could have big lights around the side of the marquee? You know, like big fairylights, ordinary sized bulbs but multi-coloured? To give it an English summer fête feel.'

Surely this isn't why Henri has just phoned me? When I'm at work.

'Um, is that all?'

'Yes, I was just thinking about it, and it hit me, literally like a lightbulb,' she says, laughing at her pun.

'Right. Why don't you make a list of these "lightbulbs" and we'll discuss them in the evenings?' I whisper into the phone. 'I mean, there's a lot to do before we get to the lighting side of things.'

Like actually hiring a marquee to hang the lights on.

'OK, Penny. That's a great idea. I'll make a list and email it over to you.'

'Great, I'll, um—'

I look up as I've become aware that there's a shadow over my desk. There, standing in front of me, is Giles. I almost drop the phone in horror.

'I'll call you later.'

I hang up and fumble the phone across the desk as I try and compose myself.

'Sorry, Giles, I had a bit of a personal issue,' I say, lowering my voice.

Giles, like Shelly, avoids eye contact.

'Right, um. Well, if you need to take some time to get anything sorted then, um, feel free.'

This black eye's amazing. Maybe I could get Mark to actually give me a quick nudge every so often. Before I even digest what I've thought, the image of Mark's face after people think that he's a wife-beater pops into my head. I never want to see that look on his face ever again, he looked so hurt.

'Thanks, Giles, but I think I'll soldier on,' I say in my melodramatic soap actress voice. I'm surprised that I didn't take the back of my hand to my forehead and mock faint into my pile of papers.

'Very noble, Penny. I've just had a word with Gunther about the team-building event and he's very pleased you've managed to organise it. In fact, he wants to come too as he's over in the UK that week for some meetings. I thought I'd let you know in person as I knew you'd be pleased.'

I'm actually in danger of fainting into my pile of papers for real now. Gunther is coming to Wales? Gunther, the CEO of the company, is coming? Gunther, who grew the company from his father's basement when he was a teenager?

'That's, um,' Penny, think of an adjective that *isn't* a swear word. 'That's, um . . . wonderful,' I manage to spit out.

'I know. It will be great. An excellent opportunity for impressing him,' says Giles.

I'm wondering if he means for him or for me. As the trip of doom is going to have the morale of an excursion to an abattoir, the only thing that will be impressive is if I'm not lynched by the end.

'Great,' I say in a squeaky I'm-having-trouble-breathing-type-of-way.

Giles disappears as quietly as he came over and I'm left trying to process the information. If only I still had the paper bag I used to carry round when I was having panic attacks during my gambling days, it would have come in handy, right about now.

'Are you OK, Penny?' asks Shelly.

I know the colour must have drained from my face.

'You know what? No, I'm not. I think I need to take a moment.'

I know it's going to take more than a moment to sort myself out. I glance down at my watch, it's not even ten a.m. yet. I've got a sneaking suspicion that this is going to be a very long week.

chapter eight

princess-on-a-shoestring friend or foe:
Table Centres

Choosing centrepieces can be tricky. They can make your table look beautiful and really allow you to put your personal stamp on the venue. Yet, at the same time, they can be ridiculously expensive, time-consuming if you make them yourself, and if they're too big and elaborate then they block guests' views of one another round the table! Why not speak to your wedding venue before you start planning, as don't forget they'll hold other functions there too and they might have candelabras or vases that they can use for your tables. I personally think they're a foe - but what do you think, do you have any tips for turning them into a friend?

Tags: table centres, obstacles, dilemma.

I don't think I've even got the energy to open my front door. If ever there was a time when I should have taken a duvet-week (that's right, a duvet-week), then this was it. The signs were all there first thing Monday morning and the tone for the rest of the week was set.

Giles has started popping over to my desk with alarming frequency. It seems that Gunther wants to know all the details about the trip. He wants to know everything from what we'd be carrying on our back to what the toilet facilities would be like. But although I'd recoiled in horror at the replies the scary sergeant major had given me, Giles expended a little yelp of delight and would exclaim, 'Gunther will love it!' I'm beginning to form an interesting view of just what kind of a sadistic bastard Gunther is.

And, if that wasn't bad enough, I had all those lovely graduate applications to sift through, so most days I've been at my desk at eight a.m. and I've still been there eleven hours later. It's been practically dark when I've left, and it's nearly summer.

Then there's Beth. Or, at least, there should have been Beth, only I haven't managed to see or speak to her all week. I've been nipping by her house every day and she hasn't been in once. I've had a lot of tea with her mum, and although she seems nice enough, the two of us having a pleasant chat isn't exactly going to solve her daughter's problem. I finally got a reply to all the texts I've sent and she's promised to meet me this weekend. Which is just what I need after the week I've had.

And, if that all wasn't enough to deal with, I don't think I have the mental energy to even think about the lists that Henri has been sending me. When I told her to email her thoughts regarding the wedding, I hadn't really meant for her to email her every thought. I've learnt a lot this week about Henri and, mostly, I've learnt that she needs to filter what she's thinking. On Thursday she started an email thread about whether she should have stockings and a suspender belt or whether she should have hold-ups. I put an end to that after telling her that we needed to get her a dress first. I've got that joy to come one day in the unfortunately not-too-distant future.

If I thought that shopping for wedding dresses with my mum was bad, then I think I'm in for a huge shock. Although my mum didn't bat an eyelid about shopping on the high street for a wedding dress after she found out that Money Saving Expert recommended it, I don't think that Henri's got the same sort of respect for (aka a crush on) Martin Lewis.

Remember when I said planning Henri's wedding would help with my blog? I've spent so much time writing emails that I haven't managed to put up more than a Penny's top tip on the blog in two weeks.

But, all I can say is, TFI Friday. The end to a crappy, crappy week. I phoned Mark as I was leaving the office and he said that he was making his triple-cooked chips. I don't know what he's cooking with it, as I stopped listening after he mentioned them. If you've ever seen an episode of *The Simpsons* and seen how Homer dribbles over doughnuts, that's pretty much what I'm like when it comes to Mark's chips. And doughnuts too, come to think of it. If only Farnborough had a Krispy Kreme drive-thru, like they have in the US.

Thinking of the chips makes me dig deep and find the energy to open the door.

'Hello,' I call out in what can only be described as a pathetic little-girl voice.

'Hey, I'm in the kitchen.'

The smell of the chips hits me as I walk in and, like the old Bisto advert, I let my nose lead me to Mark.

'Hey, honey,' I say, I shielding my eyes from the bright kitchen lights. Mark loves our kitchen lights. As if they weren't already so bright that I genuinely worry that the planes landing at Farnborough airport will get confused and accidentally try and land in our garden, when Mark cooks he puts the lights under the cupboards on too. I actually think I might need sunglasses.

He comes over and kisses me, before handing me a large glass of wine.

'No need to ask how your day was,' he says, returning to the hob to stir something in a saucepan.

'Pretty much like the rest of the week. Thank God that's over.'

'And now you can relax, it's the weekend.'

'I know. I feel like I've earnt it today. I'm knackered.'

'I'm proud of you, you know, Penny, working so hard for this promotion. You know you're going to get it.'

'Thanks, honey, that means a lot. So, how was your day?'

'Yeah, good. I got an email from Nan.'

Wow. An email; Mark's Nanny Violet is getting all twenty-first century.

'How's she getting on?'

'She's having a lovely time. She sends her love.'

That makes me smile. This time last year Nanny Violet almost ruined my chances of marrying Mark, and now she's sending me her love. Bless her. She's on a cruise right now, somewhere in the Mediterranean. Sounds heavenly. She's gone with an old friend, Ted. She insists he's just a friend, but I secretly hope that there might be more to it. You're never too old for a bit of romance in my book, and she's practically a spring chicken at eighty-nine.

It makes me chuckle that this is the same Nanny Violet who made Mark and I plan a wedding in three months because she thought she might snuff it. And now, here she is, gallivanting around Europe getting a tan.

'Anything else exciting happening?' I say, sitting down and helping myself to an extra-large gulp of wine.

'Not really. Clive gave me another one of his clients, so that's three this month. I'm sure it's so that he can get his golf handicap down before the summer.'

'So you need a good rest over the weekend too?'

'I certainly do. I think I'm going to give golf a miss tomorrow. Stay in bed.'

'Ah, I was thinking of giving the museum a miss tomorrow.'

'Are you thinking what I'm thinking?'

I'd love to say yes, but what normally happens when we both reveal what we're thinking is that we find we're on totally different pages. The last time Mark asked me that question, after I'd said I was feeling like something naughty, I went to grab my saucy underwear and he went to the kitchen drawer to retrieve our favourite curry house menu.

I was kind of hoping that when we got married we'd develop some sort of telepathy, but so far we're not quite tuned in. But, this time, I'm hopeful Mark is thinking the same as me.

'Staying in bed all morning for snuggles?' I say hopefully.

'Almost,' says Mark.

Well that's pretty good, eh? As long as Mark doesn't end the sentence with the words three-mile run, we'll be on to a winner.

'I bought these, so we can have breakfast in bed.'

Mark's holding up a packet of croissants. Croissants, you won't be surprised to know, are up there with triple-cooked chips in my book.

'Croissants and fresh coffee. I might just orgasm.'

'Well, I might be able to help with that tomorrow morning too.'

So we were thinking the same thing. Maybe we're getting more in sync after all.

'Right, are you ready to eat?' says Mark. 'I'll just put the steak on.'

'Steak, croissants? Monsieur, you are really spoiling me.'

'Well, you can spoil me tomorrow by bringing me breakfast in bed.'

'Hey, that's not fair.'

Bugger, how did I get the short straw?

'You can do the washing up tonight if you like and I'll do breakfast.'

I have a quick look at the kitchen. As per usual when Mark's been doing the cooking, he's used nearly every pot and pan in the house.

'OK, I'll do breakfast.' How hard could it be? It isn't like I'm going to have to cook a full English.

Mark places a plate of food in front of me and the sight of it makes me dribble like a dog: steak and chips with peppercorn sauce. My favourite.

'I think you're going to have to roll me out of bed tomorrow. My belly's already getting really big.'

It really is. I haven't been to the gym this week and it's practically ballooned.

'It's not that big,' says Mark taking his seat.

I stop cutting my steak. 'Not that big? Does that mean you think it's a bit big?'

'Um, I didn't mean it like that.'

'But you said it, you must be thinking it.'

I can feel the tears prickling behind my eyes.

'Penny, don't cry. Come on, you know that I didn't mean it like that.'

'Well then, how *did* you mean it? You called me fat!'

'I did not call you fat. You're blowing this all out of proportion.'

Mark's starting to sound cross, which makes me even more upset. A fat tear rolls down my face and lands in my peppercorn sauce.

'You said my belly was big.'

'No, you said it was big. I just said it was a bit bigger than normal. There's nothing fat about it.'

'But you agree that it's bigger,' I say, sobbing.

'Penny, for heaven's sake, you're going to ruin your chips.'

'I know, but I can't stop crying.'

'You've just had a long week at work. You're over-tired and that's why you're crying.'

'Don't tell me why I'm crying,' I say hiccuping as I try and stop.

I know I'm overreacting but I honestly can't help what I've started.

'Penny!'

'I'm sorry. I know, I know, I'm being irrational, I can't help it.'

Mark puts his fork down and comes over to give me a hug.

'I'll make you breakfast tomorrow, I think you need your sleep.'

'I should probably make it. After all, I need the exercise.'

Mark sighs loudly and walks back round his side of the table.

'I'm sorry. I just don't like being fat,' I say.

'You're not fat,' shouts Mark. 'And what are you going to be like when you're pregnant?'

'If I ever get pregnant.'

When this month's period arrives, we will have been trying for eight months. This month's period: there's something to look forward to.

I put down my fork.

'Mark, what's the date today?'

'The twenty-third.'

I get up from the table and run over to grab my phone from my handbag.

'Your chips will get cold. What are you doing?'

I can't reply, I'm too busy working out the dates. I'm sure my period is late. With all that's been going on lately I haven't even thought about it. I flick up my calendar app and start counting. My period's late: three days late.

'What's going on?' asks Mark. He's got concern written all over his face.

'My period's late,' I say with the thought slowly sinking in.

'How late?'

My eyes lock with Mark's and I can see the hope in his eyes.

'Three days.'

'Three days? That's not a lot, is it?'

'Well I'm usually as regular as clockwork.'

I could actually be pregnant. I mean, my belly is huge and it's been rumbling all day. And now that I think about it, my boobs are feeling a little bit tender.

'Is it too early to take a test?' asks Mark.

'I think you can do it from as soon as your period is due.'

A smile breaks out across his face and he looks so happy.

'If only we hadn't had the wine, we could have driven to Asda to get a test. Do you think the garage down the road would have one?'

'Probably not, but we can go to the supermarket first thing tomorrow,' I say, trying to keep the excitement out of my voice. I know we've been trying for ages, but I can't quite believe that it could be true.

'Imagine, this time next year there could be three of us living in the house,' says Mark.

'I know,' I say. And then it hit me. We could actually be having a baby. What about the trip to Wales? I'm having trouble breathing. I wouldn't be able to go on the trip in July. The sergeant major was very insistent that we make sure that there are no pregnant women there as a lot of the activities are fairly physical and their insurance doesn't cover it. What with Giles and Gunther coming, how would that look if I didn't participate? I'd have to tell them that I was pregnant and then I wouldn't get my promotion. Why couldn't I have just got the overhaul of the appraisal process instead? No one would have been any the wiser.

'What's wrong?' asks Mark. 'Aren't you excited?'

'Of course I am. It's just my promotion, I mean, what if I don't get it because of the bump?'

'Well, firstly I think you of all people should know that you can't discriminate against pregnant women and, secondly, who cares? We never planned for you to get the promotion anyway, it's not like we're counting on the money.'

'But what if I wanted the promotion? I mean, I know I could do it.'

'Of course you could. We always thought that if you looked for a job the next rung up the ladder, you'd get one. It's just that I thought you were waiting until after the children.'

'I was. Or I am.'

My mind's suddenly in a muddle. I've got thoughts of the promotion and Giles and Gunther combined with a little baby flashing round my mind.

Mark leans over and strokes my hand.

'Penny, we might have reached stage six.'

I giggle. Stage six. The holy grail of our life plan. I've been waiting for this ever since stage one, when we rented our tiny shoebox flat, stage two when we moved into our terrace, stage three when Mark passed his accountancy exams, stage four when we got engaged and finally stage five, which happened last year when we tied the knot.

'We might have indeed.'

I go to reach for my wine glass and instead pick up the water glass next to it. Just in case, I, Penny Robinson, may be an expectant mother. I chuckle at myself. Heaven help the child.

*

How I managed to get any sleep last night, I'll never know. I was so excited about the possibility of being pregnant. But not only did I manage to fall sleep, I also dreamt I was so pregnant that Mark had to roll me around everywhere like I was a giant wheelbarrow. After wolfing down croissants at early doors this morning (so much for our lie in), Mark's gone out to get a pregnancy test.

I've been trying not to wee before he gets back so that I'm able to perform on demand, but it's no good because I'm absolutely busting. I'll just have to go and drink a big glass of water after. As I sit down on the toilet, I realise just how close I'd been to wetting myself. Good job I got out of bed after all.

I glance down and see a familiar sight in my knickers: a tiny spot of blood.

When I was in my late teens, I loved that sight. The tiny thing which said I hadn't got up the duff although, to be honest, the way that my first boyfriend and I had sex, that probably would have been a bit like the immaculate conception. But today, I feel that someone's punched me hard in the stomach.

It's funny, you spend your life being told to always be careful and that accidents can happen, and yet when you start trying for a flipping baby you realise just how lucky you need to be to actually have sex at the right time and for

ANNA BELL

everything you don't have control over to work perfectly for it to happen.

A tear rolls down my face and I wonder how many more months I'm going to have to go through this. Last night I was so convinced that I was pregnant. All those symptoms, those hormonal tears; they were all premenstrual, nothing more.

I know last night I was freaking out about being pregnant, but I didn't really mean it. I do really want a baby. I do.

'Penny?'

I hear Mark calling up the stairs. How the hell am I going to tell him? He was up at the crack of dawn this morning making my breakfast and running out to the chemist. He's usually only a morning person if it involves watching sport or playing golf.

'Up here,' I say.

I walk out of the bathroom and bump into him on the landing.

'I didn't know which type to get. So I got the one that tells you how many weeks pregnant you are and then I got a twin pack so that you can make doubly sure of the results. I spoke to the chemist and she recommended some vitamins and I bought those—'

'Mark, stop it. I'm not pregnant.'

Mark looks like I've just told him that I drown puppies for fun.

'Are you sure?'

'I just got my period.'

Mark isn't saying anything and it just makes it so much worse. Then, before I know it, he's wrapped his arms around me and he's pulled me into a bear hug which is exactly what I need.

'There's always next month, Pen.'

I try and blink back the tears. Of course there is, there's always bloody next month.

'I'm so sorry, Mark,' I say.

'Why are you sorry? It's not your fault.'

'But I got your hopes up, if I hadn't have worked out my dates yesterday, then neither of us would have been any the wiser and I would have woken up, got my period, and everything would have still been normal. And we wouldn't have spent last night going to bed picking baby names.'

'Well, that did teach us a valuable lesson. We're not using names from *Tatler* magazine for inspiration.'

'But Chandos is such a great name,' I say, pleading. 'You can just imagine Chandos being a brain surgeon or running for prime minister.'

A small smile returns to Mark's face and I start to smile too. So it might take us a little longer, but when that day comes, Mark is going to make the best dad.

'So now that we're up when we were supposed to be having a lie-in, do you fancy doing something?'

'We could go over and see Lou.'

'Are you sure you want to do that this morning?'

My best friend Lou gave birth to a wonderful little boy called Harry last year. I say wonderful: he is eighty percent of the time, but the rest of the time I wonder whether they should have called him Damien, after the boy from *The Omen*.

'I think it might make us temporarily thankful for the lack of babies.'

'That's true. And I think there's some cricket on, so me and Russell can watch that.'

'Great, I'll go give her a ring.'

It's probably for the best anyway, this whole not being pregnant thing. What with the possible promotion and Henri's wedding and all. It will be nice to perhaps get the summer out of the way before I get pregnant. Much better on the old timing.

It's one thing for me to tell myself that, but it's another to make myself believe it.

chapter nine

princess-on-a-shoestring
Ask Penny!

Dear Penny,

My hubby-to-be (HTB) and I want to have a DJ for our reception. We can't really afford it and so HTB suggested we make our own iPod playlist. Only he's into death metal and I'm into really cheesy pop music (think The Saturdays). I have no idea how we're going to make a playlist without killing each other. Any ideas?

Pop Princess

Dear Pop Princess,

Being your own iPod DJ is becoming more and more popular these days. A great way to make the playlist is to put a card in with your invitations asking your guests to suggest a song that reminds them of you or your HTB. That way, each song that comes on is guaranteed to be liked by at least one person – and it's bound to be a trip down memory lane for you both too.

Have a fab wedding!

Pen x x

'Henri, will you calm down? All will become clear in a minute,' I say, for what feels like the billionth time since picking her up this morning. We're marching along Oxford Street, which is fairly empty as the shops are still locked.

OK, so I may be bringing Henri's anxiety on myself as I have practically abducted her and not told her where we're going. I've been a bit secret squirrel. I made her book a day off work and then I picked her up in a taxi at 6.15 a.m. and we caught the early train to Waterloo. We then had all the fun of the fair by being squished like sardines on the Tube to Tottenham Court Road.

Really, she has nothing to worry about. We're on a mission to get her a wedding dress and that is all she needs to know. I knew if I told her in advance, it would have led to a barrage of emails.

'But I just want to know where we're going. I mean, is it Browns? Or Selfridges? This is the way to Selfridges, isn't it?'

The tone of hope in Henri's voice is just like a small child when they're asking Santa for a new bike at Christmas. I don't want to point out that we'd need her entire budget to buy a dress from Browns. And I don't want to burst her bubble and tell her that we're not going to Selfridges either. I think it's better to leave her in the dark.

'Just trust me. I'm your wedding planner.'

I've used that line a lot recently. It seems to be the only phrase that calms her down. 'OK. But I don't like not knowing.'

'Your objections are noted. Look, we're almost there.'

Perhaps I should have bought a blindfold for Henri to wear as we'll have to do a lot of queuing outside the shop. No, Next haven't started doing wedding sales. We're off to TK Maxx as they've started doing designer wedding dresses. I managed to sign up to a website that tips me the nod when new stock comes in and, hey, here we are at eight a.m. Only one hour to stand in a queue along with about thirty other people. Not bad at all.

'TK Maxx?' says Henri Confused.

I can see her looking down the queue of people inspecting them. She looks as if I've suggested we're going to Primark. At least everyone is dressed nicely and, good news for me, Henri hasn't done the wrinkle nose yet.

'Yes, they do designer wedding dresses and some of

them are up to sixty percent off. They might be last season, but they're really beautiful. If you want the type of show-stopping designer dress with feathers and ruffles, like I think you do, then this might be the right place.'

Henri's pouting. I've learnt this is a good sign. If she rambles on, then she's not impressed. But by pouting, it's her way of saying that I might be right and she's considering the idea.

'What kind of designers?'

I almost punch the air with glee. Henri's interest has been successfully piqued. 'I've seen dresses from Dolce & Gabbana, Armani and Valentino on their website before.'

I struggle to think of any more off the top of my head, but I can see that Henri's pupils have started to dilate.

'And they've all got sixty percent off?'

'A lot of them,' I say, nodding.

'Well, I guess it can't hurt to look.'

'That's what I think. Now, why don't you queue up and I'll go get us some coffees and Danishes.'

'Not for me, thank you very much. If I'm going to try and squeeze myself into a size ten I don't think I can afford to be eating anything like that.'

Henri's practically a bean pole and, to be honest, I think she's more a size eight. I hardly think one pastry is going to make an impact. I'll buy an extra one anyway and then, if she really doesn't want it, at least I'll have something to snack on as she tries on dresses.

We're on a bit of a roll with the wedding planning, we've got the venue and the local village church booked. And the church have said yes to Archie the dog being ring-bearer, and with Henri's mum's house being just opposite the cricket ground where the reception will be, he can be dropped off after the ceremony – before he ravishes the marquee and eats everyone's dinner. We just need to sort out the entertainment and the catering. I know they're pretty monumental, but it doesn't appear to be to Henri. All she's worried about is the dress, ergo, I thought we'd get that done next. Then maybe I won't have my mobile beeping at inappropriate times at night when Henri's had an anxiety dream that she's had to walk down the aisle in just her knickers.

By the time I've got back from the bakery, Henri is chatting away animatedly to two women in the queue who I think are mother and daughter. There are smiles and laughter; have I actually succeeded? Is Henri happy? I give myself a virtual pat on the back as I hand Henri her coffee.

'Thanks. This is Penny, my wedding planner,' says Henri.

'Oh, your wedding planner,' coos the girl. 'I'd love to have had one but we just couldn't afford it.'

'Well, I'm sure Penny won't mind me saying, but she

works with brides on a *budget*,' says Henri, still whispering the word.

'You do? Wow,' says the girl. 'Perhaps that's what we should have done, eh, Mum?'

Her mum's eyebrows rise in a way that makes me think that their wedding planning experience hasn't been a happy one.

'Well, you can go to her blog, Princess-on-a-Shoestring, there's loads of budget wedding tips on it.'

'Oh my God, is that your blog?' says the girl. 'We've used that loads, haven't we, Mum?'

'Yes, we have. That tip about the statement flowers was brilliant. We've shaved about £400 off the bill.'

'It's so nice to hear that people read it.'

'I read every post. I've got an RSS feed and everything,' says the bride-to-be.

'Wow.'

People read my blog! In my head I'm doing a little jig. It feels like the very early days of the blog when I used to clock my stats and see that people other than me and my mum were reading it.

'I'm so excited to meet you. I comment as CrazyBride,' says the girl.

'I've seen your comments,' I say, excitedly. I wonder if this is what it's like to be famous. I can feel my cheeks tingling in embarrassment – in a good way.

'Are you going to blog about these dresses too?' says the girl.

'Yes, hopefully, if Henri will be good enough to model for me.'

I notice Henri pat her hair down and stand up a little straighter.

'Can I be in a photo for your website too? Oh, I would die if I was on it.'

I can't believe that I've bumped into my number-one fangirl.

'Of course, that would be amazing.'

The sales assistant unlocks the door.

'I'll look out for you in the fitting room,' says the bride-to-be. As we shuffle into the store after them, her mum gives my arm a squeeze and tells me to keep up the good work.

Much to my relief, the scene that unfolds is nothing like the episode of *Friends* where Monica goes to a sample sale. There are only about a dozen women in the queue actually looking for dresses, once you've taken out the fact that most brides-to-be have got friends or mothers with them. Although there might be the odd elbow, and I might have just stamped on someone's foot, it's all pretty civilised.

I end up with three gowns in my hand for Henri to try on.

Henri herself was a little overwhelmed by the experience and she just clung onto the first dress she saw which, in her defence, is a beautiful dress.

There's something really exciting about being in the fitting room area when everyone in it is trying on wedding dresses. There are people crying with happy tears all over the place. Except in cubicle number four, where there's a lot of squeezing and poking of flesh to desperately make a dress fit. As much as I'm rooting for the poor girl, matching front-and-back cleavage is never attractive.

'Ta-daa!' says Henri.

Oh my. I clasp my hand to my mouth in shock. Henri has quite the dress on.

'You look like a princess,' I say, gasping.

She does. Like an actual princess. I wonder if I can describe it in a way that makes it sound as beautiful as it looks in the flesh. It is exquisite. The dress has a strapless bodice that leads into an explosion of tulle and taffeta in a big, massive bouffant. She spins round and I can see the train that's gathered behind it. It has a train! The dress has a gold-orange hue to it and it sets off Henri's auburn hair brilliantly. I know you've probably got some sort of mental image of a Big Fat Gypsy Wedding dress, but it's miles away from that.

'I think this is the one,' she says excitedly.

I stand up and grab the price tag. It's only £599, with a recommended retail price of £1,995. Even with my rubbish maths, I can work out that that equals a bargain. And whilst I'd probably have thought that Henri could have got a cheaper dress elsewhere, for a designer-label queen like her, nothing else would have done.

'Try on the Armani I picked out, just in case,' I say, just because it's Armani and under £600. God, I love TK Maxx. I must remember to have a quick look at the shoes as we're here. I mean, if something has sixty percent off, it doesn't really count as being naughty, does it?

By the time we leave the shop two hours later, Henri has not only bought herself a wedding dress, the first one she tried on, but she's also purchased three bridesmaid dresses. I did advise her against buying bridesmaid dresses without the girls trying them on first but, as she pointed out, her sister and her niece weren't going to be in the UK until a week before the wedding, and her friend Liz would apparently wear what she was given. And with Henri and her hypnotic eye powers, I don't doubt that.

The bridesmaids dresses were an absolute bargain and, all in all, totting up the RRPs, Henri saved over £1,500.

And it wasn't only Henri that got a bargain. I bought a pair of Kurt Geiger heels for under thirty pounds. Mark will be very proud as I did desperately want a pair of Chloé wedges but, despite them being £300 cheaper than usual, they were still over a hundred. I'm not out of the doghouse quite enough yet to be splashing out on expensive designer shoes.

Henri's dress is so big and awkward that we treat ourselves to a taxi back to Waterloo. Well, we did just save all that cash on the dresses and shoes.

'Thanks so much for that, Penny. I can't believe what just happened. I mean, you actually made my dreams come true. When Nick told me we'd have to plan the wedding on a . . . you know, the first thing I thought was that I wouldn't be able to have a wedding dress that would make everyone gasp with amazement. But you found me one, Penny. I'm going to be a princess.'

'A princess on a shoestring,' I laugh.

'Exactly. Penny, you know you're wasted in your day job, don't you? I mean, I think you were made to be a wedding planner.'

'Thanks, Henri. But you know, I really enjoy working in HR.'

Or at least, I usually enjoy working in HR. I haven't liked it so much lately, but that's because I'm busting my balls trying to prove myself to Giles. But it's my career; it's what I do.

'I know you probably do, but you've got a real gift for weddings. I heard you talking to that bride-to-be and her mother about the veil ideas as I was trying on the Armani.'

I can feel my cheeks going pink with the praise. I don't naturally like to be complimented; I'm far too British for that.

'I just get ideas from when I write blogs. It's not hard if you learn to look in the right places.'

'But that's the thing, Penny, people don't know where to look. I mean, I'd never in a million years have known that TK Maxx did wedding dresses.'

'It's pretty new—'

'But you'd heard about it. Have you not thought of setting up a wedding planning business properly, rather than just the odd wedding?'

'Not really. I mean, professional wedding planners charge big fees and have their work cut out for them.'

'Yes, but I'm sure you could do different packages. Maybe you could tailor it. I mean, most fancy-pants wedding planners are there to make the day run smoothly; to orchestrate the day itself. What you seem to be best at is all the stuff beforehand: negotiating the discounts and finding the budget way to do things. Maybe you don't need to be there on the actual day. You could set it up so it runs itself like a wedding without a planner.'

'Maybe.' My mind's whirring at the thought of running Princess-on-a-Shoestring full time. Imagine getting to see women's face's light up as they find their in-budget dream dress on a frequent basis. And then I think back to Mark. He hates my wedding blog. I think whenever he thinks of me and my obsession with weddings, he can't help but think of my gambling, and who can blame him? I lost £10,000 playing bingo in order to try and buy a Vera Wang wedding dress.

And it's not like it's a *Dragon's Den* idea, is it? I mean, it's not a viable money option. From £1,000 fees, I'd have to plan thirty weddings a year to make the same amount I do now. That's potentially thirty bridezillas: imagine.

'You should think about it. If you ever wanted an investment to set it up, then I'm sure I could talk to my father about it. He's always looking for opportunities to invest in.'

Henri hasn't really talked much about her father before. I know she's very close to her mother and that her parents divorced when she was young.

'I'll bear it in mind. So, is your father excited about the wedding?'

'I think so. Although, I'm quite scared about him coming. He likes the finer things in life and he'll judge it based on how expensive it looks.'

'Could he not have given you any money?'

Henri shakes her head. 'He offered to pay for the whole thing when we first announced our engagement, but I refused and told him Nick and I wanted to do it on our own. My dad keeps trying to make up for the divorce by throwing money at things. Take my lovely shoes and my designer clothes. He sends them to me regularly, even though I tell him not to because, to be honest, I'd much rather just see him for lunch instead. But he's always out of the country or, if he's in the country, then he's too busy.'

I don't think I'd mind not seeing my dad as often if he sent me current season Miu Mius. But then again, given the option between not seeing my dad and the Miu Mius, I'd probably pick my dad. Or at least, I'm ninety percent sure I would.

'Of course, I refused before Nick told me we were going to do it on a budget.'

'Would you have taken the money if you'd known about the budget before?'

'No, I don't think so. But the problem is that now this wedding will be a reflection on Nick and how successful he is. I don't want my dad to suspect that we're not as well off as we should be.'

We're stuck on a bridge across the Thames, and Henri looks out of the window of the cab at it. I'm about to launch into a spiel that sometimes it's better to get everything out in the open and to tell her my experiences of how nice it was to be truthful with Mark and both of our families, but I manage to stop myself in time. I desperately want to confide in her as I know from personal experience how much it helps in these situations. It's all right for us addicts; we have our support group to help us through. Yet our loved ones have just as much crap to go through and who do they have to turn to? I often joke with Mark that he should set up his own 'I-married-a-gambler' support group.

'We'll just have to make sure that your dad doesn't realise that it didn't cost many magic beans then,' I say.

Henri smiles at me and, right there, I see the sadness in her eyes, which is the true cost of what gambling debt does.

'Thanks, Penny. I don't know what I would have done without you.'

In that single moment, the crazy phone calls and the hourly emails all seem worth it. Sure, to an outsider, Henri might just have a few bridezilla overtones but, then again, I've yet to find a bride who doesn't have a slight whiff of it at one point or another.

It's also the first time that I feel I've connected with Henri on a non-business level. She's far from the self-assured, confident woman she usually is.

'It's going to be an amazing wedding, just you wait and see. It will even knock your dad's socks off.'

I make a mental note to remind myself in the week to

sort out some catering options for her wedding as, at the moment, all we've got is a lot of hungry guests. The same wave of fear washes over my body that I had when I was planning my own wedding in a bit of a hurry, but then I take a deep breath. Mine all worked out just fine, didn't it? There's absolutely no reason Henri's won't as well. I've just got to keep all thoughts of her father out of my head; for some reason he's morphed into an *EastEnders* baddie. I won't let Henri's dad get under my skin at all.

chapter ten

princess-on-a-shoestring cost cutter:
Saver Favours Part 1

Almost always the cheapest option for wedding favours is to make them yourself in the form of an edible treat. This option is not for the faint-hearted as you usually need to prepare them a day or two ahead of your wedding or entrust one of your nearest and dearest with the task. Great favourites for this are homemade fudge (just watch out as each batch needs a lot of stirring and is quite time-consuming!), gingerbread hearts or shortbread. Head online to find the cheapest packaging and ribbon. If you want to be extra savvy, you can tie name labels onto the favours and then you've got your place settings and favours in one.

Tags: favours, food, edible, cheapskate.

I glance nervously at my outfit and wonder if I should have put something other than my jeans and baggy jumper on. I definitely wouldn't get stopped in the street today for one of those stylish-on-the-high-street photoshoots for a magazine. I don't usually have such little self-confidence but I feel like I've been transported back to my teenage years as I walk through the gates of the local college.

My favourite little delinquent missed the group session last night. I didn't want go through another week of us not speaking, so I made her agree to meet me today, hence why I'm walking into her college at lunchtime. It wouldn't usually be my first choice of venue, but I figure that if Mohammed won't come to the mountain, then the mountain will come to him.

I uneasily navigate my way through the corridors, trying to avoid the students as much as I can. They don't give me too many 'she's far too old to be here looks' as I know the college does a huge range of courses, including ones for mature students. But still there's enough of the young uns to make me feel dowdy, old and uncool.

I catch sight of Beth sitting on a bench near the reception and I smile with relief.

'Hi, Beth,' I say, giving her an embarrassing mum-type wave as I approach.

She looks up from her mobile and gives me a look of

horror as if she might be worried that people might see that I'm with her.

'Hey,' she says without making eye contact.

'Everything OK?'

'I guess.'

More shrugging. Jeez, Josh had a walk in the park with me in comparison. I used to blurt out exactly what I was feeling.

'So, do you want to grab some food? Have you eaten?' I ask.

'No, not yet. We can go to the refectory, if you like.'

I think back to the food when I was at college. I can almost taste the microwaved jacket potatoes, with chewy skins and lukewarm beans; it makes me shudder.

'Are there any other options?' I secretly hope colleges have gone up market since I was at mine and perhaps now they have a Costa buried in the middle of them.

'There's the fancy restaurant.'

There we go! That sounds perfect.

'Great, shall we go there?'

'It's quite expensive.'

'How expensive?' I ask.

'It's eight pounds for three courses. The people on professional catering courses cook it.'

'Three courses? Eight pounds?' I repeat.

'Uh-huh.'

'That sounds like a bargain to me. How about I treat you?'

'S'pose that would be OK.'

I can see a hint of a smile on Beth's face, but it's only a flicker before she goes back into sulky teenager mode.

Beth leads us upstairs, to what looks just how she described it: a fancy restaurant. After enquiring about a table, we're taken to one in the corner.

'Wow,' I say, reading the menu in disbelief.

'It's supposed to be pretty good,' says Beth. 'I think the chefs go on to work in top restaurants.'

'Amazing,' I say, as I try and decide whether to go with the salmon with Thai chilli dressing or the pork in Calvados with apples.

'So, have you given any more thought to what you're going to do when you leave? Are you going to apply to university?'

'I think that's what my mum wants,' says Beth.

I can't believe it. She's put her mobile away in her pocket and she's actually looking up at me.

'But is that what you want?'

Beth shrugs. 'I guess so. I mean, it's easier to get a job when you've got a degree.'

I try not to wince at this comment. After spending the last few weeks sorting out the graduate scheme, I'm not entirely sure that that statement rings true.

ANNA BELL

'What course would you want to do?' I ask, steering the conversation away from jobs.

'I haven't really given it much thought.'

Just when I think I'm getting somewhere, I feel like we're back to pulling teeth. I wonder if this was what I was like as a teenager? No wonder my mother used to despair; I barely spoke to her between the ages of fifteen and eighteen.

'What subjects are you doing now?'

'English Lit, Media Studies, History, Psychology and Politics.'

'Wow. Are you some type of super-genius?'

'No, everyone takes five AS-Levels, I drop two subjects next year.'

'What are you dropping?'

'Politics and Psychology, they're well hard.'

The thought of taking either sends shivers down my spine. I can't quite blame Beth for dropping them.

'Would you not want to do one of your other subjects at uni?'

Beth shrugs again. 'I like English.'

'There you go!' I say a little too enthusiastically. 'I think that would be lovely. A nice, solid degree.'

'Ha, you sound like my mum.'

'I guess that's what happens when you're as old as me.'

Beth stifles a laugh and before I continue with my comic

154

genius, the waiter comes up and takes our order. I settle on an onion and goats cheese tart to start, followed by the pork and then we'll decide on the dessert later. Not a bad lunch for a dreary Wednesday lunchtime. It beats the salad sandwich that I probably would have had in the canteen at work.

'Have you been looking at any courses yet? You know, seeing what grades you're going to need for them, what facilities they've got there?'

Beth's fidgeting more than Mark's four-year-old niece.

'A little. I've got a meeting with our careers advisor before the end of term, so I'm sure they'll help.'

'Great.' I think that Beth is probably seeing right through my plan, and she clearly doesn't want to tell me about her plans. I mean, if I think back to my murky youth, I picked my university based on how new the student union was, and the ratio of men to women. I wanted good odds of being able to have a drunken snog on a night out.

I decide to change the subject to what we're really here for.

'So, are you having any luck with trying to stop the gambling?'

I figure there's no point in beating around the bush. She's fidgeting in a way that suggests she's just as uncomfortable with this line of questioning as she was when we were talking about the future.

'Yes.'

I'm not sure I believe her. She's exhibiting all the trademark signs of lying. She's looking round the room and avoiding all eye contact.

'So you've gone cold turkey? No more Vegas games?'

I have to admit that, when Mary first told me that Beth was addicted to Vegas games, I had no idea what they were. The only Vegas games that sprung to my mind were the kind that Prince Harry played – strip billiards. But it turned out that it didn't involve any removal of clothing, and instead it was playing casino games on your computer or mobile. It seems that Beth had a particular weakness for both slot machines and roulette.

That's why everyone was so worried when Beth had visited an actual casino, as there was that fear that she could go somewhere and pay in cash without there being paper trails. I know I can't talk as I played online bingo, which is as synthetic and contrived as you can probably get, but I can't imagine what buzz you'd get from playing a virtual slot machine.

'Really?' I say. 'No gambling at all? Not in any way? I'm not just talking about on your phone. No playing on the fruit machines when you're out? No playing pub quiz games?'

'Pub quiz games? You mean like The Colour of Money? They're not gambling, are they? Everyone plays them.'

Before the steam comes out of my ears, the starters have arrived. I start to salivate as the waiter puts down the plates. They look like they could have come out of a gourmet restaurant, not from a local college.

'This looks amazing,' I say.

'Yeah,' says Beth.

At least we have food in common, that's something.

'Going back to the quiz machines, do you play them?' I ask as I take my first delicious forkful of food.

'Yeah, when I'm in the pub. I never thought they were gambling.'

'Well, anything that involves inserting money in order to play with the possibility that you'll get more or less money back than you started with, is gambling.'

'I hadn't really thought about it like that,' she says, through a mouthful of pâté on toast. I would have had major food envy if my goat's cheese tart wasn't so delicious.

'OK, so let's put that aside because you didn't realise they were gambling. What about fruit machines, have you been playing those?'

'Only with my mates, not on my own.'

'Have you had any more visits to the casino?' I think a week of prepping for the graduate interviews has left me in interrogation mode; I'm taking no prisoners now.

'No,' she says, shaking her head. 'Mum's given me a curfew and my friends go to the casino after I'm in.'

'Do your friends know about your problem?'

'I don't have a problem. They all do it too. I'm just the only one that got caught.'

'Really? All your friends do it? All your friends rack up £5,000 on their mum's credit card?'

'Well, no, but maybe they don't lose as much as I do.'

'No one's that lucky, Beth. I'm guessing they perhaps dabble, but they don't play as much as you. I mean, how many hours a day would you spend playing?'

Beth shrugged. 'Depends, really.'

'On a normal day. Let's just say that in my hey-day of bingo, I'd play an hour a night at least every night. Sometimes two hours.'

'OK. I'd play usually between lessons. If I had ten minutes to spare, maybe in my break times.'

'What about hanging out with your friends?' I'm slightly aware that post-nineties teenagers don't 'hang out', but I'm not up to speed with the new lingo.

'Not all my friends have breaks at the same time.'

'So you do it when you're lonely?'

Beth shrugs again. I bite my tongue not to shout at her in frustration, but I instead take the shrug as a yes.

Our waiter appears and removes our plates, and I wait for him to leave before continuing.

'Why don't we talk about why you started to gamble in the first place? When was your first time?'

I feel like a cross between an agony aunt and a slightly embarrassing mum so I try to remind myself that we're talking about gambling rather than boys.

'I dunno.'

'Come on,' I say with a hint of frustration. 'You must remember the first buzz.'

'It was a slots. I saw an advert as a pop-up on the computer and I clicked on it. I've always wanted to go to Vegas, and I guess I thought I'd see what it was all about.'

'That's it? There was nothing else special about that day?'

'I was bored. I was waiting for my dad. He was, like, a few hours late to pick me up.'

Finally I feel like I'm learning something real about her. I can see how her disappointment at her father letting her down might lead her to gambling.

'Do you gamble a lot when you're bored?'

'I suppose so.'

'Can't you fill your time on Facebook instead?'

'Yeah, I used to play games on Facebook, too. Bejewelled Blitz and that kind of stuff.'

'And you just saw the Vegas games as an extension of that?'

'I guess so.'

By the time our main courses arrive, we're actually getting somewhere.

'Beth, I know this is a bit blunt, but do you actually want to stop gambling? I mean, do you realise how big a problem it is?'

'It pisses my mum off.'

'Right, but what about with you? I mean, you could have landed yourself in real debt and that would have really impacted on your future. It could have made it difficult for you to get bank accounts, a mortgage when you're older. It could even have made you more likely to get involved in crime.'

I may be overreacting slightly, but I've been doing research on teenage gambling, and they reckon that about six percent of teenagers have a gambling addiction, and those teens are far more likely to turn to crime to support their habit.

'I haven't hurt anyone,' says Beth. 'I've just been playing some games. I didn't mean to upset my mum and I'm not going to be nicking stuff, if that's what you're saying.'

'No, I just meant that it could lead there, if you don't get it under control. We've got to get you to stop playing. Do you not find it helps to come along to the group and listen to other people's stories?'

'I guess, but everyone else has had these big problems, and I don't think mine is the same.'

I feel like Beth and I are continuously taking one step forward and two steps back. She's just about admitted that she's got a problem, and yet she can't really understand the ramifications of what she's done.

It's really frustrating for me as I've lived this. I know how easily these habits can spiral out of control and ruin everything. I came so close to losing Mark last year, but so many of the other gamblers in our group have lost a lot more. Some did lose partners, houses, or life-savings like Nick did. But Beth is so young, and she doesn't really feel the consequences of her gambling. It was her mum's money she lost, not hers.

'Look, I'll stop playing the games. I won't play the fruities or the game machines in the pub. Yeah?'

'That would be great,' I say, knowing full well that it's an empty promise. It's exactly what I used to be like when I was a teenager, I would have said anything my mum wanted to hear just to have an easy life.

The problem with gambling is that it's dead hard giving up even if you want to, and it's a hundred times worse if you don't. And it doesn't go away when you stop either. Although it landed me in a whole lot of trouble, even now I'm sometimes tempted to escape to a bingo site and get lost in the games and the banter of the chat rooms.

'I've got to go. Thanks for lunch, I've got English now.'

Beth gets up and grabs her bag.

'I'll see you on Tuesday?' I say hopefully.

'Yeah, I should be there.'

I watch Beth as she hurries out of the restaurant and the waiter swoops in to clear our plates.

'That was absolutely delicious,' I say.

'That's good to hear. I'll let the chefs know.'

'Yes, please do. Tell them I thought it was cooked by professionals. Do you do this every lunchtime?'

'We do it three days a week and then Tuesday and Thursday nights.'

'You do it at night?'

'Yeah, only it's twelve pounds a head.'

I smile at the students describing a three-course meal and thinking it's expensive at twelve pounds. Maybe I'll bring Mark here the next time it's my turn to pay for dinner. What? That's not being tight, that's just me being a savvy-saver. Mark would probably be dead proud.

'That's great. So do you do other things with the catering? I mean, do you cater events?'

'We do, occasionally. College events, balls and fundraising dinners.'

'What about weddings?'

That food was seriously as good as the food I've had at any a reception.

'I think so, but I don't know too much about it.'

'Is there someone I could talk to about it?'

'I could get the tutor to come and talk to you if you like?'

'Perfect,' I say.

'I'll ask him to come and see you. Now, have you made up your mind about the dessert? If your friend isn't coming back you get to have hers too . . .'

By the time I get back to the office, after my slightly longer than usual lunch break, I feel a bit sick, but in a full up with lovely food way. I had an Amaretto cheesecake and a chocolate mousse. I know I probably should have just had the one, but I am, after all, a self-confessed pig if food is in front of me.

'Henri, it's me. I might have found us a caterer.'

I pull the phone away from my ear as I hear a scream of delight.

'Tell me more,' she says.

'Well, how about you pop round and see me tonight and I can talk you through it as I'm at work.'

'Fabulous, I'll see you at around seven? The suspense is going to kill me.'

'All will be revealed,' I say, giggling.

I hang up the phone just as I turn the corner into our office and I bump straight into Giles.

'Ah, Penny. There you are, I was just looking for you.'

My cheeks flush as I've probably been away from my desk for a noticeably long absence.

'Is everything OK?' I ask.

'I've just got off the phone with an engineer in the Design Department and he wants to report that one of his colleagues is running another business in company time. I'm going to need you to investigate it with me. I'm not up to scratch with current legislation in the UK for dismissal, so I want you to lead on this. I'll be overseeing it, of course.'

My mouth drops open. Giles's view on moonlighting has put me in a state of shock.

chapter eleven

princess-on-a-shoestring top tips:
DIY Wedding Items

This might sound like I'm telling you to suck eggs, but don't leave your DIY wedding items until the last minute. The day before your wedding is going to be stressful enough making sure everything's delivered to the venue, and that you're pampered, preened and ready for the big day. You don't want to be printing orders of service or writing place names before you go to bed. If you can, get all the stuff you're making out the way early on. Give yourself deadlines and if it looks like you're going to struggle to get it done in time, ask for help. It's better to find out three weeks in advance that you need an extra pair of hands rather than the day before. For more inspiration on just what you can make, check out my DIY section.

Tags: wedding, organisation, planning.

I open the door of our terrace and I immediately hear cackling. My heckles rise. Just who is Mark entertaining? All I want to do is have a long, hot soak and watch *Keeping up with the Kardashians*. It's been a long afternoon of meetings and investigations into the moonlighter.

'Pen, is that you?'

I'm about to reply no and ask him just who else he thinks has a key, but I realise I'm just being mean and tired.

'Yep,' I call out instead.

Mark walks out of the kitchen door. He still makes me swoon sometimes when I see him. Tonight he's dressed in a work shirt, no tie and he has a tea-towel slung over his shoulder. He comes over and gives me a kiss on the head.

'Henri's here, I've just served her up some dinner. I wasn't sure what time you were going to be back, and you weren't answering your phone.'

'Oh my God, Henri! I'd forgotten that I'd asked her over. Has she been here long?'

With all the meetings and investigations into the woman running her own company, Henri coming over had completely slipped my mind.

'About half an hour.'

'Mark, I'm so sorry,' I whisper.

'Don't be, it's fine. We've been having a chat.'

'Great.' I'm wondering just what they've been talking about, but as long as he doesn't mind that I've left him alone with a crazy bridezilla then I'm happy.

'Hi, Henri, I'm so sorry to have kept you waiting,' I say, walking into the kitchen. Henri's sat digging into what looks and smells like fish pie.

'Don't apologise, Mark has been keeping me fed and watered. Tell me, is Mark the catering option for the wedding? Because, seriously, this fish pie is to die for.'

'If only. At one point I thought about trying to get Mark to cater our wedding, but it's a bit much to get the groom to do it!'

'That's a shame. But your food sounded wonderful, Mark's been telling me all about it.'

'Just the food?' I say, my voice a little shaky.

'About the wedding in general.'

I look up to Mark and I guess he understands what I'm hinting at.

'I was telling Henri how you thought it would be sweet to organise the wedding as a surprise for me. And I was telling her about the little details that made it memorable.'

I breathe a sigh of relief. For a minute I thought Mark might have mentioned my little faux pas with the gambling and my real need for the 'don't tell the groom'. It might have been a bit too close to home for Henri.

'It sounds like a lovely idea. I'd have loved to have done something similar for Nick, but he does like to know everything that's going on. Keeps an eye on just what I'm up to. Not in a scary doesn't-let-me-do-anything kind of a way though!' she says laughing.

'Of course not,' I say, suppressing a smile. I can't imagine that any man could stop Henri doing what she wanted. It does, however, make me think that perhaps she doesn't realise what an effect her puppy-dog eyes have on him. Perhaps, I'll keep that as another one of his secrets.

'So, Pen, what's the big mystery? Henri and I have been guessing.'

I look up at Mark and wonder who this man is and what he's done with my husband. Clearly Henri's magic works on more men than just Nick. Mark's interest in my wedding planning is practically non-existent 'So, today I went for lunch at the college.'

'What were you doing there?' laughs Henri.

Oh, shit. What was I doing there? I would have thought with all the lying I'd done last year that I'd be able to think on my feet, but I really can't.

'I was . . . I was meeting with one of the tutors; we're thinking of helping them with an insight into industry day. You know, get some workers to go in and get the students interested in business.'

Wow, I've impressed myself, and actually that isn't a bad idea. It would make a nice little puff piece for the local rag, they always love those kind of 'big business does good' stories. Maybe I'll suggest that to Giles, once the moonlighter situation has calmed down. I imagine Giles would like the idea; it's right up his street. Who knows, it could get me a step closer to the promotion.

'That sounds great, is that all part of Operation Brown Nose?' asks Mark.

'What's that?' asks Henri.

'Penny's up for a big promotion at work.'

'Penny, that's amazing. Why didn't you say?'

I'd like to say that it's because I can't get a word in edgeways with Henri and her wedding talk. But, if I'm being honest, it's because when I'm with Henri and talking weddings I forget all about my actual life and it's as if they're completely separate. And I love the planning so much that I almost don't let the HR stuff, and the real world, intrude. Instead, I pretend I'm a full-time wedding planner.

'Penny's probably being modest,' says Mark before I can answer for myself. Mark is positively beaming and he looks so proud of me. I feel a bit guilty about all the time I'm spending *not* working towards the promotion. 'Well, Penny, good luck.'

'Thanks, so I was saying,' I say, desperately trying to change the subject as I don't want to think about work any longer. 'I had dinner at the college and the food was divine.'

'Really?' says both Mark and Henri in a way that suggests that I said that I tucked into to a meal of contaminated needles.

'Yeah, they have this fancy restaurant on the top floor and basically the trainee chefs on the catering courses cook the food, so you get amazing quality really cheap. I had three courses,' I say. I wonder if, technically, I had four courses as I did have two desserts. We'll just ignore that, Mark doesn't have to know everything. 'And it came to eight pounds.'

'Wow, that's great value,' says Henri.

'Yeah, it really was. I had the most delicious pork in brandy dish.'

If I wasn't currently eating a yummy fish pie, I'd probably be wishing I was still tucking into it. Quite how I am still eating after the amount I ate at lunch, is anyone's guess. I had meant to phone Mark this afternoon to let him know not to cook for me but, like most of my plans for the day, they got swept into oblivion after I spoke to Giles.

'So come on, what has that got to do with my wedding food?' asks Henri impatiently. 'Are the college going to do my food?'

'No,' I say, shaking my head. 'I spoke to the course tutor to see whether they could cater your wedding, but they can't do it. Something to do with insurance; they're only covered to prepare food on the college campus, so unless you want to have your wedding there, they couldn't do it.'

'Please tell me that this story has a happy ending, or else I'm going to force your husband to cook us fish pie on the day,' says Henri, pointing her fork menacingly at Mark.

'The tutor told me that although the college couldn't do it, he could. Apparently he runs a small catering company on the side: he's the chef and he often uses a couple of the students as his sous-chefs. It just means that the costs are slightly lower than they would be through a mainstream catering company. He also gets a lot of his students to do the silver service as well.'

'Isn't that like child labour?' asks Mark, laughing.

'I think he called it CV building. And at least he's paying them and not calling it an internship,' I say.

Mark nods. Of course he does, he knows his wife is always right.

'OK, do you think they'd be up to the job? I mean, students . . .' says Henri.

'I thought you might be a little sceptical.'

Actually, I thought Henri would be a lot sceptical, and that she would need much more convincing. But she's making fewer wrinkle noses than I thought she would.

'So, we could go and try the food there. We could either go for lunch, or they do dinner on Tuesdays or Thursdays. Then we could have a proper chat with Brett the tutor and you can see what you think.'

'Ooh, great. Tomorrow, then? Can we do tomorrow?'

'Um, I'd love to but we've got Lou and Russell, our friends, coming over for dinner. How about next week?'

'Do you think we can wait until then? I mean, it isn't long until the big day.'

'No, I guess it isn't.'

'Maybe Lou and Russell would want to come along too, it could be fun,' says Mark.

Hang on a minute, does Mark think he's invited? I'd only intended it to be Henri and me.

'Um, I thought it would just be me and Henri, you know, as it would be boring talking about wedding stuff and sorting out details with the caterer.'

'Nonsense,' says Henri, waving her fork around in a much less threatening way. 'It would be so much better if everyone came along. We need all the guinea pigs we can get! And I'm sure your friends won't mind.'

'But what about Lou and Russell getting a babysitter? I told them they could bring Harry to sleep upstairs.'

'Pen, you know as well as I do that Lou's mother always babysits at the drop of a hat.'

I shoot Mark an evil look, which he misses as he's started to clear away the plates. He obviously doesn't know that I'm trying to see as little of Henri and Nick together in order to preserve my nerves. But there's a bigger problem. Nick appeared in my very public apology video. I made Mark a video where I discussed my gambling habit and then other people in my gambling group, including Nick, told their gambling stories in order to help him understand what I had been going through. I just don't want Mark to recognise Nick and say something publicly. Ideally, I didn't want Mark and Nick to meet at all, only now Henri and Mark have become new BFFs. This is just perfect.

'Great, so that's your friends sorted. Do we need to phone and book ahead?'

'I think so.' Perhaps I could pretend I've phoned and they're fully booked, but Henri jumps in.

'Right, well I'll phone first thing when I get into work tomorrow and reserve us a table. What time shall we say, seven p.m., or do you think a little later might be better? You know, for your friends with the baby. They might want to put him to bed first, mightn't they?'

Get Henri thinking about the baby's routine.

'Um, I think maybe I should give Lou a call to check that her mum can babysit and—'

'I'm sure with Lou and Russell's rocking social life with the baby that, even if they couldn't get a babysitter, they wouldn't mind rescheduling until Friday night,' says Mark.

'Great, so I'll say a table for four possibly six then, at eight p.m. Oh, I can't wait.'

I look between Henri and Mark and I wonder what has gone on without me. I feel a bit uneasy that we've changed Lou and Russell's social plans without them being consulted. I know Mark is right and that, since baby Harry arrived, they haven't really been out much in the evenings. But I feel a bit annoyed that Mark and Henri think they can rearrange their evening without a second thought.

'I suppose I'll phone Lou then,' I say sulkily. I'm too tired to assert any control over this situation. Anyone would think Henri was the wedding planner, not me. In fact, if she only turned her bossiness and hypnotic control into wedding planning, she'd have this whole thing whipped into shape in no time. It's moments like this that I find it strange that she's using me at all.

'Right then, now all that is sorted, I'd best get home to Nick. Mark, I'd love for you to meet him, you'll get on like a house on fire. I just know that you'll have loads in common.'

More than you can ever imagine, I think to myself.

'Can't wait,' says Mark.

Blimey, Henri is a hypnotist. I often have to drag Mark out to meet new people. He was practically kicking and screaming the time we went to Lou's house to meet the new friends they'd met at NCT classes. He'd huffed around the house all weekend and then, when he got there, he'd had a really great time. All the guys did was talk about sports, apparently. It was me that should have been dreading it. All that talk of nipple shields and stitches, it was enough to put me off having babies. In fact, maybe that's why I haven't become pregnant; maybe my uterus was scarred for life.

'I'm sorry again, Henri, for not being here when you arrived. I promise I'll be on time tomorrow night.'

'Don't worry at all. And I'll look forward to tomorrow. I'll just have to find something to wear. When you say fancy, just how fancy are we talking? A little black dress or is it more smart jeans and a nice top?'

I walk Henri out of the kitchen and down the hall to the front door, not really listening to her prattle on. For all I know, she is talking about pigeon racing I'm that tired. I'm almost surprised I'm not seeing two of her.

'I'm glad we've got that sorted then. See you tomorrow.'

I tune into the end of the conversation as Henri air kisses

me goodbye and I hope that means that we've sorted out her wardrobe dilemma.

'So, she seems nice,' says Mark as I walk back into the kitchen. I slump down again on a chair and watch Mark stack the dishwasher. I'd usually do it when he's cooked, but look how neatly he's stacking it, and he's doing all the pre-washing of the plates so they won't get crusty bits. I can't possibly interrupt that.

'Yeah, the more I've got to know her, the sweeter she seems.'

'She's not at all what I pictured, I somehow imagined her to be highly strung.'

I almost say give her time, but instead I just murmur a yes.

'I hope this Nick guy's all right. At least Russell will be there too.'

Nick. My stomach is starting to churn a little uneasily. It could be something to do with the fact that I've eaten three days'-worth of food in the space of about six hours, but I think it's more likely to be because I'm feeling uncomfortable about lying to Mark. I mean, surely he'll recognise him instantly and make the connection. Deep down, I know I should care more about trust in my relationship with my husband but, for some reason, I can't seem to bring myself to tell him. Is it better that I tell him the truth now so that he can preserve the illusion to Henri that we don't know the secret?

'He's a really nice guy,' I say, meaning it. After all, he was there for me last year when I needed him.

I open my mouth to tell him, but then I close it again. I could be worrying about nothing, after all, I have to remind Mark constantly who's who when it comes to my friends' boyfriends. Is Richie the guy with the pit bull? No, that's Robert, I'll reply, Richie is the guy with the vegetable patch. And I've met him? Mark will ask, despite the fact we'll have gone to their house for dinner the month before.

Yes, I'm worrying over nothing. There's no way that Mark will remember Nick from the video he saw once, under duress, on the day of our wedding. I'm sure he had much bigger things to concentrate on than Nick.

I hope Lou and Russell can come. It would certainly take a lot of the heat out of the situation.

'So, how come you were late home from work? Still working on that graduate scheme?'

'I wish,' I say like an involuntary spasm. 'An engineer tipped us off that one of his colleagues has been running a business during office hours and Giles wants me to handle the investigation.'

'That's great,' says Mark.

I'm trying not to laugh at the fact that he's turned round from the washing up and he's wearing my Marigolds.

'Yeah, it is. From what I can tell, it seems that this woman, Indy, has been running an Italian cheese importation business.' I can't believe that after everything I've eaten today, talking about it is making me crave cheese. 'It's just really tricky trying to prove that she's been working on it whilst she's in the office. And we have to do it in secret because if she gets an inkling about what we're up to then she'll probably cover her tracks.'

'Sounds very cloak and dagger.'

'I know, it is. Giles thinks, from what the engineer has told us, that it's ground for instant dismissal, so we've got to make sure that we have everything checked and in place before we confront her.'

'Giles doesn't take any prisoners, does he?'

'No,' I say, feeling slightly sick that he would take a dim view on my wedding planning too if he found out. But it's not like I'm in Indy's league. I mean, I only have one client and I'm not in contact with her very often when I'm at work.

'When's the big confrontation going to happen then?'

'Probably later in the week, or early next week. Giles wants to strike while the iron is hot.'

'Hopefully this will score you some brownie points for the promotion.'

'I hope so.'

Mark comes over and gives me a kiss on the top of the head and I realise how lucky I am to have such a lovely husband. I haven't spent nearly enough time with him lately.

'Are you going to be all right to come tomorrow night, or do you think you'll be late home from work again?'

Tomorrow night. I'd almost forgotten that. The thought that Mark might realise I've lied about Nick turns my stomach.

'Yes, I'm sure it will be fine.' Hoping against hope that it will.

chapter twelve

princess-on-a-shoestring top tips:
Food Glorious Food

The first rule of wedding catering is that you will probably never please everyone. There's always going to be someone who only eats green beans or fish fingers. If your venue offers food choices like a hot or cold buffet, then that's a great way of catering to different tastes. Likewise, a hog roast with different vegetable and salad options often goes down well. No matter what you have, people will judge you on your food choices so don't worry about it. As long as you and your fiancé like the food, then that should be good enough!

Tags: food, wedding breakfast, judgemental guests.

'Hey, lovely. Wow, look at you all dressed up,' I say gawping at my best friend who is tottering across the college car park in a little red dress and killer heels. You would never have guessed that she had a whopper of a baby last July. Flipping heck, in a line-up trying to work out who's given birth, you'd pick my pot-belly first off.

I'm feeling slightly like the eighth and ninth dwarves who, in my head, are Frumpy and Dumpy. I got back from work late, again, and I didn't have time to wash my hair or shower. So with hair that hadn't been washed for two days slicked back into a severe bun (with generous helpings of dry shampoo), I slipped on a pair of skinny jeans, a lacy top and ballet pumps. Now I wish I'd made more of an effort.

'Hiya, I've finally reached my goal weight, so thought I'd show it off.'

'Well, you'd better be careful with Russell later, or you'll be making another baby. Look at him, his tongue is practically hanging out,' I say as I link arms with Lou and walk into the college, leaving the boys to catch up behind us.

'There's no chance of that. One baby in the household is plenty at the moment, thank you very much. Speaking of which, any luck with you?' asks Lou.

I shake my head.

'Don't worry, Pen, there's always next month.'

I bite my lip a little. If anyone else says that to me, I

might actually punch them. Yes, there is always next month, but the agonising wait for that month between periods is awful. Spending four weeks hoping that you're about to embark on the most special time of your life only to discover that, yet again, you're not pregnant, well, it's heartbreaking.

'Yes, next month,' I say, hoping that will be the end of the conversation. 'So, I'm excited about you meeting Henri, she's really lovely.'

'From what you've told me about her already, I'm surprised that you're not introducing her to Jane, it sounds like they'd get on like a house on fire.'

'I know. Mark did text Phil to see if they wanted to come, but apparently she's not going out of a fifteen-mile radius of her doctor, and we're just too far out here!'

'Oh, the horror!' says Lou, laughing. 'She's only, what? Six months' pregnant?'

'Seven months, so she's worried that the baby could come prematurely.'

'But even if she did go into labour this early she'd have loads of time before she needed to see her doctor. She could go to Birmingham and back!'

'I know that, Mark knows that and Phil knows that, but we all know what Jane is like.'

Neurotic and a complete snob. I'm sure she'd have fainted

if Phil had suggested she visit the local hospital here in an emergency.

'I guess that's true,' agrees Lou.

'There's Henri.'

I spot her a mile off in the lobby and now I really feel underdressed. She's dressed in a little blue lace dress that wouldn't look out of place if she was going for dinner somewhere fancy in London.

My stomach's starting to tie itself up in knots as this is the moment that I've been dreading: Mark and Nick meeting.

'Ah, Penny,' says Henri doing a delicate feminine hand-wave. It's the kind of handwave people do when they go to the opera or they're trying to be discreet. It's the polar opposite of the handwave I'm doing that makes me look like I'm an over-excited toddler who is in danger of wetting her pants after having spotted Peppa Pig across the room.

'Henri,' I say as we get close enough to air kiss.

I ignore the fact she gives Mark a massive hug, and she pauses in front of Lou and Russell for an introduction, which I give.

'Nick's just gone out to make a work call,' says Henri. 'He said to go on up to the table and he'll meet us there.'

I'd sort of hoped we'd have Mark doing the 'don't I know

you' sketch before we got to the restaurant, just in case there was a scene, but that is just my luck.

'Great,' I say.

'So I can't believe it, we're going to be eating dinner with a famous writer,' says Henri.

'I'd hardly call myself famous,' I say.

'What's that?' says Lou looking at me, her brow furrowing.

'Penny's been approached by *Bridal Dreams* to write an article.'

'Oh my god, Pen, that's huge!' says Lou.

'That's news to me,' says Mark, looking straight at me.

'It only happened this afternoon, and I was emailing Henri at the time so I slipped it in. What with the rush to get here after work, it slipped my mind.'

'Isn't it amazing though, my wedding planner writing for *Bridal Dreams*.'

'It's a one-off, nothing to get too excited about.'

Actually, inside I'm doing a happy dance. *Bridal Dreams*, the third bestselling bridal magazine in the UK want me, Penny Robinson, to write an article.

'Nonsense. We'll have to toast you when we get drinks,' says Henri.

We walk into the restaurant and I see my friends' eyes light up. The ambience of the restaurant was nice when I was here for lunch, but now the candlelight makes it feel warm and inviting.

'I thought you were wearing a dress?' says Henri as we sit down.

'Really?'

'Yes, I asked you last night, and I said that it would be a nice outing for your new Kurt Geiger shoes.'

'You've got new Kurt Geiger shoes?' asks Lou.

I widen my eyes in a don't-speak-so-loud voice, as Mark is sat right next to me. I'm just hoping that whatever rugby/football/cricket team the men are talking about now is so engrossing that Mark's ears didn't prick up at the mention of new shoes.

'Yes,' I whisper across the table. 'But they're TK Maxx, so they were dead cheap.'

'Well, now that I can fit into my little dresses again maybe we could go for a night out, heels and everything,' says Lou.

'Sounds good to me, perhaps when work calms down a bit.'

'Uh, work. It always gets in the way, doesn't it?' says Lou. 'And to think I go back full time next month.'

'What do you do, Lou?' asks Henri.

'I'm a civil servant, I work for the MOD.'

'That must be nice, all those men in uniform trotting about,' says Henri.

'Actually, I work in an office mostly with other civvies, so I rarely see the boys in gre—'

I look up at Lou, whose mouth is wide open. I follow her gaze and I see Nick walking across the restaurant to us.

I look between Lou and Nick and the penny drops. In all my worrying about whether Mark would recognise Nick, I didn't for one minute think that *Lou* would recognise him. Not only did Lou see the video, but I'd completely forgotten that Lou met him while we were filming the thing.

I try and use my best-friend psychic-ness to tell Lou not to say anything.

'Ah, honey,' says Henri spinning round. She's obviously noticed Lou's jaw drop and sensed his arrival. 'Come and meet everyone.'

'Hiya,' says Nick, giving a friendly little wave.

'You've already met Penny, of course, and this is her husband Mark, and these are their friends Russell and Lou.'

Nick shakes the hands of both of the men as they stand to meet him. I get kisses on both cheeks and when he goes to kiss Lou, I can't help but see a flicker of recognition in his eyes. His relaxed stance disappears and instead he looks just a little twitchy.

I'm wondering if Lou's going to say anything, but she's

busy adjusting her cutlery to make sure it's all perfectly in line. It seems that Lou has realised who Nick is, and she isn't going to make a big thing of it.

'Good evening, everyone, my name is Billy and I'll be your waiter for this evening. Can I start by giving you the menus.'

He hands them to us and at least it gives Lou something else to stare intently at.

'So, Nick, Russell and I were just talking about the Lions tour. Are you a rugby man?' asks Mark.

'Certainly am, I went to see the Lions in South Africa a few years ago.'

Mark and Russell look like I did when I saw Henri's current season Miu Mius on her feet. I see the beginning of a bromance here.

'Penny, this menu is so impressive! It all sounds delicious. I'm going to have the pear and walnut salad to start. I'm so excited about talking to Brett now. Do you think we have to wait until we've had the food?' asks Henri.

'Yes, I expect he's busy supervising in the kitchen, plus you'll have more to talk to him about. And you may not even like it.'

Whilst Henri starts to talk about the wedding favours she now wants, which are personalised wine corks that, quite frankly, she's never going to be able to afford, I'm vaguely aware that my phone is buzzing in my bag. I'd usually ignore it, as it's normally only my mum or Mark's, but I'm conscious that I told Beth that she could call whenever she's tempted to gamble. Although it's unlikely she'd turn to me, I can't let her down.

I sneakily pull it out of my bag only to see it's a message from Lou. I look up at her in surprise but she still looks engrossed in her menu. She must have her phone positioned underneath it.

As I glance down at my phone, my left ear is focused on Henri talking about place mats and matching napkins and, to my right, I could have sworn I heard Nick suggesting that Mark and Russell join him in the Caribbean to watch cricket. Clearly Nick is just as out of touch with the reality of how much everything costs in the real world as his soon-to-be wife.

HELP!!! I've snogged Nick before . . .

I drop my mobile in surprise and it clatters noisily to the ground. I swoop down to grab it and say a mental prayer that it isn't smashed to smithereens like it was the last time I dropped it. I breathe a sigh of relief as the screen looks intact and scratch-free and then I bang my head on the table as I get back up.

'Ow,' I say, rubbing my head.

'Everything all right?' asks Henri. Everyone at the table is looking at me. Aside, of course, from Lou who is leaning on her elbow and shielding her face with her hand.

'Yes, everything is fine,' I say, remembering what the text message had said. When exactly has Lou snogged Nick? She's only met him once before and she was six months' pregnant. Not to mention I was with her. It may have been a time in my life when I was suffering emotional distress, but I'm sure even then I might have noticed if my best friend had her tongue down someone other than her husband's throat.

'Penny, I can't believe that you're actually on your phone at dinner, after all the stick that you give me if I even glance at mine,' says Mark, laughing.

'That's because you're surgically attached to your mobile with your sports monitoring. I'm sorry but delaying by half an hour the score to some random sports game is not an unreasonable request.'

'Oh, you get that too? I get that all the time,' says Nick in a manner that reminds me of Beth.

'I just don't understand why you need to know right that second,' I say.

'But it's a live game,' says Nick as if he's giving the definitive answer.

'You're on to a loser,' says Mark, 'Penny doesn't get sports.'

Contrary to popular belief, I do 'get' sports. I know my offside rule from my LBW and I know more than I would care to admit about stats, players and sporting grounds. What I don't get is why men care so much about this stuff. Mark, of course says the same thing to me about why I buy gossip magazines, but at least celebrity lives are real life.

Before World War Three erupts, Billy, who's clearly sensed that there appears to be a split between the blue and pink personnel at the table, wisely comes over to distract us.

'Can I get you any drinks to start off with?' he asks.

'We haven't even discussed the wine list,' says Henri, 'Who wants what?'

'Red wine, I want red wine,' calls out Lou from behind her menu. 'A bottle of Shiraz, please, for me.'

'Just for you?' says Russell laughing nervously. 'I'll share that with you then.'

'I'll have red as well,' I say.

In the end we settle on one red and one white, and then we order the food. Given how fidgety Lou is now that the safety net of the menu has been removed, I'm guessing we'll be ordering another bottle of red wine before we know it.

The sports versus women argument seems to have faded away and it's been replaced by Russell recounting the latest development in Harry's little life, which is that he's pulling himself up on the sofa to stand. Both Henri and I might have had little uterus-skipping moments, and even Nick and Mark cracked a smile. But that might have been more to do with Russell's comic delivery.

By the time the wine appears, Lou is seriously on edge. She practically downs the whole glass of wine in front of the waiter, and she asks for another bottle then and there.

I notice the look between Henri and Nick and I can just imagine what they're thinking. Something along the lines of alcoholic.

'Making the most of your night of freedom, hey, Lou?' says Mark. 'See I told you, Penny, it isn't a picnic having kids.'

'How many kids do you want?' asks Henri, smiling at me.

One would be a start. 'I'd love a whole football team, but I'm guessing two or three's a nice number.'

'Could you imagine two or three of Harry?' says Russell raising an eyebrow at Lou.

Lou smiles weakly and drains the half glass of wine she'd just poured from the now-empty bottle.

'He's not that bad.' Most of the time, I add in my head.

'He's pretty good,' says Russell, 'It's just occasionally that he's a terror. But, I wouldn't have it any other way, I love him to bits.'

I smile at Russell as I think how far they've come from the little 'accident' that led them to be parents earlier than planned. But just as I knew they would, the two of them took to parenthood like ducks to water.

Henri asks Russell about his one day a week at home with Harry, and I take my chance to lean over to Lou.

'What's going on?' I ask.

'I need the toilet,' says Lou standing up and almost announcing it to the entire restaurant. I'm guessing the red wine has gone to her head at lightning speed, given that it's on an empty stomach.

She stands up and gives me a look which suggests that I'm to join her in the bathroom and I realise that she's not going to leave the table until I get up to go with her.

'I might nip to the loo, too,' I say, standing up to follow her.

'Ooh, girls' trip to the toilet. Don't leave me out,' chirps Henri, standing up and following us.

We're reminded that we're not in a fancy restaurant when we get into the toilets which are six cubicles in a line, with far too many strip lights and lots of white plastic. Henri goes over to the mirror and gets out her make-up from her clutch bag.

Lou and I each go into a cubicle. As Henri starts talking about the boys and how well they're getting on, I go to get my phone out of my bag, and I realise that I haven't got it; I obviously left it on the table after the whole debacle with dropping it on the floor. I do, however, have a receipt and a pen.

When did you snog Nick? I write.

I wave it under the toilet cubicle whilst trying desperately to pee. I'm not good at going under pressure, but I don't want Henri to think something weird is going on.

I feel the pen and paper being snatched away from me.

'And then I said to Nick, if you want to take me to St Lucia for a honeymoon, then that's fine, but don't expect me to go to some cricket match,' continues Henri.

As I play noisily with the toilet roll dispenser, I wait for the receipt to appear.

Dunno, before Russell. Looks dead familiar. HELP!

It takes me a couple of reads to realise what's happened; Lou hasn't snogged Nick at all. She merely recognises him. Thank goodness for that. I go to write on the receipt for her not to worry, but before I get a chance to hand it over I hear her door open and she and Henri start talking by the sinks. Why hasn't she waited for my response?

'Have you been with Nick long?' asks Lou.

I walk out and try and make eye contact with Lou, but she's not paying attention; her eyes are wild and glazed over from too much wine. In fact, it's that look of danger that flashes over someone's eyes when they're well on their way to being trollied. I don't think Lou has really recovered after giving up drinking during pregnancy and breastfeeding.

'About seven years,' says Henri.

'Blimey, that's a long time. And you've been together all that time, you know, no gaps?'

'Lou!' I say loudly. 'Sorry, Henri.'

'It's fine, Pen. Yes, we've pretty much been together all that time, bar a few weeks a couple of years ago. I know what you're thinking.'

Believe me, Henri, you have no idea what Lou's drunken mind is thinking.

'Nick's taken his precious time getting me up the aisle, and you'd be right.'

I take my lead from Henri, who's laughing, and I laugh uncomfortably too.

'We better get out to the boys before they wonder where we've got to,' I say.

Henri goes out first and I try and whisper to Lou. 'You've got it wrong.'

'What?' she hisses.

'What's that?' asks Henri looking round.

'Nothing. I just had toilet paper on my shoe,' I say, lying.

We walk back over to the table just as the starters are beings served.

'I'm starving,' says Lou as she sits down.

I silently say a quick prayer that Lou will sober up and not blurt out her amorous suspicions about Nick and start my food.

'This looks fantastic,' says Henri. 'It's like something you'd get in a Michelin-starred restaurant. I just hope it tastes as good as it looks.'

I know that look in Henri's eyes, it's the one I used to get when I was planning my budget wedding: the 'please work out as it's all I can afford' look.

'Oh my God, it's delicious,' says Henri after her first mouthful.

'It certainly is. If the rest of the food is as good as this, then perhaps we've found our wedding caterer,' says Nick. 'Well done, Penny.'

I blush at the compliment. Mark gives me a smile and then I catch Lou out of the corner of my eye and she's just staring at Nick, not eating.

'Is your food all right, Lou?' I ask, trying to jolt her into remembering where she is.

'It's fine. Thank you. How's your food, Nick?'

'It's lovely, thank you,' he replies.

'Great, do you like things on the side then?'

I almost drop my fork in horror.

'I'm sorry?' says Nick, looking up at her.

'I said, do you like things on the side,' repeats Lou. 'You

see, you've got your salad on the side,' she says, pointing at his plate.

The rest of the table are squinting at Lou, trying to work out what on earth is going on.

'Oh right, yes, Lou. I like salad on the side,' says Nick in clarification.

'So Mark was telling us yesterday about your DJ set at their wedding,' says Henri, clearly trying to change the subject.

'DJ Loopy Lou, in the house,' says Lou posing in what can only be described in a rapper pose pulled by your mum.

I subtly try and move Lou's wine glass out of reach, but she's on it like a rocket. She grabs it out of my hand and the next thing I know she's thrown red wine all over the starched white tablecloth.

'Oops,' says Lou. She lunges for Henri's white wine glass to do the classic counteract, but I intervene, grabbing Lou's hand and summoning over Billy the waiter. After some wiping down with damp towels, the heavily stained tablecloth is no longer dripping all over the floor.

'I can't wait to see what my main is like after that,' says Mark putting his knife and fork down, pretending that catastrophe hasn't just hit the table.

'Me neither. I'm especially excited about the dessert,' says Lou.

'Me too, I've gone for the passion fruit panna cotta,' says Henri. 'Sounds heavenly.'

'What about you, Nick, or let me guess, you're going for the tart?' says Lou, snorting with laughter.

'Lou, honey, did you want to check on the babysitter?'

'I'm sure my mum will be fine, Russell,' says Lou laughing him away. 'Honestly, you fuss more than I do.'

'Actually, Lou, I think we should phone her, just to make sure. Why don't I come with you?'

'I think she's fine,' says Lou, shaking her head to the rest of the table as if Russell is the one acting like a crazy person.

'Louise, outside now,' orders Russell. I haven't seen him get this authoritative since the time that Lou and I got really drunk and we tried to put butterfly clips in his hair. It was all Lou's fault: she told me he let her do it when it was just the two of them at home.

With Lou away, the conversation naturally gravitates to Henri and Nick's wedding. It warms the cockles of my heart just how much Nick dotes on Henri. By the time Lou and Russell come back from their phone call, Lou looks a whole lot better. The fresh air and a stern word seem to have done the trick as she's now as quiet as a mouse.

Billy the waiter soon brings over the main courses and just as we're about to tuck in, I'm worried that Lou's little outbursts are back.

'Fish and chips,' she says, pointing at Nick's gourmet presented plate.

'Yes, Lou,' says Nick nodding.

Finally, I can see it's clicked in Lou's mind and she looks horrified. She must have remembered where she met him – after we'd finished filming the video he went and bought us fish and chips. She goes to open her mouth and I manage to catch her eye and shake my head gently. She seems to get the message and she goes back to her lamb. Hopefully I won't have to be on tenterhooks for the rest of the evening.

By the time we make it home, I'm exhausted. It's gone midnight on a Thursday and I've got a busy day at work tomorrow to get through. The good news is that Brett and Henri hit it off, so he's agreed to cater the wedding. I just need to arrange a meeting at the cricket club to finalise out all the details.

'So why didn't you tell me that Henri's Nick is from your gambling group?' says Mark out of the blue. I stop wiping the make-up off my face and look at him in horror.

'You knew? All along?'

'Of course I knew. I don't have that bad a head for faces.'

'I didn't think you'd recognise him. It's just that Henri doesn't know that I know about Nick's gambling.'

'So Henri doesn't know that you're a gambler?'

'Nope.'

'Don't you think you should tell her that you already know Nick? We of all people know how dangerous it is to keep secrets.'

'I know, but Nick's adamant and it's not my secret to tell.'

'But Henri knows about Nick's gambling, right?'

'Right. You're not going to say anything, are you?'

'No. You could have told me though. We are supposed to trust each other.'

'I know, I just didn't think it was my secret to tell.'

'Well, I respect your loyalty. I won't mention anything to Henri, but maybe you should get Nick to tell her. It's not nice being kept in the dark. I should know.'

'I guess,' I say. I know Mark's right, that Henri should know too. The more I've got to know her, the more guilty I've felt about being privy to something so personal to her. I feel we're almost becoming friends, and I'm not so sure that I should be keeping secrets from her.

chapter thirteen

princess-on-a-shoestring cost cutters:
Flower Power

Cut out your floristry fees by growing your own flowers. If you're organised and work out your flowers and what's in season when you're going to be married, you can plant them in either your own or a family member's garden. Imagine a lovely, colourful bouquet of handpicked sweet peas. This option is not for the fainthearted - the blooms have to be picked the day before, and they do need tending to and a little bit of TLC in the run-up to the wedding. This is where a mother-in-law with green fingers comes in very handy. For more info check out the Green Fingered Brides' Blog.

Tags: green fingers, growing, flowers, garden.

'Hello,' I say into the phone. My heart is racing as I try and talk through my nose to disguise my voice.

'Hello, is that Linda?'

'Yes,' I say lying.

'It's Indy here from Bella Cheese Imports. I understand from your answerphone message that you wanted to place a large order?'

I look at my watch. It's 3.42 p.m. I can't believe she's phoned back now. I know she's at work today. We also checked with her manager before leaving the message to see what her hours are today, and she's due to be here until five p.m.

'That's right. I've been on your website and I'm especially interested in the Romano cheese.' My mouth is practically watering. I'm going to have to nip to the supermarket to get some cheeses tonight, I hope Mark's in the mood for a cheeseboard dinner.

'That's one of our most popular products. When you say that you wanted a large quantity, how much are you talking?'

Bugger. I have no idea.

'Um, hang on a second.' I cover the mouthpiece and count to five. 'Indy, would you mind if I called you back in a bit? One of our suppliers has just turned up and I'm the only one here.'

'Yes, of course. I'll speak to you soon.'

Sooner than you think.

'Great, thanks, Indy.'

I end the call and instantly feel awful for having been deceitful, but we needed to confirm that when Indy was disappearing round the corner to answer calls, that they were relating to her business.

I walk over to Giles's office to tell him the news, waiting patiently as I knock.

'Come in,' he barks.

I walk in the office and sit down on the uncomfortable plastic chair.

'Indy just phoned me back about my cheese order.'

Giles whips his glasses off and I see a smirk appear across his face.

'Excellent, so we have her phoning you on your mobile number, which we can get the call record for. And it's not even four. Right then, there's nothing else for it. Time to go over and confront her.'

I look up at Giles. It's four p.m. on a Friday afternoon. What a crappy day and time to go and fire someone. Not that there's ever a good time to fire someone.

Personally, it sucks for me as there goes any hope of me sneaking out of work early. I felt like I needed it after crawling into bed after midnight last night. It might have been a great dinner at the college but I'm not used to going out on a school night.

I watch as Giles picks up the phone and arranges for Indy and her manager to meet us in one of the conference rooms.

'Right, Penny, go and get your files.'

I nod and make my feet cooperate. I pick up the huge wodge of paper spilling out of a manila file and follow Giles across to the conference room. We settle ourselves into our chairs and it isn't long before Indy and her manager turn up and join us.

'Hello, Martin, Indy, thanks for coming,' says Giles.

I look up at Indy and she's still smiling happily. She's clearly oblivious to what's coming her way.

'Indy, it's come to our attention that you have your own company and you've been working on it during office hours.'

I watch Indy's smile fall from her face. Her bottom lip drops and I can see it wobbling as her eyes widen in surprise. But she remains silent.

'I'm sure you're aware that we take a rather dim view on that type of thing here.'

I swear Giles is enjoying this.

'We have pulled your IT records and have reason to believe you've used your computer for personal use on a frequent basis. Other people in your department have also reported absences where you've been on your mobile for long periods of time too. Now might be a good time for you to say something.'

Indy rubs her eyes and I'm not sure if she's blinking away a tear or not. She shakes her hair back and tries to compose herself.

'I don't know what to say,' she says, looking down. 'I mean, I do a good job, don't I?'

She's looking up at her boss with desperation in her eyes. Oh God. That could just as easily be me sitting there, pleading with Giles that my wedding planning doesn't interfere with my job. I mean it doesn't. Unlike Indy, I've only taken a few personal calls at work and answered a couple of Henri's emails. But my cheeks are still starting to burn and I'm starting to perspire.

What if I'm just like Indy? What if that's how it starts? The odd email here, the odd phone conversation there and suddenly we're staring at a huge file of evidence from IT. Mark would kill me if I got fired.

'Indy, we've never been unhappy with your work, but even I've noticed that your focus hasn't been there lately. You've been late to meetings, which is unlike you and you've gone close to the wire on the last two deadlines,' says her manager.

'But other members of staff don't even turn up to meetings sometimes.'

'I know, but it's out of character for you. Plus, when you add that to the paper trail that Penny and Giles have put together, it is pretty damning.'

'But I haven't done anything wrong. I mean other people check websites all day long, how come I'm being singled out?'

Why is she looking directly at me? It's like she can sense that I'm a frequent web surfer. Although I'll freely admit that I won't be surfing anywhere near as much now I know what IT records. I mean, I knew they were all-seeing, but they record absolutely everything. And it's amazing how those little fleeting glances to websites add up timewise over a day.

'You're not being singled out, Indy. It's not a little slap on the wrist over some web surfing, although you should know from our IT policy that you're not allowed to do that.'

'So if it isn't a little slap on the wrist, what exactly is this?' asks Indy in a quiet voice.

'I'm afraid, Indy, that we have grounds for dismissal,' says Giles.

Indy's face crumbles.

'Over a little bit of web surfing?' she says, struggling to maintain her composure.

'Come on, Indy, we both know it's a bit more than that. It states in your contract that you're supposed to declare any second jobs or business interests. At the very least you should have told us you were running your cheese importation company.'

'So can't I just declare it now? I mean, I run it jointly with my husband in my spare time. I don't do anything relating to it when I'm at work.'

'We've got records from IT to suggest otherwise,' says Giles. 'Plus we know you've been answering your phone during office hours.'

'Well, my mum's been ill, I've been on the phone to her, that's all.'

'Actually, you made a phone call to Penny here just a few minutes ago.'

I look up at Indy and her eyes are burning into me. I can see Giles out of the corner of my eye, nodding at me as if I'm supposed to elaborate.

'Yes, um, Indy, I'm afraid I'm Linda, the one that phoned about the Romano cheese order.'

'You're Linda? Surely this is entrapment?'

I wonder if it is, but it was merely for us to be sure we were right.

'Look, Indy,' I say. 'I know this is hard, but we've got enough grounds for dismissal from the evidence we've collected from IT. We only left you the voicemail to see whether you did respond to them during your working hours here.'

'I don't do it all the time,' says Indy. 'It's just that the company grew so quickly. It was only supposed to be a few clients and we'd be able to manage it in the evenings. But lately it's gone crazy. I didn't mean for it to interfere with my work. I honestly thought it hadn't.'

Indy's tears are falling thick and fast now and even though this is the first time I've met her, I want to reach across the table and give her a big hug. Obviously I'm not going to as that would be weird and unprofessional, but I really want to.

Being involved when people are getting fired is one of the major downsides to my job. No matter how awful the person is or what they've done to mess things up, I always feel terrible for them. But this time, with Indy, it just seems so much worse. It's like I've got too much empathy with her. Although I have to keep reminding myself that I'm not her. Yes, I haven't declared my wedding planning business, but that's because mine's not really a proper business, is it? I've only had two clients and I'm not taking on any more. My situation is completely different to Indy's.

But as Giles reads over the process for dismissal and her rights regarding appeals, I can't help feeling hot under the collar and like I'm the one being dismissed. The only thing I can do is take this as a wake-up call and make sure that I keep my business separate from my day job. I don't want to be sitting on the other side of that table with Giles dismissing me.

From now, on I'm going to have to put my foot down with Henri and her emergencies and make sure that I don't give Giles any reason to start investigating me.

chapter fourteen

princess-on-a-shoestring friend or foe:
Chair Covers

Now, I actually love chair covers. I love the bows, I love the clean lines and I love the look it creates before anyone comes into the venue. But do you know what? By the time people sit down and you lose that clean look, you don't notice them. I mean, can you tell me what weddings you've been to that have and haven't had chair covers? They're one of those little extras that are a nice icing on the cake but not essential. And for us budget brides, you don't want your chairs to be more dressed up than you are! What do you think about chair covers: are they a wedding essential or a wedding extravagance?

Tags: chairs, ribbons, covers.

'Keeping you up, are we Penny?'

I look up mid-yawn to see Giles hovering over my desk – I hadn't noticed him come out of his office. I think that perhaps being up until the small hours last night writing my article for *Bridal Dreams* has caught up with me.

I still can't believe they picked me to write for them. They're re-jigging their magazine from next month and they're going to create a different themed section each issue. The first theme is dedicated to vintage weddings; I can't wait for that to come out. But, more excitingly, for me, the second month will be about low-budget weddings and keeping down the costs. I've written them an article about my blog and my top ten budget-busting tips. I've had a few weeks to write it, but as the deadline was this morning I couldn't stop myself from tinkering with it last night.

I'm just dreaming of buying the magazine and staring at my little picture and a byline, when I remember that Giles is standing over me.

'Sorry, Giles. I had a terrible night's sleep. I was just churning over the programme for the Wales trip.'

'Ah, well, that's what I wanted to talk to you about.'

That doesn't sound like a great tone. It sounds like the tone he used when he wanted me to renegotiate the ration packs for Gunther with the scary sergeant major. Trying to explain exactly what kind of rehydrated food a vegan could eat didn't go down very well, which I'm guessing will be exactly like the food when Gunther tries to eat it.

'What about it?' I say a little curtly.

'Well Gunther can't make the fourth.'

And this is bad news? Our CEO can't make it and now the biggest thing I will have to worry about will be whether or not the sales directors attempt to smuggle booze in like they did the year before last. Pot-holing with a whisky hangover is quite possibly the most pain I've ever experienced. At least it was dark in the caves.

I'm about to do a victory lap of the office with this wonderful news when I realise that Giles has carried on talking.

'So we'll have to move the trip to another date.'

'Move the date?' I say slowly, trying to process what Giles is saying.

'Yes, Gunther can do the week after.'

Can he now? That's fantastic! Screw the fact that we've got thirty-four other members of staff coming, and we've already organised minibuses, catering options not to mention the team-building itself with the scary sergeant major. But if Gunther can do the week after, we'll just have to move it!

'Um, I don't think it's entirely practical to change it

at this late stage. I mean, everyone has agreed to come. Don't forget, people have lives outside of work and other commitments. Childcare, for instance.'

And I've got a flipping wedding to oversee the week after. I don't think Henri would be too impressed if I was MIA the week of the wedding.

'I know, Penny, I know. This isn't exactly ideal timing for me either, you know. But Gunther's asked us to look at it, and as the CEO, we sort of have to do what he says.'

'But what if it can't be moved?'

'I think you've got to get it changed, Penny. Gunther's very keen to come.'

'But what if—'

'Penny, I think you should give it a go, you never know it may not be as difficult as you might imagine. And, besides, if you were an HR supervisor then you'd have to deal with problems like this and overcome them all the time.'

Is that Giles trying to give me a kick up the arse – do this or don't get the promotion? I know he's right. I'm just over-tired and sulky.

I look up at Shelly as I can see she is keeping a straight face, but there is just a hint of a smug smirk break-ing out across it too. In contrast to my dismal planning, Shelly's appraisal overhaul is going well. She's got the design team doing a pilot scheme, and so far the feedback's been encouraging.

'I'll get on it right away,' I say.

'Excellent. Just come and let me know how you got on.'

'OK,' I say, sighing.

Just when I think I'm getting somewhere, I seem to have to take three steps back. The Wales trip was just coming together nicely and now this happens. I don't want to phone the scary sergeant major, in case you haven't already guessed; he scares the bejesus out of me.

'What are you going to do?' asks Shelly.

'I've got to get it moved,' I sigh.

'Aren't you tempted to just say you tried but you couldn't move it?'

'I'd be lying if I said that hadn't crossed my mind, but I've got to try, what's the worst that could happen?'

I flick through my contact book and bring up the SSM's number. I dial it, hoping that he's out in the field and I'll just get his answerphone.

One ring. Two rings. Three rings. My heart rate starts to slow down as the possibility of the answerphone seems more likely.

'Yes, Penny?'

'Oh, um, hello, Baz,' I say with a stutter that I haven't

had since I was a teenager when I tried to talk to hot boys at school.

'I'm just running an orientation exercise, so signal might be a bit dodgy. Now, you're not phoning about any more vegetarians, are you?'

If I wasn't so terrified, I'd stifle a giggle at the way he said vegetarians, as if they were some type of diseased individual.

'No, no more vegans or vegetarians. In fact, no dietary amendments.'

Yet, I add in my head. If we move weeks, the likelihood is that we'll have to have a change or two, as I'm guessing we'll be substituting some personnel as not everyone will be able to make it still.

'Bloody glad to hear that. What did you want then?'

'Well, there's been a little change of plan.'

'What kind of change?' says Baz.

Uh-oh, there's the anger in his voice coming out.

'Well, you know our big boss, Gunther, is coming.'

'The one who only eats leaves?'

'The vegan, that's the one. Well, he can't actually make it.'

'Right . . .'

'He wants us to move it to the week after, and I told them that it's probably impossible for you to do as it's such short notice and I know that it isn't that simple.'

'You want to move it to the week after? At this late stage?'

'I know, I know. Look, if you can't do it, then we'll have to keep it. But if there is, you know, any possibility that we could move it on by a week, we'd be so grateful.'

I've realised I'm twirling the phone cable around like I'd twirl my hair if I was flirting. I can't believe I'm trying to use my feminine powers of persuasion to sweet-talk SSM into changing it.

'Oh, right then. Well, if he can't make it, then we'll have to move it. Don't worry about anyone else and that all the arrangements have already been made.'

'To be honest that was exactly my reaction at first.'

'And yet you're still phoning me to see if I can change it?'

'Yes,' I say.

Something flashes through my mind, maybe it's my inner HR supervisor coming out. Maybe the little talking to from Giles gave me earlier on has stirred something, but whatever it is, I'm suddenly not going to be walked over, SSM or not.

'Look, Baz, it's costing us quite a lot to bring all thirty-five of us. We're paying for your gold package, after all. We're quite happy to walk away and lose our deposit. I'm sure we'll find another company that we can do some team-building with.'

There's a silence on the end of the phone and I'm praying he doesn't actually call my bluff.

'I'll see what I can do. I'll be back in the office in half an hour, I'll call you then.'

'Great, I'll look forward to it.'

I put the phone down and my hand is ever so slightly shaking. I look up and see that Shelly is staring at me wide-eyed.

'That was impressive,' she says, before going back to her typing.

'Thanks,' I mumble. It really was quite skilful, wasn't it? I even impressed myself.

And now all I need to do is twiddle my thumbs for half an hour until Baz calls back.

I've got myself into a bit of a pickle. I'm now potentially going to be away the week of Henri's wedding. It's not exactly great timing. But, at the same time, even though I'd rather put Princess-on-a-Shoestring and the wedding planning first, I've got to remember that I need to plan the most amazing away trip in order to get the promotion. Like it or not, this is my career and this is what pays the bills. Still, I know that doesn't help Henri and that I'm going to be going AWOL before her wedding.

I'm sure Henri, being the level-headed bride that she is, will be understanding. I'm only going to be in Wales, right? It's not like I'm going to Timbuktu, or anywhere in a different time zone. I'll be fully contactable and only a couple of hours away in the car if there was a serious emergency. Yes, I'm sure that Henri will understand.

As I reply to a couple of emails on my computer, my hand sneakily swipes at my phone to check my personal emails. I have been trying to resist the temptation to do this during work hours. I glance over the inbox on my phone and I can feel my heart start to race as I see there's one from *Bridal Dreams*. This is a real heart-in-mouth moment, will they have liked my article or are they writing to tell me that they've got someone more qualified to write it?

I'm about to click it open when my office phone rings, making me feel extra guilty that I've been caught doing something I shouldn't at work.

'Good morning, Penny speaking.'

'Penny, it's Baz. Good news, you can do the week after.'

'Great, that's perfect. Thank you so much.'

'But there are a few changes,' says Baz.

'Right,' I say, not liking the sound of the word 'changes'.

'The first thing is that we can't do it in Wales, it will have to be at our South Downs centre, in Sussex.'

'Well that's great for us, it's much closer,' I say, thinking that it may be a couple of degrees warmer too.

'Right, so it will be the Thursday and Friday.'

Friday? I've got to be back on Friday to set up the marquee

in the late afternoon. Henri really will kill me if I'm not there.

'Er, is there any way that we can do it slightly earlier in the week?' I say, wincing.

'Penny, you're bloody lucky that I've been able to move it at all. We're chocka for the rest of the summer with kids' groups, so you'll have to take it or leave it.'

I'm torn between Henri's wedding and pleasing Giles and Gunther. In the end, it's Mark's voice I hear in my head and I know what I have to do.

'Take it,' I shout. 'I'll take it. Thanks, Baz. I'll let you know if there have been any changes to personnel and I'll get the relevant new consent forms and dietary requirements sorted out.'

Baz's sigh nearly bursts my ear drum.

'Penny, just pick people that eat normal things. No one with allergies, no more vegans, all right?'

'I'll try my best.' I try and imagine the email in my head. Staff wanted for team-building away trip on South Downs. Must be free to come 11–13 July. Must be willing to put yourself through hell. Must be good at taking instructions and must not have any special dietary requirements or allergies. I'm sure that's not breaking any discrimination laws at all.

'Speak later.'

The dial-tone rings through my ears and I place the receiver down.

'Success?' asks Shelly.

'Yeah, not ideal in terms of dates for me, but I'm not the important one, right?'

Shelly smiles at me in solidarity and I get up from my desk to go and deliver the good news to Giles.

I knock on the door and wait to enter the office.

'Come in,' he bellows.

I open the door and Giles looks up.

'So, Penny, do you bring me good news?'

'I do, Giles,' I say in a smug voice, sitting down opposite him.

'Excellent. Gunther will be happy with us. Is it still Wednesday and Thursday?'

'Unfortunately that wasn't possible. It will be Thursday to Friday.'

'Oh right, that's not great for me.'

Me neither, I scream in my head. If Giles wants me to change it to suit *his* bloody plans, he's got another thing coming. If I'm ruining my plans, then he is too.

'Well, it was all they could do. Baz, I mean, Barry, the man who runs it, says that they are fully booked from then on with children's courses as it's the school holidays.'

'Ah, of course. I'm sure it will be fine. I might just drive up in my own car and sneakily leave a little bit earlier on the Friday. That would be all right, wouldn't it?'

'I'm not entirely sure what sort of message that sends to everyone on a team-building trip away, that one of the company directors drives themselves and leaves early when other people probably would want to too.'

'I know, you're right, Penny. But that Saturday is my daughter's wedding.'

'Oh right,' I say. I start to break out in a cold sweat as I have this crazy thought – what if Giles is Henri's dad? 'Where's she getting married?'

'A big hotel in the country,' says Giles, grinning.

I sigh with relief and I almost laugh at myself at how ridiculous an idea that would have been.

'How are her plans coming along? Only a month to go, is she all sorted?'

'I think so, to tell you the truth I've kept well out of it. She's got one of these fancy wedding planners from London, very hard to get, you know the type.'

I do indeed. The type that would laugh at any of my Princess-on-a-Shoestring reader's wedding plans.

'Sounds like it's going to be quite the wedding,' I say.

'I'm sure it will be. Harriet's got excellent taste, just like her old dad.'

I smile at Giles. Every so often he goes slightly soft around the edges, but I try and make the most of it as it never lasts long before he goes all business mode again.

'Well, if it's anything like the lead up to my wedding,' I say with rose-tinted glasses, 'It's the most exciting time. Everything falling into place and the anticipation.' The fear that your husband-to-be isn't going to turn up to the ceremony as he finds out you've gambled away the wedding budget and that you've been lying for months. 'A magical time,' I say.

'I'm sure it is. Right, so can you email Gunther's PA and tell her about the new dates? Then I take it you're going to check everyone else can still come?'

I swallow at the fact that I'm being allowed to liaise directly with Gunther's PA, as so far Giles has been keeping that privilege at arm's length. I start to feel a warm glow come over me; does this mean that Giles is beginning to trust me?

'Absolutely,' I say, nodding. 'I'll email everyone now.'

'Excellent.' The glasses are back on and I'm well practiced that this is my cue to leave.

All I have to do now is break the news to Henri. The event finishes at three p.m. on Friday and, as long as we're on the road by five, we should make it back for me to get to the little village where Henri's having the wedding by seven. That'll be all right. I may be a little exhausted from two days of hiding from the sergeant major, but I'll be there, that's the main thing. I'm sure that if Giles is desperate to get home, he'll probably try and make sure that everything is chivvied along as quickly as it can be.

I sit down at my desk and start to compose the email to those staff members who are supposed to be coming, then I remember that I have an email from *Bridal Dreams* waiting for me:

Penny,

Loved the feature! Thanks for sending it over.

We've been talking in the office, and how would you fancy doing a regular column, a sort of agony aunt feature? Brides write in with an expensive idea for their wedding and they ask you how they can have a cheaper alternative, and you provide said alternative?

It would be about two hundred words a month, so at our freelance rate of twenty-five pounds per one hundred words you wouldn't get rich, but we would add your blog links etc.

Let me know what you think and we can start it off in the same edition as your article.

ATB

Jane

I have to read the email twice to make sure that I've read it correctly. *Bridal Dreams* want me, Penny Robinson, to be an agony aunt. I start to feel light-headed and I desperately want to tell someone, but it's another hour until lunch, and I can't risk calling Mark whilst I'm at work in case Shelly bat-ears overhears.

'You look happy,' says Shelly.

'Yeah, you know it's great when your hard work pays off,' I say.

Shelly's nodding knowingly.

I take a deep breath and go back to my email about the former Wales trip. This is all going to work out fine. I'm an agony aunt now, a proper grown-up dispensing advice. I was getting worked up over nothing about the away trip and Henri's wedding clash. I'm still going to be there Friday evening. And, to tell you the truth, the week before the wedding there's probably not a lot to do in terms of planning, because as long as I do my job properly, it will all have been done by the time it gets to that stage anyway.

In fact, I probably don't even need to tell Henri until nearer the time. There's no point in upsetting her now, is there? After all, I want to keep her as calm as possible and make sure her inner bridezilla doesn't rear its ugly head too much. Yes, it will be much better to tell her in a few weeks when everything is running like clockwork and, that way, she'll realise it isn't a big deal.

chapter fifteen

princess-on-a-shoestring top tips:
Don't Neglect your HTB

As a bride-to-be it's very easy to be all consumed when planning a wedding. Especially if you're doing it on a shoestring and always surfing the net trying to find the cheapest option available. But one thing to remember is that you don't want to turn up on your wedding day and realise that it's the closest you've stood to the groom in a while. Make time for each other in the run-up to the wedding, and make a pact not to talk about the big day on your dates. Instead, enjoy each other's company and remind yourself why you're getting married in the first place. If the planning gets stressful, those little dates will make it seem all worthwhile.

Tags: keep romance alive, date night, neglect.

'Are you nearly ready, Pen? I thought we could go for a drink first if you are.' Mark shouts up the stairs to me.

'Almost.'

Mark's eyes are going to pop out of his head when he sees me. I've gone all-out wearing a special outfit for our date tonight. Earlier this week, Mark put in a formal complaint to me that he hadn't seen a lot of me lately. It's true, I'm failing miserably in the wife stakes. Back in our pre-married days, we decided that we were going to have a weekly date night, only I can't remember the last time we did it.

I've been up to my eyes and ears at work. I've been working with the health and safety manager to create risk assessments for the escape-and-evasion trip, which include things like risks of drowning, broken bones, falling from great heights and claustrophobia. I'm now considering writing a risk assessment for myself on the subject of writing risk assessments, as they seem to be bringing me out in a mild panic attack each time I look at them.

I've also got Beth, my little gambling charge, to worry about. She's started attending the support group more frequently now, which is a good thing. Although I still get the impression that she's not being entirely honest with me.

Then there's the blog, and whilst Henri's wedding is fairly time minimal at the moment, I'm still spending a lot of time online. It takes a surprising amount of time to keep up-to-date with what's going on in the wedding industry and with the article in *Bridal Dreams* coming out in a couple of months, I need to make sure that the site looks as good as it can. The magazine sent me my first couple of agony aunt questions through and I spent a lot longer than expected on the responses, as I wanted to make sure that my answers were perfect.

I walk down the stairs and into our living room where Mark is waiting for me.

'What the hell are you wearing?' he asks.

I do a quick spin for him so he can get the full effect.

'What? Don't you like it?' I ask.

'Um, Penny, we're going bowling.'

'And that's what I'm dressed for. Haven't you ever seen *Grease 2*?'

'No. Why on earth would I have seen that? I can't even believe they made a second one.'

'Well they did, with Michelle Pfeiffer, and it was a classic. There's this big scene where they go bowling, and one of the characters wears trousers like these.'

For everyone that isn't Mark, I'm wearing skin-tight gold trousers just like Paulette's. Unfortunately, I don't have a pink lady jacket, so I've teamed it with a pink cardigan.

'Didn't you buy those for a fancy-dress party?'

'What's that got to do with anything?' I pout.

'Well, doesn't that make them not wearable in everyday life? I don't go around wearing my Superman costume, do I?'

'No, but you should.'

I'd forgotten that Mark had that tucked away somewhere. I can still remember the tautness of the fabric on his bum. Hmm, maybe we should do fancy-dress bowling.

'Penny, why don't you go and change? We've got an hour before the lane's booked anyway.'

'I'm perfectly fine in these,' I say.

An hour and a half later, and I'm not perfectly fine in these gold leggings, but I daren't tell Mark. No one likes to hear 'I told you so'. Not only are the leggings forcing my thong into places that I'm going to need tweezers to remove, but every time I go to shoot the ball down the lane I worry that they're going to split at the seams.

The motive had been to get Mark to notice my lovely curvy behind, but actually it's backfired and now I'm worried that *everyone's* going to notice my lovely curvy behind when it comes flying out from behind the safety of my leggings.

'We should do this again,' says Mark as he comes back from throwing a ball.

'Yes, we should.' And next time, I'll wear more appropriate

clothing. And perhaps get a bit fitter. I'm actually working up a little bit of a sweat rolling the balls. It might be due to the fact that I'm almost dying from heat exhaustion as these Lycra leggings are taking no prisoners, and for a mid-June night it's actually surprisingly hot. 'Or we could have a Wii tournament, save us leaving the house,' I say. That way we really could do it fancy dress and then Mark might wear his sexy Superman costume and I could wear my Princess Leia outfit again.

'I guess. Either way, it's just nice to spend some quality time with you,' he says.

'But you see me all the time.'

'I know, but you're always on the computer, or knackered from work.'

The pins have re-set and it's my go. As much as I want to defend myself, I also want to kick Mark's arse. I take my turn as quickly as possible, eager to get back to the conversation. Surprisingly, I hit more pins hurtling the balls down and hoping for the best, than I usually do.

'I can't help it if my work's busy at the moment; you told me that I should prioritise the promotion,' I say as I walk back to Mark. I try to not fall off the plastic seats as I sit down, my bum sliding across the shiny plastic and my sweaty Lycra leggings offering no resistance.

'I'm not talking about your work, but you're not resting

when you come home because you're always doing your blog or wedding stuff.'

'I've got to build up the website before the edition of *Bridal Dreams* with my article comes out.'

'You don't have to do that. You do it for fun.'

I watch as Mark goes up and rolls his penultimate ball. I can feel my heart start to beat faster as he's beginning to piss me off. There's something slightly annoying about having a difference of opinion when you're bowling as one person has to get up and stand just out of earshot and bowl whilst the other sits watching, slowly fuming about what's just been said.

The only upside is that it turns me into a better bowler and in my last two goes I get a strike and a spare, meaning I beat Mark. Perhaps not the best strategy when I'm trying to appease him.

'Do you want to go to the pub across the road and grab a drink?' asks Mark when we've finished.

'Yes.'

I'm relieved to be leaving the bowling alley, and the stinky shoes. I'm amazed that I'm leaving with my trousers in one piece and if I could just relieve my bottom, then that would be perfect.

We walk into the pub. It's of the family Beefeater type and I haven't felt as exposed in an outfit since I went out for Halloween dressed in a boob tube that barely kept my modesty. The fact that it was supposed to be a bikini top might just clue you in on how small it was.

I'm entirely sure that it isn't my imagination, and that people are actually staring at me.

'Mark, are people looking at me?'

'Probably, Pen. Your trousers look like they've been spray-painted on.'

'Thanks for being so blunt about it.'

'What do you expect me to say? I said you might want to change before we left the house but you told me you wanted to look like Pauline.'

'Paulette,' I say.

This is not how I want our night to go. Our first date night in weeks and we're fighting. I'm wishing that I'd stayed at home, and that's not what I should be thinking when we're spending quality time together.

'Whatever. You're just lucky you've got a cute bottom.'

'Thanks,' I say, smiling. I'll take any compliment at this stage.

'Now, sit your bum down and I'll get us a drink.'

When Mark comes back, I feel that the tension from before has gone and, for a while, we stick to safer conversation topics like our shared excitement about the impending *The Apprentice* final and we talk about where we might want to go on holiday next year. Me: Maldives, Mark: Canada. Slightly different in terms of wardrobe needed, but we'll get there eventually.

'Have you sorted out which suit you're going to wear to Henri's wedding yet? I'm getting my dress dry-cleaned so I'll take the suit at the same time if you like.'

I'm thrilled that since Mark hit it off with Henri and Nick, they've invited us both to the wedding. It will be so much better than Lara's, where I had to bugger off when all the fun started. Although it will mean that I'll be on-call if anything goes wrong.

'I'm going to wear my Ted Baker, I think.'

'Nice choice. You'll have to try it on to check it still fits. In fact, you should probably try it on when we get home.'

'Oi, are you saying I've put on weight?'

'No, I just thought you might want to. You know you look hot in that suit.'

'Oh, I see. Between your trousers that are leaving nothing to the imagination and me in my suit, I see what you've got planned, Mrs Robinson.'

'Well, we are trying for babies.'

I lean over and give Mark a quick kiss. I don't quite mean for it to be as slow and sexy as it turns out and I come over all hot and flustered. Then I remember we're in the middle of a family pub. I probably already look like a hooker; I shouldn't go acting like one too.

'I'm looking forward to going to the wedding with you. It'll be our first wedding together since ours.'

'Let's hope it has a better start,' says Mark smiling.

'I think Henri would physically kill Nick if he wasn't there when she arrived. Anyway, not much chance of that; don't forget Henri knows all about Nick's gambling.'

'Speaking of secrets, Henri and Nick's wedding is going to be the last one you're planning, right?'

'Yes, I promised you it would be,' I say sadly. I know it was a bit of a nightmare to start with and it didn't quite go to plan with my no-contact-during-office-hours rules, but actually I've loved helping Henri realise her dreams.

'And then you're not going to get sucked into another one?'

It takes all my resolve to say no. I'd love to take on one or two weddings a year, but I know I can't.

'Good. I've enjoyed meeting Henri and Nick, but I don't think you'd be that lucky to get such a laid-back bride the next time.'

If only you knew, Mark, I think to myself. I have to admit that I might not have told Mark just how many emails I used to get from Henri in the early days of the planning.

'And then are you going to scale back the blog?'

'I don't know why you hate it so much. I mean it's much better than me gambling.'

'That's like saying it's OK smoking a little hash as you're not shooting up heroin. All I'm thinking is that you might want to do less work on it.'

'Why would I do that?' I ask taking a sip of my wine.

'I thought you weren't going to do it for ever. It's been over a year since our wedding, I thought it was supposed to be helping you ease the transition from planning the wedding to normal everyday life.'

'It was at first. But I can't stop it now, it's just getting big and with the column coming out and the magazine article, I'd be foolish to stop it now.'

'Do you not think it's too much? I mean, look at us, it's been weeks since we last went on our date night.'

'We went out on Saturday night.'

'For dinner, with my boss and his wife, that's hardly the same thing. And it wasn't what I'd call an enjoyable experience. I'm talking about us actually doing stuff as a couple.'

'You sound like a big girl,' I say laughing, attempting to lighten the mood.

'Penny, I'm being serious. Are you going to keep your wedding blog going even if you get the promotion? Look at how much longer your days have got and you haven't even got the extra responsibility yet.'

'But I find the blog relaxing, it's not like work. I don't want to go back to not having anything to do in the evenings. Don't forget that you were doing your accountancy stuff in the evenings for years, and you never used to think about me having nothing to do. Perhaps you're the one who's bored and you miss studying? Maybe you should set up your own blog.'

'What, neglected husband dot com?'

'Mark, you're sounding ridiculous,' I snap.

'I know, it's just . . . it's just that a wedding nearly ruined our lives once, I don't want the same thing to happen again.'

'Mark—'

'I'm serious, Pen. I just think that you're spreading yourself a little thinly, and what about your mentoring? You've been late home from work twice this week because you've been to see your gambling friend.'

'I can't let B down, Mark.'

'I'm not saying you have to. I'm just saying that perhaps you need to think a little about what you are doing. At the moment you're making time for Henri and for this B character, but you're not making time for me.'

I hadn't really thought of it like that. I couldn't be resentful towards Mark when he was doing his course as he was doing it to better himself for our future happiness. What am I doing Princess-on-a-Shoestring for? To distract myself from gambling? To fill my time? To help brides on a budget get their princess day?

To be honest, I don't know why I love blogging, but I do. I love weddings. I thought it would fade after my own but it hasn't. In fact, it's got stronger. It's like by getting married and realising what a wedding should be about, I've got a greater degree of clarity. And I want to share that vision.

But I guess Mark is right, it's not like I'm doing it to kick-start a second career or anything. I can see why he thinks it's eating up my time.

'So do you think I should give up blogging then?'

'I don't want you to give it up, I just think you need to spend less time on it. Can't you get help? If your site is getting so big, why don't you take on some contributors? Delegate some posts?'

I don't know quite how I feel about sharing my little baby, but I guess that would be a compromise. I've never thought of asking someone else to come on board, but that's not a bad idea.

'I guess that could work.'

'Look, Pen, I don't want to be the big, bad husband, but these last couple of months have been really shit for me at work, and I've needed you and you haven't been there.'

That's news to me. I mean, I know he's looked a bit more tired and black around the eyes and he has been getting back from work later than usual, but he hasn't said anything.

'What's been going on?'

'Clive gave me another one of his clients and I'm drowning. I can't work out what's going on, but I feel like I'm being punished for something.'

'Like what?'

'I made that mistake with the Hiscock account last year, I guess it could be that.'

'Surely they'd just tell you if there was a problem.'

'Clive has a vindictive streak, you know. The only other thing I can think of is that he's trying to force me out.'

'Mark, that's crazy. They love you over there. Clive wouldn't have taken us out for dinner if he was trying to get rid of you, would he?'

'I guess not,' says Mark.

'Mark, you should have told me about this, you know I would have made time for you.'

'I know, but you were never around and then when you were you always seemed so knackered I felt bad bringing it up.'

I feel terrible that I've missed this and that Mark's been getting steadily more and more pissed off with me. It's typical him, he keeps everything to himself until eventually it snowballs and suddenly it's a huge issue.

'Mark, you've just got to tell me what's going on.'

'I know, and I'm sorry to be so down about your blog. I'm proud of what you've done, really I am. And I'm sure that Henri's wedding's going to be brilliant. I just want to make sure that I see you, too.'

'I probably shouldn't be upset that my husband wants to spend time with me. Does this mean that you're going to watch less sports then, if I'm going to put the computer down in the evenings? If we're going to have quality time together, then we need to have the TV off.'

'Well, I wouldn't go that far—'

'Mark, if you want my undivided attention, then I want yours.'

'I guess I walked into that.'

'I think you did.'

'I'm sorry, Pen, for being a grumpy bastard.'

'And I'm sorry for neglecting you.'

I lean over and give Mark a kiss. 'What shall we do on our date night next week then?'

'Anything that doesn't involve skin-tight trousers. We've been getting odd looks since we got here.'

I give Mark a playful punch on the arm.

'What about going to that new Japanese restaurant?'

'OK.'

'I love you, Mark.'

'I love you, too, Mrs Robinson.'

'So how about we go home and you get me out of these trousers.'

'Penny, I've been trying to do that all night.'

As we get up and leave, I take Mark's hand and squeeze it hard. I might have to give up my dream of having the best wedding blog ever, as this is what's important; right here in my left hand.

chapter sixteen

princess-on-a-shoestring:
Ask Penny!

Dear Penny,

I can't afford to hire a photographer and I've asked a relative to do it instead. Other friends have told me I'm crazy and I'll regret it. Are there any other solutions?

Clueless one

Dear Clueless one,

I too didn't hire a photographer and got my hubby's brother to take our photos. The pictures were lovely as he's a pretty good amateur photographer. I'm sure your friend's photos will be fine. You can always set up an account on a wedding photo-swapping website, they're free and, once registered, people can upload their photos to the site. Simply place a card with your wedding details on each of the place settings and then all your guests can upload their best photos. That way I'm sure you'll get some crackers.

Good luck!

Pen x x

I was supposed to be meeting Beth and Cat, Mark's cousin, fifteen minutes ago. I thought it might be good for Beth to meet someone who's still at uni to try and inspire her. Only it's not going to plan as I'm sitting here alone outside the coffee shop. I'm beginning to wonder whether I've got the date wrong, when a girl comes up in front of me.

'Hey, Penny,' she says.

I do a double-take. There, in front of me, is Cat, only she's changed a lot since I last saw her at Christmas. Her ash-blonde hair has been replaced by dip-dyed black-and-red shoulder-length hair. Her arms are covered with the most intricately designed tattoo sleeves that I've ever seen up close, and where once she had dainty child-like earlobes, she now has massive tunnels.

'Cat,' I say, in shock.

'You've got the same look on your face that Mum had when she came to pick me up last week.'

'It's just a big change from what you looked like before.'

'Hmm, those weren't my mum's exact words,' says Cat giggling mischievously.

'Do you mind?' I say, pointing to her arm. Cat shakes her head and I take her arm to study it in detail. The artwork is amazing, all full-colour; there are flowers and people and abstract shapes, and it really is a work of art. But why she would want to get it done is beyond me. She's always going to have them; Cat's nineteen-year-old arms will stay encapsulated like this for ever. I squint and try and imagine what her arms would be like if she puts on weight or got bingo wings. Or, heaven forbid, in a wedding dress. I know, I'm sounding old before my time.

'They're lovely,' I say. I hope that I'm doing the right thing introducing Beth, the impressionable teenager, to Cat. I'm failing miserably as a mentor trying to get Beth to stop gambling, I'm sure that her mother would be even less impressed if I managed to plant the idea in her head that she should get tattoos and ear tunnels.

'I'm just dreading going to see Nanny Violet,' says Cat.

Now that, I'd like to see. Mark's got a little tattoo on the side of his arm, it's a tribal symbol, the type that was big in the nineties. He still never lets his Nanny Violet know he's got it. He has to make sure that when he goes to see her in the summer, his T-shirts are long enough to cover it, and if he's got his top off on holiday, I always have to stand in front of it when photos are taken.

'Good luck with that one,' I say smiling.

I look up and see that Beth is coming towards us. She's walking slowly and unsurely over to us, and I guess she's probably shy about meeting an older teen.

'Hey, Beth,' I say.

'Hey,' she mumbles.

'This is my husband Mark's cousin Cat, Cat, this is my friend Beth.'

'Nice to meet you. Penny tells me you want to hear what being at uni is like?'

Beth looks unsurely at me and I nod at her.

'Yeah, I guess,' she says.

I cringe, this is going to be like pulling teeth.

'I've been trying to tell Beth what my uni experiences were like, but I'm guessing things are a bit different now. I couldn't imagine what it's like with Facebook. When we took photos they were for the eyes only of those who saw the developed copies.'

'Oh my God. How old are you, Pen?' laughs Cat.

I give her my best stern look.

'Yeah, I guess it's changed a lot. We used to have to queue

up in the library to use the printers and the Internet.'

'You didn't even have Internet connection?'

'No. Not in our student houses off campus. I used to type my emails in the middle of the night, on the way home from the students' union, when the computers were free. My poor mother thought I had an alcohol problem as she didn't get a sober email from me for three years.'

'Beth, it's nothing like that now.'

Now I really feel like a dinosaur. It wasn't even ten years ago that I left uni, but by the eye-rolling and looks I'm getting from the girls, I know that I've got nothing to add to this conversation.

'Why don't I go grab us some drinks. Cat, you could start by talking about where you live and your friends, and then talk about your course.'

'Sure. So I, like, live in halls with three guys and two other girls.'

I drift off inside the coffee shop and let them get on with it. There's clearly a lot about Cat I don't know, and although I'm slightly dreading what she's telling Beth, I think they're better off talking by themselves. Penny the dinosaur will only get in the way.

After I deposit their drinks on the table, I excuse myself and, as we're in the town centre, I decide to pop into a hiking shop. The escape and evasion trip is approaching rapidly and, unless I want to go in my new Kurt Geiger's or old, faithful Converse, I haven't got any appropriate footwear. I threw out my walking boots the last time we went to Wales, swearing that if I ever went again I'd get boots that were actually waterproof.

Walking into a hiking shop fills me with the same fear as walking into somewhere trendy like Abercrombie & Fitch. The clothes are always so androgynous that I'm worried that I'm going to be browsing in the men's section by accident.

'Are you all right there?' asks a sales assistant, a mere second after I've walked over the threshold. Either this shop has particularly amazing American-esque customer service or he's taken one look at me in my little summer dress and flip-flops and decided that I'm lost.

'I'm looking for some hiking boots. Must be comfy and extremely waterproof.' I feel like I'm giving a personal ad for the walking boots, but after almost developing trench foot last time, I feel this is an important acquisition.

'OK, well, in that case I'd recommend that you go for something Gore-Tex, they're a little bit more expensive but you can stand in a puddle for an hour and not get wet feet.'

'Just an hour?' I say thinking back to the risk assessments from the SSM.

'That's as good as you're going to get.'

'OK.'

I slip on the funny little free pop socks and try on four pairs of boots. I examine myself in the mirror and in pair number four, I don't look too bad. I could actually pull this off as an outfit: summer dress and big boots. It looks like I'm a bit rock and roll and that I'm off to a festival. And they certainly feel comfortable.

'How much are these?'

'They're £149.99.'

I gulp and look down at my feet. I guess Mark can't get mad at this kind of shoe expenditure. But holy moley, I'm not going to think about how many pairs of nice dainty shoes I could have bought for that.

'I'll take them,' I say.

I also eye up some hiking trousers and fleeces. I know I'm clearly in the women's section as the fleeces are bright colours of pink and purple. I settle in the end with a zippy turquoise fleece and a pair of trousers. Apparently we're given army fatigues to wear during the escape and evasion task day, but we need something to wear the night before.

I take my purchases up to the till where I'm reunited with my walking boots and I try not to let my jaw drop too much when the cashier asks me for £210.

'Would you like to buy any of these items for half price?' says the man waving his hand over the shelf behind him.

Now usually, I love these kinds of promotions: new scarf, giant chocolate bar, salon products. But as I look at the selection on offer: Deet mosquito repellent, hiking socks, waterproofing lotion, head torch, I shake my head. When would I ever use them?

'No thanks, I'm fine.'

I enter my pin into the machine and wait for the 'please remove your card instruction', only it doesn't come.

'I'm sorry, but your card has been declined.'

'Declined?' I say in surprise. I rack my brains to think what I've put on it lately, but I can't think of anything. I haven't used it for months, I've been trying to be good and actually save up for things I want. 'Can you try it again?'

'Yes, of course. Sometimes these things happen.'

The cashier takes my card out for me and puts it in again, and we go through the same process with the same outcome. I'm aware that there's a slight queue behind me, and I'm mortified that it looks like I have no money.

'I don't know what's happened there,' I say deliberately loudly so that the other people behind hear.

'Sometimes the phone lines to the bank go down and cards are declined like that. It may be nothing to do with your card whatsoever,' says the cashier.

'That explains it then.'

I'm not too sure how much money I've got left in my

current account, so I use the debit card to the joint account instead. I'll just have to remember to tell Mark and to put the money in on payday. We've always got surplus money in the joint account just in case we have a domestic emergency: blocked drain, massive electricity bill or, more often than not, a takeaway before payday. What? It's a domestic bill as it's food for us both, and it's an emergency as we obviously don't want to cook.

I walk away with my giant bag of purchases and hope that by the time I get back to the girls that Beth still has perfect, tattoo-free skin.

'And you only have to go to fifty percent of your classes anyway, so it's not that bad,' says Cat.

'Hey, guys.'

'Hey,' says Cat, perking up. 'We were wondering where you'd gone.'

'Just had to do some work shopping. So how did it go?'

'Yeah, good,' says Cat. 'I've been telling Beth all about uni life.'

I'm not too sure I like that Cat's winking conspiratorially at Beth, or that Beth has cracked a smile in return. I think I'd rather not think about what they talked about. All I care about is trying to get Beth interested in her future, and then hopefully that will give her a focus other than gambling.

'Great, thanks so much, Cat,' I say.

'It's fine,' she says, shrugging. 'Anyway, Beth find me on Facebook if you want. I've gotta run as I'm meeting some friends.'

'Thanks,' says Beth.

'I'll see you at Nanny Violet's sometime,' I say laughing.

'Ha, I'll be the one in a burka.'

I laugh and turn back to Beth, who looks like she's been punched in the stomach.

'Beth, what's wrong?' I ask.

I think Beth is actually going to cry. The plan was to give her a kick up the bum by showing her what she could have, not to make her feel worse.

'I thought that might help you,' I say.

'It's just . . . Never mind.'

'What, Beth?'

She sighs in the way only a teenager can.

'I'm never going to make it to uni.'

'Don't say that. Your mum said you're a good student.'

'Ha, yeah. My mum thinks I am.'

'What do you mean?'

'Do you, like, promise you'll not tell anyone? Including Mum, or that Mary?'

I wonder just what promise I'm about to keep. But if I say no, then none of us will know.

'Promise,' I say. I'm about to do the Brownie salute, but I get the impression that it will probably be lost on Beth.

'I can't go to uni.'

'Why not?'

'I'm failing, Penny.'

'Failing? What, at college?'

Beth nods her head sullenly.

'And you haven't told your mum?'

'No. I did well in my mocks at Christmas, but lately I've been doing really shit.'

'How come?'

Beth shrugs again. 'I just can't focus on the work.'

'Are you gambling when you should be working?'

I'm taking the guilty look written all over Beth's face as a yes.

'And I feel kinda bad about the money.'

Now this is something that transcends the age divide.

'I know all about that. I felt so guilty about the money I lost. I still do. And I try and put any money I make from my wedding planning into our joint account to try to make up for what I lost. Have you thought about getting a summer job?'

'Yeah, but there aren't any. And I've got no experience. I've got no chance.'

'That's not true. Couldn't you try and get a supermarket job or shop work? When I was younger I worked at Asda and it was great. We were all about the same age.'

'I tried everywhere last summer, and I've kept my eyes open for them since. There's so much competition for them these days that they always take on older, more experienced, people.'

I feel like telling Beth not to keep playing in the bitter-barn, but I've been there. When you're low from gambling, everything seems to be against you.

'Is that why you play your games?'

'I'm doing badly because I'm playing my games.'

'Then why don't you stop?'

'Because it's the only thing I'm good at.'

'Even if it's ruining the rest of your life? I mean, what are you expecting to do? Go and work in Vegas as a croupier?'

'Wow, that would be awesome.'

'Beth!' Gosh, I am so ready to be a mother. 'Look, you're at a really delicate age. If you mess up your life now it's going to be really hard to sort yourself out and it could affect everything. You're a smart girl, why are you doing it?'

'Why did you do it?'

'Because I was an idiot. But I did stop when I realised what damage I was doing.'

Beth's silent and I think she's gone into full-on teenage sulking. I've tried to be nice to her. I've tried being her friend. I've tried to rub a magic lamp and show her what her future could become – in the guise of Cat – but none of it has worked. What Beth needs is some tough love.

'How are you even getting the money to gamble anyway?'

Beth's still silent and keeps fidgeting.

'Beth?' I say, scaring myself at how much I sound like my mum.

'I had some winnings. And I'm winning now.'

I'm always doubtful when people say that they're winning. No one ever wins all the time.

'Can't you give that money to your mum and then stop?'

'I don't think I can.'

'Not even after hearing about Cat's experiences? You've got a year left to go, you could still get to a good uni if you work and catch up.'

'I dunno.'

I try and channel my inner peace to work out what I can do. The incentive of going to university doesn't appear to have done what it was supposed to.

'What about if I help you get some work?'

'Where?'

'Well, I'm organising a wedding in a few weeks and one of the tutors from the college is doing the catering. He uses students to do the silver service, and maybe I could see if I could get him to take you on.'

'Like waitressing and stuff?

'Yes, posh waitressing.'

'But I've never done that before.'

'Well, I'm sure you could learn. Is it something you might be interested in?'

'Yeah, if it was paid.'

'It would be. But I'm only going to help on one condition.'

'What's that?'

'You're not allowed to use the money for gambling.'

'That's it?' asks Beth, as if it's some sort of trap.

'Yep.'

'You're not going to make me stop gambling?'

'No, you're going to do that yourself.'

'I am?'

'Yes, you are. You're going to turn your grades around. You've got half a term left. You're going to work your arse off cramming for your exams. You'll do your best and see if you pass. If not, you're going to have to repeat next year.'

'Repeat? What about my friends?'

Ah, so that's something that bothers Beth.

'Well, if your friends have their shit together then they'll go into their final A-Level year and after that they'll probably go off to university.'

The tears start to roll down Beth's cheeks, making me feel guilty but I know I've got to keep playing tough cop.

'I just wish I'd never started playing.'

'Well, it isn't going to get better until you stop. Do you think you might be able to do it?'

'Maybe.'

'Good, well I'll phone Brett and see what I can do about the wedding.'

Beth seems to crying even harder than she was before.

'Beth, you can stop crying, you're going to get through this. I'm going to help you.'

'Why are you being so nice to me?' snuffles Beth.

'Because I know how awful it is to be where you are, and I know how much the guilt can affect you, and how you feel like you're alone. Well, you're not alone. I'm going to be here for you.'

Beth wipes her tears away and looks round self-consciously.

'Thanks, Penny. I'm going to get going, OK?'

'OK. You've done really well. See you later.'

Beth waves as she walks off. I feel like I might have finally got through to her. I start beaming with pride; I, Penny Robinson, might just have turned someone's life around.

chapter Seventeen

princess-on-a-Shoestring cost cutters:
Saver Favours Part II

There's no doubt that eBay is a budget bride's best friend when it comes to wedding favours. You can usually pick up anything from organza bags to old-fashioned sweets much more cheaply than you could in other online shops. My top tip for wedding favours would be to buy mini packets of Love Hearts in bulk from eBay or Amazon. Then you can buy labels on eBay that you can have personalised, usually with the bride and groom's names on. They send you sheets of the printed stickers and all you have to do is stick them over the top of the original wrappers. Finish by placing in an organza bag.

Tags: sweets, eBay, organza, favours.

It's 10.41 a.m. How long do you think I've been in the office for? Well, I'll tell you: three hours and forty-one minutes. That's right, for those with speedy maths skills, I got here at seven a.m. It was so early when I left the house that no one had even updated their status on Facebook. And just what could have dragged me from my bed, my bed which is the most comfortable bed on the planet, at that un-godly hour? Work. No special conferences, no VIP guest, just your average-Joe workday.

I have several friends who have more high-powered jobs than mine and it's not uncommon for them to be in the office at six or seven in the morning, and they'll leave twelve hours later, and that's a good day – often it's more likely they'll leave around midnight. I have never wanted to be one of those people. And yet here I am. The reason work is even worse than usual is that it's only a week to go before the team-building trip and I'm making sure that I cross all the 'i's and dot the 't's. I know I'm only going to be out of the office for a day and a half, but with Shelly in charge of the department in Giles's absence, I don't want her to have to do any of my work in my absence.

I stand up from my desk and make my way to one of our larger meeting rooms. I'm holding a briefing for all the staff lucky enough to be my guinea pigs on the trip. It's a chance for me to tell the chosen ones (aka the sacrificial lambs) what they're in store for. I'm going to give them a briefing on their conduct (no hanky panky), what clothes they should or shouldn't bring (bikinis are out, thermals are in) and what to expect (that it will be cold, wet and miserable).

The way I see it is that this briefing will set the tone for the rest of the trip. As I'm trying to impress the pants off Giles and Gunther, I need it to make myself look as professional as possible, by being in control and authoritative. And when I say impress the pants off, I don't mean literally, as from what I've discovered of Gunther the vegan, he'll probably be wearing hemp underwear.

Lucky enough, neither Gunther or Giles are attending the briefing as Gunther's not over in the UK until next Thursday and Giles is on annual leave today. Which means that I can brief everyone else and then it will be like a well-oiled ship when we depart next Thursday afternoon.

One of the things I've got to do is to put people in teams. But I'm going to save that joy until later on, after I've explained the fun time ahead. There isn't really a best bit about organising this crappy away trip, but I like to think that there is always a silver lining, and today's silver lining is that I get to pick the teams. This means I can put Giles and Gunther in any team but my own. Bonus.

At exactly five minutes before anyone's due to arrive,

I load up my presentation and, amazingly, after much cursing and colourful language, the projector is behaving itself and actually working. All I need now are for the people to arrive.

You can tell a lot about people by how early they turn up to these things. As people start to trickle in, I wonder if I could mentally rig it so that I mix up the teams to have a few early birds, and then those that file in a couple of minutes past eleven, 'the sorry I'm laters' to even them out.

'Right then, everyone,' I say. I always have to bite my tongue at this point as I went to a school where we had assembly every day and it got drummed into me that we say 'good morning, everyone', and everyone chants it back. When I first started working here, I did actually do that a couple of times at our whole staff training sessions. That year our departmental approval rating went down, and people muttered about incompetent and patronising staff. Now you might think I'm being paranoid about this, thinking it was all about me, but there was even a sketch about it at our work Christmas party that year.

'Thank you all so much for coming. I know that we're taking a lot of your time up next week, but we felt that it would help a lot if we could have half an hour now just to check everyone knows what we're getting ourselves into.

'So, has anyone ever been in the Army or done anything with the TA?'

I see a rogue hand go up at the back. Perfect. That one's going to be in my team.

'Well, you'll know what to expect, but for the rest of us, it might come as a bit of a shock. Essentially, they'll be five teams of seven. We're hoping to do the usual, mixing managers and different departments. It should be a good opportunity to get to know colleagues that you usually wouldn't get a chance to meet.'

Oh, dear lord, I can hear what I'm saying and yet I'm still saying it. I am that person from HR that everyone wants to kill.

'As you know from the medical forms and disclaimers you had to sign, this is going to be fairly physically demanding. Now, I don't know any more than you do about the content of it, but I have been told that if you want to get something out of the day then you have to put something in. This is a team-building event. I want you to bond with your group and I want you to help everyone along.

'The way it works is that each team is taken to a different location. We'll all have maps and we'll be told another location that we have to get to – we'll all be trying to reach the same point. We'll be given an hour and a half's head start before six 'chasers' try and catch us. Every time they catch your team, you are given penalty points, but after that you're given half an hour's grace to get going before the chasers can look for you again. If you make it to the central location without being caught, you'll get bonus points. You can also try and get bonus points by picking up flags along the way, but these flag stations will be favourite hang-outs for chasers. There is also an elite chaser that will hunt all teams. Apparently he is ex-special forces and a top tracker. If you manage to avoid him, you'll get bonus points. You can also receive them for special tasks that you must take photographic evidence of, such as shelter building, survival eating et cetera.

'You will be scored as teams rather than individuals, so this is an opportunity to work together. If you're caught and you're missing any members of your team, you'll get penalty points.

'So, if there are no questions about the team-building part, can you have a quick read of the things you'll need to bring with you and then let me know if you have any questions.'

I look up and see a man waving his hand in the air.

'Er, yes?' I say pointing at him.

'It says here we have to wear army fatigues. I'm afraid that offends me as I don't believe in armies.'

I wrinkle my eyes in confusion. I understand that he

might not believe in Santa Claus or the Easter Bunny, as they may not actually exist, but I'm pretty sure that the Army exists. The fact that we work about five miles down the road from Aldershot, the Home of the British Army, is a slight giveaway.

'When you say you don't believe in armies . . .' I say as diplomatically as I can.

'I don't believe in what they stand and for, as such, I don't want to be dressed like them.'

'Right,' I say. Now I'm not exactly pro-war and I did in fact go on an anti-war march for the Iraq war. We'll skip over the fact that I had seen this guy I fancied on campus getting on a bus and, with it being midnight, I mistook it for a party bus on its way somewhere infinitely more exciting than the students' union. I passed out somewhere south of Leeds and was awoken at dawn in London.

'The thing is, the idea is that we all wear the same thing. That way everyone in your team is equal and if you don't wear the fatigues then that already stands you apart,' I say.

'But what about those who are vegetarians or have special dietary requirements, they don't have to eat meat just to fit in with the rest of the team, do they?'

Oh, great. We have an office of five-hundred-and-sixty people, and after taking a random five per cent segment of the staff we managed to get Mr Know-it-All. He is not going on my team. And I certainly can't have him on either Giles or Gunther's teams.

'Good point. But unfortunately you're going to have to wear them because you signed the contract in which you agreed to follow the rules, and one of the rules is to wear the fatigues.'

Ouch, take that, awkward man. Today's lesson: read what you are signing. It seems to have done the trick as Mr-I-Don't-Believe-in-Armies is looking glumly at the floor.

'Any other questions?' I ask hesitantly.

'When it says we have to carry our own bags, what does that mean?' says a woman at the back.

'We get given rucksacks with all our kit and vital supplies and we have to carry it.'

'So we don't have Sherpas or anything?'

'Um, we're not going up a mountain, we're trotting around the South Downs countryside. I'm sure the distances involved are short and you'll be able to manage your bag. And I don't think there are too many hills,' I say, crossing my fingers behind my back. Baz did send me an Ordnance Survey map and I'm not a geographical expert, but many of those contour lines looked tightly packed together.

'Anyone else?'

At least four hands go up.

'It said on the risk assessments that we may get wet, yet there's no mention of swimwear. Do we need to bring some to go under our wetsuit?' says a woman at the front.

'Um, no, as you won't be wearing wetsuits. Everyone will be issued with army fatigues and that's what we wear all the time, apparently.'

More hands shoot up – every question seems to prompt another. Thank God Giles and Gunther aren't here because this is fast turning into a shambles.

'How about I go through the list, and then perhaps we can do questions at the end if you still have them? We've established that you'll be given fatigues, but you'll have to supply your own footwear. Ideally these should be hiking or walking boots rather than trainers as the terrain will be rocky and muddy. They advise you to take a change of clothing, especially underwear.' Clearly in case you shit your pants, I think to myself. 'In case, er, they get wet during the day.'

There's a collective murmur at this point. I'm wondering where the flags are going to be placed and whether we're going to be swimming or making rafts to get to them.

'You also need comfortable loose-fitting clothing to wear after we've finished and for the awards ceremony.'

I share the puzzled look on people's faces as to why we have to have loose-fitting clothing for the presentation of the awards. Surely we won't be doing power lunges on the way up to the podium?

'All personal items that aren't essential should be left at our initial rendez-vous point. Now I'd advise against taking any valuables with you as we'll probably have to lock them in the minibuses. So, if we're all happy with that, I'll commence with the programme of events.'

I ignore Mr I-Don't-Believe-in-Armies, whose hand has shot up. I'm wondering just how much his manager told him about this trip before he signed up.

'We will be leaving here at 1600 hours sharp on Thursday and travelling to the South Downs in our minibuses with designated drivers, you know who you are, and we should arrive at the scout hut around 1730. We will then be given our kit and a safety briefing before dinner. We get some tips on escape and evasion from our chasers that night, and we will be sleeping in a scout hut. Females will be in one dorm, males in another and never the twain shall meet.'

There are a few chuckles and grins around the room as we almost do a silent salute to the manager and his secretary who did the dirty on the final infamous Wales trip.

'I don't know what time we start the escape and evasion on Friday, but apparently we have to be at the final point by 1600 hours, so at 1530 your chasers are called off and you make your way there. We then head back to the scout camp to get changed and for the presentations. Any questions?'

'Are there any facilities at the scout hut?'

'Um,' I say, stalling for time. 'I'm not entirely sure. I know there are toilets. I think it's a dormitory, so I'm guessing camp beds.'

'So it will be like camping?' another person asks.

'Sure, like camping,' I say. 'In fact, remember to bring a fleece as it will probably get chilly in the evening.'

'Will there be fresh water for me to wash my hands? I'm going to have to take my contact lenses out,' shouts out someone else.

'Yes, I've been told that there will be food and water. I've also heard the words "cook-out" used,' I say enthusiastically. I think I read too much Enid Blyton as a child, but cook-outs still hold a bit of a magic for me. I can just see us now putting jacket potatoes in foil, and toasting marshmallows. If only Mark was coming as well, it sounds so romantic.

'Right, if there are no more questions, I think that takes us to deciding teams. I'm going to call your name and give you a number and then that will be your team number.'

I start reading out the names first, then assigning numbers. I may have done a couple of swaps. Believe it or not, Mr I-Don't-Believe-in-Armies was supposed to be in my team. Instead he's now in team five and I managed to swap him with a quiet-looking man.

When I finish I look round the room and, for once, there are no hands up. I give myself a quick pat on the back. I'm clearly a born organiser after all.

'Right then, if we quickly introduce ourselves to our teams and then we'll have to get back to work. And between now and next week if you have any questions at all, you can either come and see me or email me.'

We break away into our little group of seven. I have to say that my team looks like a motley crew. If I'd been more foresightful then I would have been more selective in my choice of team, going only for the likely winners. Not that I'm competitive or anything. Really.

But no, it's not about that, is it? It's team-building, and it would probably look dodgy if my team won anyway.

'So, obviously I'm Penny. Why don't we go round and introduce ourselves?'

'OK, I'll start, I'm Annie, from Finance and I'm so excited to be coming. I've been in training for weeks now to get fit for it.'

'Great, thanks, Annie,' I say. I was worried that everyone was going to be really quiet and I'd be the only one talking, but it looks like Annie's nice and friendly.

The rest of the group introduce themselves, and I think

we've got a pretty good team. It consists of: Martin from Sales who looks pretty fit (in terms of for escape and evasion, not as in looks), Tim with the army experience – our star member, Jack and his manager Tess from Design, and Matt from IT.

As I say goodbye to my new band of brothers, the room starts to thin out.

I start packing away my stuff and I'm aware that there's a young woman waiting for me.

'Hi,' I say looking up. 'Have you got a question about next week?'

'Oh, no. I just came up to say congratulations about *Bridal Dreams*.'

I look up at her in horror and I frantically look round to see whether there's anyone else left in the room. The last two stragglers are just leaving and I turn my attention back to the woman.

'How do you know?' I ask.

'I'm a subscriber, so I got my copy in the post. I was flicking through it this morning when I was eating my breakfast and I saw your picture.'

'For the agony aunt piece?'

'Yes, and the bride-on-a-budget piece. I didn't know you were a wedding planner as well.'

'I'm not. Not really, I've only done a couple. I can't believe you saw it. It's not supposed to be out until August.'

'But it's the August edition. They usually come out about six weeks before.'

'That's great,' I say, hyperventilating. I remember when I sent the article off, thinking that I couldn't wait to get my hands on a copy. I imagined myself racing down to the newsagents to see it. But I hadn't for a moment considered the idea that anyone from my work world would ever read it. It's not like I wrote an article for *HR Magazine* or anything. I hadn't thought that there might be others at the company who would be getting married and reading *Bridal Dreams*.

'I was pretty sure that it was you, but having come to the meeting it confirmed it. I absolutely adore the magazine, and I can't believe you're one of their monthly agony aunts. It must be a dream come true.'

It's actually starting to feel more like a nightmare and I'm too stunned to reply.

'Listen, um . . .'

'Meg.'

'Meg, do you mind if we keep this a bit quiet at work? I mean, it doesn't look good for me to be talking about my hobby as I'm here.'

'Of course, Penny. Mum's the word,' she says tapping her nose. 'Right, well, I best get back to my desk.'

'Yes, I'll see you next week then.'

I watch Meg go and then I sit myself down in a chair before I fall down. I better hope that Meg's good to her word and doesn't tell Giles, or else I can kiss the promotion and maybe even my job goodbye.

chapter eighteen

princess-on-a-shoestring top tips:
Don't forget to pack for your wedding night and the next day

Yes, I've known this to happen. A bride who shall remain nameless turned up to my hotel room the morning after her wedding in her wedding dress and a T-shirt after failing to pack anything to wear on her bottom half. If you're staying somewhere the next day, take a couple of changes of clothes. Think about an outfit to wear the next day, and maybe also one for late in the night if you'll be drinking after-hours in the hotel later (especially if your wedding wasn't there). And don't forget to take some special undies for the night of your wedding, just in case you're one of the few couples who actually gets round to consummating their marriage on their wedding night.

Tags: wedding night, next day, clothes, packing, consummation.

I am a supreme packing goddess I chant over and over in my head as I walk into my house. Why oh why did I leave packing for this work trip until the night before? I've just got back from supervising the construction of the marquee and now I've got to pack before bed. I've been putting it off all week.

'Honey, I'm home,' I say cheerfully as I walk through the door.

'You're back! How did the set-up go?'

'Really well. The wedding's going to be beautiful,' I say proudly.

There's something different about Mark tonight and I can't quite put my finger on it. He's just a little bit perkier than usual and his eyes are practically twinkling. He's also fidgeting like he's dying to tell me something.

'What's with you? Is everything OK?'

'More than OK.'

Now he's broken out into a full-blown smile.

'You're looking at Brown and Sons' newest manager.'

'What?' I say, a matching smile appearing on my face. 'Mark, that's brilliant. Congratulations! So much for you being worried that Clive was going to fire you, huh?'

'I know. It turns out he's semi-retiring in a couple of months and they wanted to give me some of his clients to see how I coped and to see if I was ready for the promotion.'

'That's amazing. I'm so proud of you.'

I wrap my arms around his neck and give him a proper good snogging in congratulations.

'I got a bottle of champagne on the way home from work, I'll go and grab it.'

'Great,' I say screwing my face up as he goes. I can't tell Mark that I need to be packing rather than celebrating. After all, I mean how often does he get a promotion like this? I'm sure it's not going to take me that long to pack. As Mark comes back with the champagne flutes, I decide I'll just get up extra early tomorrow morning to pack instead. It'll be easy, chucking a few things in a backpack, it's not like I have to pack things neatly or worry about creasing.

'Is that what you're taking?' asks Mark.

I sense he's laughing at me.

'Yes, it's the bare minimum.'

'Right. I used that rucksack for my backpacking trip round Asia for twelve weeks. And it wasn't that full.'

'Well, I am organising the trip, so really I need to make sure I have something for every eventuality. I've got extra jumpers and tracksuits bottoms, two first-aid kits, emergency Snickers bars. You know, the essentials,' I say shrugging nonchalantly.

'Hmm.'

It turns out I'm not the queen of packing after all. Far from it being easier to shove things in a rucksack, it's actually a lot trickier than packing into a rectangular suitcase where everything's out in the open and you can rearrange things easily. I'm currently sitting on the bag, determined to get it done up. I had to scale up from my rucksack, which was never going to fit everything I needed.

Now, you'd think as I delivered the briefing that I would have known exactly what to pack, but I seem to have found a lot of grey areas this morning.

I mean what constitutes an essential? Tinted moisturiser? It's not make-up and it has SPF in it, so I think that counts. Small vest? In case it's boiling and I have to de-layer. Travel pillow? In case the pillows provided aren't comfy enough. Flip-flops to walk around the camp in?

There also seem to be a few essentials that I seem to be missing. Remember when I was wondering why anyone would want a head torch or hiking socks? Well it turns out that both are listed under kit you should have. I've borrowed a couple of pairs of hiking socks from Mark, and they may have holes in and be a fair few sizes too big, but I'm sure it's better than wearing my thin-as-a-pin Little Miss Sunshine socks.

And, as for a head torch, the closest I could find was a wind-up torch I carry in my car. I can't quite mount it on my head, but at least I may be able to find my way to the loo in the middle of the night.

I stand back from the rucksack and give it a final look up and down. It's as good as it's going to get.

'Do you want to give me a hand taking it down stairs?' I say as I stand up from it and the sides that looked relatively compressed have immediately bulged out.

'Don't you need to be able to carry it?'

'Yes, that's why you should carry it down the stairs, you know, to preserve my arm muscles.'

'Right. Can you actually lift it?'

'Of course I can,' I say as I clasp it by the straps and attempt to pick it up. OK, so it takes both hands to get it an inch off the ground, and I'm not entirely sure that I'm going to be able to swing it over my back, but at least I can lift it, right?

'Come here,' says Mark, picking the backpack up with one hand and throwing it on his back in what looks like an effortless motion. 'Bloody hell, Pen. What on earth have you got in here?'

'I may have to take some stuff out when I get there. Maybe I can dole out the Snickers to everyone tonight instead.'

'That might be a good idea.'

As we walk down the stairs, I can't see Mark or his cute bum as it's eclipsed by the bulging bag. Perhaps I have packed too much.

'Right then, shall I put it in the car for you?'

'Yes, that would be great, thanks.'

All I need to do now is transfer it to the minibus and then I can dish out the chocolate which will drastically reduce the weight.

'I'll just grab my handbag.'

As I meet Mark outside by the car, I look up at the blazing July sunshine. I just hope that the weather is like this for Henri's wedding on Saturday. I've given up hoping that it will stay this hot for our escape and evasion. I've seen the weather forecast, I'm a realist. But at least there's no rain forecast.

'Hope you have a lovely time,' says Mark as he closes the boot.

'Thanks, honey.'

He pulls me towards him for an early-morning kiss. With freshly brushed teeth it's all minty and lovely.

'Just remember, you're in charge,' says Mark. 'And you'll be fine.'

I'm not sure SSM will agree.

'Thanks, honey. I'll try and give you a call tonight.'

'Great stuff. And, maybe this time next week, you'll be the HR supervisor.'

'Oh, don't speak too soon. It's going to be a long thirty-six hours. But imagine if I got it, both of us being promoted.'

'Yeah, that would be fantastic. You'll be great, Pen, everything will work out fine.'

'Thanks, honey. Well, don't forget, I'm going to go straight to the cricket club after the trip, to set up the marquee, so I probably won't see you until late on Friday night.'

'OK, I'll see you then.'

Mark kisses me again and I get in my car. Today is going to be a good day, I start to chant over and over in my head.

I'm still trying to chant that mantra in my head as I go through my work day. This leaving at four p.m. isn't the best idea. It means that the office is full of people sneering at those of us dressed in combat trousers as they know what horrors are to greet us. And those of us dressed in said combat trousers seem to have that 'off on a school trip' feeling that seems to make it impossible to do proper work, as you know you're leaving any minute.

I'm trying to look busy when actually I'm killing time until I get to meet Gunther. He's due here at midday and then he's going for a lunch meeting with Giles. I've got to give them both a mini briefing about the trip, although without the fun of giving them a packing list as I emailed it to them both last week. And, hopefully, as this trip was Gunther's idea, he won't have any objections to sleeping in a hut, wearing army fatigues, or carrying his own backpack.

I'm just adding the finishing touches to my out-of-office reply (it takes time to get it just right) when my mobile rings.

I peer over it, and see it's Henri.

I have a quick look at my watch. 11.41 a.m. I've got just under twenty minutes before Gunther arrives, but what if he's early? I'm not going to make the best impression if I'm sat here on my mobile. But, on the other hand, it's T-minus two days until her wedding, and I'm going off to deepest-darkest Sussex and deserting her. Hardly what a super-dooper J-Lo-type wedding planner would do.

'Hello,' I say, answering the phone as quietly as I can. I run out to the stairwell and take refuge in the ladies loos.

'Penny, there's an emergency. I repeat, an emergency.'

'OK, Henri, just breathe. Now, we've been through this before, haven't we?' I say, trying to use calming and soothing tones. 'Is this in the same league of emergency as the paper-cut you got from the table plan? Or like the napkins being too thin?'

In case you can't tell, Henri and I have been having a lot of fun this week with the phone calls, emails and even tweets to my @princess_shoestring account. There's really nothing for Henri to worry about, the marquee went up yesterday and it looks lovely. It won't take long on Friday night to do the decorating, as it's only really the homemade bunting and the battery-powered fairylights in jam jar centrepieces that can be put out the night before. The rest: helium balloons to scatter round the ceiling of the tent, tablecloths and all the paper bits (things like seating charts and name places) can't be done until the morning of the wedding because they'll go damp overnight. But Henri has been worrying about everything. She even wanted me to check to see if the vicar marrying them was making sure he was taking Vitamin C so he didn't get ill.

'Worse, Penny, worse!'

'OK, calm down.' I wonder if the knives aren't the right weight or the strawberries are too small for the Pimms. Unfortunately, Henri is suffering from a touch of the bridezillas. It's mean of me to say, but I'm slightly looking forward to going out of the area for a day and a half. 'Just talk me through the problem.'

'It's my sister's bridesmaid dress. It doesn't fit.'

'What do you mean it doesn't fit? Too big, too small?'

'Too small. My sister must have been in denial when she told me she was still a UK size twelve. She can't get the zip anywhere near done up.'

'Is there any bit of the fabric that could be let out? Maybe you could take it to a local tailor.'

'We've already tried. My sister put the dress on and the seamstress laughed. She said, short of putting an extra panel of fabric in it, she couldn't wear it. I can't not have her as a bridesmaid, and we can't get new dresses as the napkins are the same shade of orange. The chances of us trying to find another dress in the right shade are miniscule. And we can't afford to get both new dresses *and* new napkins. What do I do, Penny? What do I do?'

Henri's talking in such a high-pitched voice that probably only me and dogs can hear her.

'Just breathe, Henri. What about getting bridesmaid dresses in brown, you know they might compliment the orange.'

'It will look like a flipping harvest festival.'

I think it would look really nice, but the number-one rule of wedding planning that I've realised is that it is not my wedding. And I have to at least get the bride to like it.

'OK, what about us trying to get you another one of the dresses, have you looked online?'

'Yes,' says Henri.

Oh great, I can hear her sobbing.

'Henri, this is a little bump along the way, we'll be able to find a solution; we just need to think about it.'

'Oh my God. You don't even have a solution off the top of your head? I thought you'd know instantly what to do. I can't just sit around here and wait, how will I cope?'

'Henri, it will be fine.'

'No, it won't! My sister's going to be walking down the aisle naked at this rate and—'

'Henri, let's be realistic. Have you phoned the London store to see if they have any left?'

'What? No I haven't, but I haven't got any time to go up. How would I get it?'

'Mark could pop in after work; they'll be open until eight on Thursday.'

'He'd do that for me?' says Henri through her sobs.

'I'm sure he would. Why don't you phone them and see. They might be able to check the other stores locally too, maybe the Farnborough or Guildford stores will have them.'

'Penny, you're a legend.'

'Let me know how you get on. If I don't answer it's because I'm on my way to Sussex and I'll phone you tonight.'

'Thanks, hon.'

I hang up the phone and look at my watch. Five minutes until Gunther's ETA. I put my phone on silent and fix my hair in the mirror before leaving.

'Gunther's just arrived,' says Shelly as I sit down at my desk. 'Giles asked where you were, but I said I didn't know.'

'Thanks, Shelly,' I say. Trust her to get in on the act. 'Did they say for me to go in?'

'Giles said he'd pop out in a bit. So, I'm off to lunch, did you want me to pick anything up for you, I'm guessing you're not taking lunch as you're leaving early?'

I look at Shelly. I know I'm leaving work an hour early, but it's not like I'm going on a jolly holiday, is it? I'm going to spend the next thirty-six hours solidly at work, with colleagues. But nonetheless, I can't admit to her that I was going to take a full hour for lunch, so instead I nod and ask her to pick me up a tuna salad sandwich.

My office phone rings and I see it's Giles.

'Hello, Giles,' I say.

'Penny, great you're back. Do you want to come in and brief us?'

'Sure,' I say as enthusiastically as I can.

I walk towards Giles' office making sure that my flies are done up, my V-neck top isn't revealing too much cleavage, and that my phone isn't in any of my pockets. I'm thinking there will be many more emergencies from Henri before the day is out.

I knock on the door and I wonder just what Gunther is going to be like.

'Come in,' says Giles.

I walk in the office and both Giles and Gunther stand up.

'Gunther, this is Penny Robinson,' says Giles motioning towards me like there are multiple candidates standing in the room.

'Hello, Penny. It's so lovely to meet you,' says Gunther in a very unSwedish accent, in fact, he sounds very British. But his hair is Swedish blond and he has that Nordic cheekbone structure that makes him look confident and authoritative.

'Hello, Gunther, nice to meet you,' I say, shaking his very firm hand.

Oh dear. I had seen pictures of Gunther on the company intranet and in magazines, but I didn't realise just how tall he is in real life. What is he, six foot seven or eight? Stop staring, Penny, it's rude. But I can't help it. I think if you're over six foot seven or eight you can legally be called a giant. Amazing.

'So, Penny, Giles tells me you've done an excellent job so far organising this trip and making those tiny changes for me.'

I almost laugh; tiny changes like moving it on a week and affecting the working schedule of thirty-four members of staff which led us to have to substitute six people. Six new medical forms, six new disclosures and six new risk assessments. But I'm glad that was only a tiny change, I'd have hated to see a major change.

'Thank you, I've really enjoyed it. The logistics, the management, it's been a great challenge.'

If I don't get this promotion I'm going to investigate jobs that require you to be an awesome bullshitter. It would be a shame to waste a skill I've managed to develop.

'Great stuff. Now, can you run us through the briefing as we're off to Chez Vivant for lunch.'

Charming. They get to go to Chez Vivant for lunch whilst I eat my sad tuna salad roll at my desk. Mark's right, I need to get this promotion.

'OK, well, you've already had your emails about what to bring. I trust there weren't any problems.'

Gunther's PA had confirmed he'd read the email, but that still left room for doubt in my mind. I always prefer to hear things from the horse's mouth.

I look wide-eyed to make sure neither of them are pulling a face that suggests that they forgot vital kit. I don't really want to have to go on an emergency lunchtime shopping trip to get supplies. But, luckily for me, they both nod.

'Great, so I've split everyone up into five teams of seven. The plan is that we've got three minibuses to take us there so everyone should be able to travel with their teammates. For extra bonding.'

'I like that. That's good. Are we in your team, Penny?' asks Giles.

No, I'm not crazy, I nearly answer before I instead clear my throat. 'Actually, I thought it would be more in the spirit of inter-departmental team-building if we were all in different teams.'

'Oh, yes, good idea. We did that with the Swedish meditation training we did.'

Phew, I breathe a sigh of relief. I was a bit worried that they'd make me rearrange it so that they were in my team. Mark had wondered whether Giles would want to observe me from close quarters.

I go on to tell Giles and Gunther the rough outline for the next thirty-six hours. There is much nodding and, to my horror, Gunther is one of those people who looks at you as though he's actually listening to what you're saying, word for word, rather than working out what he's going to have for tea. This is bad news for me, as I'm trying desperately to make sure that I don't say anything about his giant status or whether he'll be able to escape and evade as he'll be head and shoulders above everyone else.

'Sounds like you've got everything under control,' says Gunther, staring at me intently. 'And you managed to sort my meals out without too much of a problem?'

To be honest, even if I hadn't sorted it out I would lie and say I had, as Gunther doesn't seem to be the type of man to say no to.

'Barry, the man in charge, said it will be fine.' I don't think those were his exact words, but I'm sure Gunther won't mind me paraphrasing.

'OK then. So, Giles, let's go to lunch. Penny, are we meeting you back here?'

'We're all meeting in the west car park, at 1545,' I say, getting far too into this whole military talk.

'Excellent! See you then,' says Gunther.

I walk back over to my desk. I look over at my phone and see that I've had two missed calls. Two isn't bad, two doesn't signify an emergency in Henri's eyes. Obviously she's only at Defcon- Five.

Giles and Gunther walk past my desk and they give me a little wave as they disappear off. No last-minute invite comes my way, unfortunately.

I wave back and pick up the phone to Henri.

'What's new, Scooby Doo?' I say, who knows why.

'Are you calling me a dog, Penny, in the week of my wedding?' shrieks Henri.

'No, no, I wasn't. Henri, I wasn't—'

'I'm only kidding, sweetie. Now, I have good news.'

I breathe out the biggest sigh of relief. I thought, for a minute, I'd sent her over the edge.

'Let's have it then,' I say, hoping that the Farnborough store have the dress in size fourteen.

'There are only three stores in the UK that have a size fourteen.'

'That's fantastic. Where are they?'

'Cardiff, Manchester or Brighton.'

'Oh blimey,' I say again. Well, I guess Brighton's only a

three-hour round journey, maybe Henri's sister won't mind a little road-trip whilst she's in the country.

'Yes, isn't it perfect? You're off there this afternoon, so you can pick it up.'

'Oh, hang on now, Henri. I can't go and get it, I'm driving a minibus full of my work colleagues on a team-building trip that I'm organising. I can't just drive into the centre of Brighton to pick up a dress.'

'I'm sure no one will mind.'

'Henri, I'm not even going anywhere near Brighton. We're going into the South Downs countryside.'

'But you have to! You're the only one that is going anywhere near.'

'Can't you or your sister go, tomorrow?'

'No, there's no time, we're in the hairdressers getting our hair dyed today, then we've got the spa tomorrow followed by the mani-pedi.'

I don't think I can really point out that maybe getting a dress to wear for her big day might be a slightly higher priority than a spa day, but as I was the person who, an hour ago, said that there would be an easy solution, I probably don't have a leg to stand on.

'What about getting the store to courier it down?'

'Apparently they don't do that. If you want them to send it between stores you have to allow at least two days and there isn't time. And I don't know anyone who lives in Cardiff, Brighton or Manchester to post it to me, I've thought of everything, I really have.'

'OK, calm down, Henri,' I say as I can hear her voice starting to go funny like she's starting to cry. 'I'll tell you what, I'll look at our route and see if we are going anywhere near Brighton.'

'Oh, Penny, you're a life-saver. A dream come true.'

'I'll phone you back in a minute,' I say.

I put the phone down, just as Shelly comes back to her desk. That would be the last thing I needed at the moment, her to find out about the Henri dress errand that I'm probably going to have to run.

'Here's your sandwich,' says Shelly, handing it between the no man's land between our desk, which is where we used to keep shared copies of *Marie Claire* and *Heat*. Only, now that we're in serious competition, they've been replaced by copies of *HR Magazine*.

I pull up the route on Google Maps and conflicting feelings of dismay and relief wash over me. We are staying in the scout hut which looks to be about twenty minutes, at most, outside of Brighton. A plan hatches in my head as I do the necessary research into where the Brighton branch is and how I'm going to navigate my way through the city centre.

I pick up my mobile and text Henri. I'm too afraid to call in case Shelly overhears.

We're on. Text me the details of where and who I pick it up from. x x

I press send, and I hope that I'm not about to do something that's going to come back to haunt me.

chapter nineteen

princess on a shoestring:
Ask Penny!

Dear Penny,

I want to have a photo booth at my wedding where people take photos of themselves and then they get uploaded onto Facebook, only I can't afford to have one as they're so expensive!

Amber J

Dear Amber J,

Don't despair, just get a digital camera and a tripod and make your own booth! Pick a blank bit of wall at your reception venue, place a table next to it with props like wigs, hats, glasses and inflatable guitars etc. Either write instructions for people to use the timer or get them to ask another guest to take the pics. Then you can upload the photos to Facebook from the memory card. So it might not be as high-tech as a fancy photo booth, but the results will be just as fun.

Penny x x

We manage to make it to the scout hut on time, which I think is impressive, considering I was driving one of the minibuses. Not only did we not get lost, but I also resisted all urges to sing classic road-trip songs like, 'Take Me Home, Country Roads', that I do to the annoyance of Mark every time we drive for more than an hour. No one was sick (which I felt was an indication of my excellent driving skills) and we only had to stop once for a toilet stop at my insistence.

I was slightly disappointed that people didn't think we should play games like Twenty Questions or I-Spy. I thought it might be fun to start the team rivalries – gee us up for the competition, but no one seemed that bothered. Instead ,they spent most of the trip with headphones in their ears or surfing on phones. Clearly they're not very excited about the prospect of tomorrow's mobile-free day. Luckily for me, next to the driver's seat and chief navigator was Annie. Who, let's just say, kept me company all the way. I think my ears are going to still be ringing tonight.

According to my instructions from Henri, TK Maxx is open until seven p.m. and Brighton is twenty-two minutes away. As far as I know, we're not doing anything special tonight, other than the cook-out which means I should be able to slip off for an hour without anyone noticing. I didn't imagine that I'd be trying to escape and evade everyone before we'd even started the competition, but I guess it's all good practice for the main event tomorrow.

I step out of the minibus and immediately lock eyes with a man who has to be Baz. He's dressed in full green camouflage and is sporting a 'tash circa 1980.

'Hello, Baz,' I say, receiving a very firm handshake which has the potential to rip my arm out of its socket. I always say that I like a firm handshake, but that was something else.

'Penny,' he says in the same way that Len says seven in *Strictly Come Dancing*. 'If you get everyone to line up in their teams, we'll get everyone kitted out, and then we'll have a mini briefing session before we go and get some scram.'

'Great,' I say, no hanging around here, no comfort breaks or a cup of tea. We are, as they say, in the Army now.

After getting everyone into their teams in almost

straight lines, we follow Baz into a large wooden hut. It's got that rustic cabin in the woods type feel to it, along with a pungent smell of disinfectant mixed with smelly feet and wood.

'Right, listen up. There are piles of kit that you will need. First you will pick up a Bergen.'

It's a good job that Baz is holding up a large rucksack as, to be honest, it sounded like he was telling us to pick up a tasty snack.

'You will then walk around the edge of the room, stopping at each pile of kit and taking it. It might not look like anything useful to you, but it might just be a vital piece of kit for tomorrow's exercise.

'The only things you will need to try on are your helmet and your boiler suit. Everything else is one size. Helmets and boiler suits are at the end there. I will call people over, team by team, to get them. Understood?'

I look round at everyone and we all nod our heads in fear as he doesn't sound like he'd be sympathetic if we said no.

'I said understood,' says Baz so loudly that the walls seem to shake and I'm sure I can see dust falling out of the roof.

'Understood,' we all say like schoolchildren.

Blimey, Baz truly is a SSM.

*

When Baz told us he was going to kit us out, he wasn't joking. I don't entirely know what I need all of this kit for, but one thing's for sure, there isn't going to be a lot of room for any of my 'essentials'. I'm thinking the tinted moisturiser, foot lotion and deodorant aren't going to make the cut.

Mr I-Don't-Believe-in-Armies is looking pleased with himself at the fact we are wearing plain khaki boiler suits. I don't want to point out to him that I'm sure somewhere in the world an army fights in this kind of outfit, but I must remember the prime objectives of this trip are a) not to get lynched, and b) to make sure everything runs smoothly so I get the promotion. Which means I have to be nice to him.

'Right then, privates,' says Baz, to much sniggering, mostly from the men. 'You will pick up your roll-mats and your sleeping bag and you will make up your bed in here.'

I look round the sparsely populated room and wonder exactly what he means. Everyone else is doing the same and then, for some reason, they're looking at me. And then I remember that I'm in charge.

'Baz, can I, um, have a word?' I ask. 'Talk amongst yourselves,' I call as I walk towards him. 'I thought that we were sleeping in dormitories?'

'Er, no. You're doing the escape and evasion package.'

'That's right, for the day,' I say nodding.

'Well it starts tonight. We have you all in one room,

sleeping on the floor so you start off tomorrow morning sleep deprived. It's the next best thing to dumping you in the woods overnight. We used to actually get people to shelter build and sleep outside, but we found that teams would sneak off and try and get a head start.'

'But there aren't any beds.'

'No, there aren't. You've got a roll-mat and a roof over your head, that's all you need.'

'But we needed separate accommodation between the women and the men.'

'Penny, we'll just split it down the middle.'

I'm starting to feel ever so slightly queasy. Gunther and Giles spent their lunchtime at Chez Vivant, how are they going to cope lying on a bit of foam? And not only that, how am I going to cope sleeping in the same room as all these men? The smells and noises that emanate from my own husband are bad enough; how awful will it be with twenty of them?

'Right,' I say nodding and wishing I'd bought ear plugs and a nose peg.

I go back over and join the line of people listening to the briefing.

'So, you will all be sleeping in here tonight on roll-mats and sleeping bags. Women down that end, men down the other. I suggest you take some time to get yourself sorted and pack your bags. Dinner will be at 1900 hours,' shouts Baz.

Perfect, I think. It's six now, I've got an hour to get to Brighton and back, that sounds doable.

'After dinner, we'll give you some tips for escape and evasion. Then I suggest that you get an early night, we will be setting out to your start locations at 0530. This means you must be up, dressed and ready in your full kit by 0530. You will need to have breakfast before you go; it can be found in your ration pack. Enjoy.'

I'm starting to imagine what kind of breakfast you get in a ration pack, as any illusion of a nice hearty full English to give us energy for the day disappears.

'There are showers, in case any of you are brave enough to use them. They are solar-powered, and hot water is on a first-come first-served basis.'

Luckily, I've bought a family-size pack of wet wipes so I'm happy to make do for a day with those.

'Right then, I'll leave you to pack your bags. Remember you will be carrying these tomorrow over rough and, in some places, difficult terrain. Only carry what you absolutely need. Now, get to it.'

I rush off almost a little too quickly and secure myself a space in a corner in the women's section of the barn. I unroll the roll-mat and throw along my sleeping bag. I'm just going to have to make time to pack my big bag later as I really need to get going to make it to Brighton in time.

I make it outside the doorway of the barn when someone calls my name.

I turn round and realise that it's Anthony, the sales director.

'Hi, Anthony,' I say, hoping that he's simply going to congratulate me on my excellent organisational skills.

'About this sleeping arrangement. I don't think that it's very appropriate for the senior managers to sleep on the floor next to the other staff, is it? I mean, Gunther Jacobson is here, Penny.'

'Well, I don't hear him complaining,' I say looking longingly over at the minibus. I'm desperate to make a bid for freedom, and every minute I'm talking to Anthony is another minute wasted not getting this dress.

'He's probably too embarrassed. I just don't understand how we're supposed to get these people to respect us and take us seriously when they've seen us sleeping.'

I wonder what is it that Anthony does in his sleep that would make people not respect him.

'Anthony, the barn has no windows in it, it's going to be pitch black. No one will see you sleeping.'

'That's not the point. I'd rather check into a hotel.'

Me too, I want to scream, but I don't. Instead, I take a

deep breath. I feel like pointing out to him that he agreed to come on this sodding trip and as a manager he should lead by example. But I'm worried that it will come out a bit snide. I'm supposed to be in charge here and I've got to find a way of resolving the situation without shouting at him, and in double-quick time so that I can go to Brighton.

'Anthony, look, I think rather than taking away respect for you, sleeping amongst the staff will *give* you it. You'll be known as one of the team, one that mucks in with everyone else. All you'll be doing by going to the hotel is alienating yourself.'

I almost do an involuntary dribble as I think of a hotel room with a comfy bed, a bath and clean fluffy towels. Sod the bridesmaid dress, I should be going in search of that instead.

'Do you think so?'

'I know so. Look, go into the barn, set up your bedding and chat to those in your team. You may find you actually have fun.'

Anthony looks at me in horror.

'OK, perhaps not fun, but it might not be as bad as you imagine. You know sleeping on the floor sometimes does wonders for the posture.'

'I guess so,' Anthony walks off slowly back towards the

barn and I give myself a virtual pat on the back for sorting out the problem.

I glance at my watch, how did that take ten minutes to sort out? I'm cutting it fine if I'm going to get there and back by seven.

'Penny!'

I turn round and see Gunther towering over me.

'Are you leaving?' he asks as I've got the door open to the minibus.

'No, no. I just thought I'd left my mobile in here,' I say looking around for it in exaggeration. 'I guess not,' I say acting surprised, despite the fact that it's in one of the myriad pockets of my combat trousers. 'I'll find it in a minute. What can I do for you, Gunther?'

'It's about my meals.'

If he's going to say anything about changing, I'm going to lose it. The number of conversations I had with Giles and Gunther's PA about it, not to mention the terse conversations with Baz. I don't want to go there again. 'What about them?'

'Well, it's just that I've been given a vegetarian ration pack.'

'OK,' I say. 'And you can't eat any of it?'

'Bits, but the main meal is vegetable Thai curry, and I can't eat that. I wonder if you could sort it out for me?'

I look longingly at the driver's seat of the minibus and I step back and shut the door.

'Of course, Gunther.'

'Thanks, Penny. I don't want to make a fuss.'

No, no fuss at all. I think to myself.

I head back into the barn where Baz is helping someone pack their bags.

'Baz, I just need a quick word,' I say.

He looks up at me and sighs.

'I promise I won't keep doing this,' I say.

'What can I do for you?'

'Remember how we were talking about the vegan?'

'How could I forget?'

'Well, it seems like he has a vegetarian pack.'

'Oh, well you'll have to speak to Knobby, he does the food. He's over there.'

I look over to see a tall, lanky guy in combats and go up to him. I don't really want to ask him if he's called Knobby, it's one thing for a butch, scary man to call you that, quite another for a little woman to.

'Um, hi. Baz sent me over to speak to you about the food. It's just that one of my colleagues is a vegan, and he's been given a vegetarian meal.'

'Right, isn't it the same thing?'

I wince and wonder just what all my phone calls with Baz were about. I feel like slapping my head in frustration.

'No. . . Vegans, don't eat any animal products, so no dairy.'

'Oh right, now that I think of it Baz did say something about that. Right then, there's a Tesco Express down the road, I'll nip out and get something like a Pot Noodle.'

'I'll go,' I say a little too enthusiastically. That would be an excellent and legitimate cover story. I could go and get the food, whatever that would be, and then go and nip to Brighton. If anyone asked, I could just say that I got lost trying to find the supermarket.

'Are you sure?' asks Knobby.

'Dead sure, I'll know exactly what to look for,' I say, about to race off before anyone can stop me. But, just at that moment, I hear and, almighty crash over the other side of the room.

'What did you just say?' I hear Baz shout in his booming voice.

'On second thoughts,' I say to Knobby. 'You might have to go.'

I run over to the other side of the barn where there seems to be a Mexican stand-off between Baz and Mr-I-Don't-Believe-in-Armies. I should have known he was going to be trouble.

'What's going on?' I hiss.

'You, outside now,' says Baz, ignoring me.

Mr-I-Don't-Believe-in-Armies stays rooted to the spot, and I have to drag him outside myself. 'Everyone else, carry on with the packing, there's nothing to see here.'

'What's going on?' I ask, putting myself in the middle of the two of them when we're safely away from the barn.

'He just called me a war-mongering butcher,' says Baz pointing his finger in a menacing way.

I turn round and look at the trouble-maker.

'Did you really?' I ask in disbelief.

'Well, I didn't mean for him to hear, but yes, yes I did say that.'

Baz almost goes to lunge at him, but I manage to throw my hands up to stop him.

'Look, Baz, he obviously didn't mean to say what he did. Did you?'

'Yes, I bloody did.'

Baz goes to launch at him again, which means, with me standing in the middle, he's coming straight towards me, but you know what? I've had one black eye this year, and that's plenty for any lifetime.

'Baz, I'll sort this, OK? You, over there,' I shout, as I march my irritating colleague over to the corner of the courtyard.

I'm fuming. Not only is this guy embarrassing the whole company, but he's also ruined any chance I had of getting

301

this bridesmaid dress, as even if I left now for Brighton, the shop would be closed before I got there.

'You can't go around saying things like that. What is your problem?' I shout. 'I know you might be anti-war, and I can't say I always agree with what's going on, but you can't shout things like that at people.'

'We've only been here ten minutes and he's already shouting at us and making us feel like we're this big,' he says, holding out his hands in a pinching motion to illustrate his point.

'Surely he can't have done anything too bad, we've not been here long enough.'

'I just hate men like him.'

'Men like what? OK, so he's a bit scary, but it's all an act. It's meant to give us that illusion of being in the Army. It's a bit of theatre.'

'I just hate it, that's all.'

I look at the rage that's burning in him, his eyes are practically on fire with the loss of control. There's something about this that doesn't ring true, he can't have taken such a dislike to someone so soon.

'Look, um. I don't know what your name is.'

'Richard.'

'Look, Richard, have you always had such a grudge against the Army?'

He's fidgeting on the spot.

'My girlfriend left me last month. The geezer was in the Army.'

'Oh, right.'

'He came round the house when she was leaving me, standing there as bold as brass in his uniform, packing up her stuff and throwing his weight around and I did nothing. I stood by as he took her away and I didn't do anything. You know who he reminded me of? My dad. He was in the Army and he was a wanker too. They're bullies and they're mercenaries. So that's why I don't believe in the Army.'

Blimey, I feel like I'm in an episode of *The Jeremy Kyle Show*.

'Sounds like you've had it tough over the last few weeks. You could have perhaps come and talked to me about it. I'm not a monster, we could have put someone else in your place.'

'Nah, my boss was stoked I was coming. I think he thought it would do me some good. He said in my last appraisal that I was a bit of a loose cannon and not a team-player.'

Note to self, read the appraisals before allocating places on such excursions.

'Well, you can't go around behaving like that here. For starters, Baz has done nothing wrong. And, secondly, he isn't even in the Army any more, it's just an act. And, thirdly, most importantly, Gunther is the CEO of this company: he is not someone you want to make a bad impression in front of.'

'You're right. Everything's just such a fucking mess at the moment.'

Oh my God. He's actually going to cry. It's difficult enough knowing what to do when a woman cries, let alone when a six-foot-one, fully grown man starts to well up.

'Maybe tomorrow will be good for you. Take your mind off things. Who knows, you might meet another woman here. People always say most relationships start in the workplace.'

What am I saying? I don't want any more repeats of what happened last year in Wales.

'Thanks for trying to cheer me up.'

'You're welcome. Look, I'll go and talk to Baz, explain the situation.'

'OK,' says Richard, wiping his eyes.

I walk over to Baz. He's been having a cigarette and watching the two of us very closely. Occasionally giving us a death-stare.

After explaining the story to him, he utters the word 'women' and goes off to talk to Richard. A minute of tense conversation later and Baz is slapping Richard on the back and the two of them are walking towards the makeshift bar.

'Penny,' says Giles striding over.

'I just wanted to say what an excellent job you've done so far with the organisation. This place is just perfect. And not only that, I've seen you sorting out the little problems. You're showing all the signs of someone with good management potential, keep it up.'

I watch him walk away and I'm stunned. It takes a minute for it to sink in that I haven't messed it up yet. The promotion is still within my grasp.

I can feel my phone vibrate in my pocket, and when I see it's Henri I send it through to voicemail. I can't face talking to her yet. I'll have to think of a new plan which will see me picking up the bridesmaid dress tomorrow. Right now, I have no idea how I'm going to be able to escape and evade a team I'm supposed to be stuck to like glue.

chapter twenty

princess-on-a-shoestring cost cutters:
Invite fewer guests

OK, so this is a bit of a no-brainer, but when you're throwing a party where things are priced per head, then reducing your guest list is a great way to reduce your costs. Do you really want Great-Aunt Margaret who you haven't seen for years there? Or what about your old work colleague that you occasionally meet for lunch? Ask yourself, if they were getting married, would you be upset if you weren't invited? If the answer is no, then that's an easy name to cross off your list.

Tags: cheapskate, guests, de-friend.

I couldn't face calling Henri back yesterday. I did what any cowardly custard would do, I texted her and told her I had

306

dodgy signal and that I'd call her this morning when we were on the move.

I thought that there was no point worrying her unnecessarily about the lack of dress as it wasn't like she could do anything about it. It was more important for her to keep calm and get her beauty sleep. Unlike me, who got no sleep at all.

I think I would have had an easier job sleeping through the London Philharmonic Orchestra's brass section rehearsing. The noise levels from the snoring last night were on an unimaginable scale. And I can't even blame the men. Annie, who I was sleeping next to can, it seems, both talk *and* snore for Britain. Then there were those that needed to traipse to the loo in the middle of the night, the barn door squeaked as it was opened and shut. Oh, and that was even before the rain started, which sounded like someone was playing drums on the barn roof. Did I mention I didn't sleep?

So when we were roused out of our bed at dawn and I had to wet wipe myself awake, I was not feeling well rested, I was not in the mood for escape and evasion, and I certainly was not in the mood for Annie; within five minutes of being let loose on the Downs, she asked me what my thoughts were on the Cumberland sausage.

Today has proved, without a shadow of a doubt, that I am

not a morning person. And that I am never, ever, taking my bed for granted, ever again.

'Let's rest up here,' says Tim, as he takes us into a team huddle behind a tree. We've been walking for hours and hours and I think that I've broken my back. My pack is ridiculously heavy, despite having stripped it down to absolute bare essentials; not even my flip-flops or fleece came with me.

'How are we all getting on?' asks Tim.

'It's pretty tough,' says Annie as she struggles to reach her water bottle from the side pocket of her pack. She looks like a dog trying to chase its own tail.

'Here,' I say freeing it from the elasticated pocket and passing it to her.

'Well, it's only going to get tougher now. The chasers will be leaving around now.'

'What?' I scream before I get a chance to compose my thoughts.

I look down at my watch and I see that it is only seven a.m. I thought we'd been walking for at least three hours already.

'Sorry,' I say embarrassed. 'I thought we'd been going for longer.'

'Me too,' says Tess.

'How are we doing on the map? Are we near any flags?' asks Annie.

'There's one here,' says Matt pointing to a small X on the map.

'And we are?' I ask.

'Just here,' says Tim pointing.

'So we're almost there, we could go and grab it,' I say.

'Is it too risky though, won't they catch us?' says Tess.

I'm having trouble taking anyone seriously. Now that it's getting light, I can see everyone's efforts with the camo face paint. In the dark, when we were applying the paint by torchlight, it didn't look like we were actually putting much on but, now in the daylight you can see how hideous it actually is. We've got a full spectrum from American footballing look-a-likes with stripes under the eyes, to full-on face covering.

'Why don't we go and get it, and then try and double back.'

We all look up at Jack from Design, he's barely said boo to a goose so far this morning.

'How do you mean?' I ask.

I'm not one for strategy at the best of times. Much to Mark's delight when we play Monopoly. But that, along with the serious lack of sleep last night, means that none of this is making much sense to me.

'Look, here's the central rendez-vous point. The chasers are going to be homing around it, waiting for us, hoping we're going to go for the early win. Why don't we go and get a flag, go back to where we started and then try and go to the rendez-vous point from there. There's another flag, look there, beyond where we started.'

'That's actually not a bad idea. We did something similar when I was on exercise with the TA,' says Tim.

'Does that mean they might think we'd do it?' asks Matt.

'Probably not, as far as they know we're all civilians,' says Tim.

'OK, then, I think that's our best bet.'

'Is that where we started? And is that the scout hut?' I say.

'Yeah, why, do you think we should double back past there?' asks Tess.

'That's an excellent idea, Penny, excellent,' says Matt. 'If we can get behind it, then we could hide there and wait. Maybe do some of our tasks.'

I pat myself on the back, as this means that it would be a perfect time for me to pop into Brighton. I've just got to work out how I can sneak away for an hour without anyone noticing, but we'll cross that bridge when we come to it. Right now I'm happy we're going to be near to the minibus, which saves me having to hitch a ride to Brighton.

You can tell that we are getting into this whole escape

and evasion thing properly now. It's light and instead of us going for big, bold walking across the Downs, we're starting to pick out routes along tree lines and we're looking over our shoulders constantly, hoping we don't bump into any of our chasers.

The ex-special forces man laughed at us all last night as he said he thought we'd all be easy to find. He told us that even the trees have eyes, so we've been making sure we've been looking up too. I keep imagining that I'm going to look up and there he'll be sitting, up a tree, swinging his legs from it like Robin Hood.

'How are we going to get across that field?' asks Annie as we reach the end of the clearing.

There's a wood about a hundred metres away that will give us cover. But between us and the wood is a field on top of a valley. If we walk across it, then anyone below us is going to see.

'There's nothing else for it. We're going to have to leopard crawl,' says Tim, dropping down to the floor.

I'm imagining that he's going to start crawling across the floor pouncing like a seductive woman impersonating a cat. But instead he's lying on his belly and half-pulling half-shuffling across the ground. It bears no resemblance to any leopard that I've ever seen.

One by one, we all drop to the floor and follow Tim. It's

bloody hard work. The grass is dewy. I usually like the smell of wet grass in the summer, but now that my nostrils are hovering a centimetre from it, it smells pretty gross and my elbows and knees feel like they're being battered and bruised with every inch I gain.

By the time I make it out to the clearing of the wood, I stand up and stretch like an old woman.

'That's it,' I say, 'I am definitely taking up yoga again.'

Everyone laughs at me; I seem to have become the joker of the pack. It's always nice when you have a skill in a team. I'd prefer it if people were laughing with me, rather than at me but, hey, I'll take any laugh I can get.

We're just getting into the tree line when I feel my mobile phone go.

'Um, guys, I've got to go for a call of nature,' I say. I spot a big hedge to the side of us, and I deposit myself behind it.

'Hello,' I say wincing at the caller-ID that says it's Henri.

'Penny. Thank God. I've been trying to call you practically all night.'

'Yes, sorry bad signal,' I say lying. 'What's up?'

'I just want to confirm you got the dress.'

Now, as I see it, I have three options. I could: 1) make swishy noises and pretend I can't hear Henri and hang up and switch off my phone. 2) I could lie and tell her I've got it, as I will have in about two hours. Or I could, 3) Tell her the truth.

'It's all under control, Henri.'

Maybe I'm learning something about being a manager. I mean, I'm not technically lying, the situation is in hand. There's no point in worrying her.

'Oh, Penny. That's such a huge relief. Now we can work out a solution to the other problems. I was speaking to Brett last night about the tablecloths and I was asking him about the canapés.'

'What about the canapés?' I don't think I want to hear this.

'Well, I thought maybe I'd been playing it a bit safe with my choices, you know mini roast beef and Yorkshire puddings, and mini fish and chips. I just can't help thinking it's a little Mum's-gone-to-Iceland.'

'But they were your idea.' I start to pull at my ponytail in order to take out my frustration.

'I know, but I was speaking to my dad and—'

'Henri, you can't change the menu the day before your wedding.'

'Well yesterday it was two days before. But that's pretty much what Brett said.'

'And he's right. Look, one of the top ten rules of weddings

is that you don't piss off the chef. So, Henri, don't piss off the chef.'

'Well, it might be a little late for that—'

'What happened?' I growl down the phone.

'I just told him that I'm the bride, and really what I want should be his top priority,' she says, defensively.

I instinctively throw the palm of my hand up to my forehead. Why is this happening when I'm sixty miles away?

'Henri, promise me you will not speak to Brett between now and tomorrow. If you want to know anything about the catering, you ask me. OK?'

'But, Penny—'

I can hear the snuffles of tears.

'Henri, I'm serious. No talking to Brett. Call me.'

I know I shouldn't really be fielding Henri's calls whilst I'm on the team-building day, as I can't afford for anything to go wrong or anyone to find out that I'm running my own wedding business. But I don't think I've got any choice. I get the impression that Mark might be catering the wedding in a minute if Henri has her way as I don't think that Brett copes well with brides. He said that was one of the reasons that he didn't do many external catering events.

'OK,' says Henri. The blubbering appears to have stopped. I know crocodile tears when I hear them.

'Right then, so no other emergencies. The napkins are sorted?'

'Yes, although I do think the windows of the clubhouse are a bit dirty and I would prefer them if they could be cleaner.'

I contemplate whether I could still do that going through a tunnel noise and hang up feigning bad signal. But I end up listening to Henri as she talks to me about her woes of unbreakable glass and the fact it looks dirty. Short of Henri replacing the windows there's nothing that anyone can do about it, and yet she still goes on for five minutes about it.

After we say goodbye, I ring Brett to calm him down, and it was just in time as he was apparently on the verge of pulling out. As I finally appease him, I'm increasingly aware that my team-mates are probably beginning to wonder where I am.

'Penny, are you all right?' calls Annie.

'Don't come round here,' I say. I walk back round the front of the bushes where the rest of the group are sat resting and tucking into their ration pack Yorkies.

'Is everything OK? You were there for over ten minutes,' says Tim looking at me.

'All I can say is that I wouldn't go round there if I was you.'

Everyone pulls a face at me. That's just perfect. I've just given myself a fake case of diarrhoea. How mortifying for no reason. Henri Scott, you better appreciate the lengths that I have gone to to plan your wedding for you.

'Well, I hope you buried it. That SAS guy will sniff us out from that.'

If I didn't feel sick from my fake stomach problem, I certainly do now after that lovely mental image. 'Don't worry, Tim, no one will ever find it,' I say with utter confidence.

'There's the flag,' says Annie with far too much gusto.

She's about to make a run on open ground to get it, when Jack pulls her back by her rucksack like she's a child in reigns.

'We need to talk about strategy. Perhaps one of us should go and get it,' says Jack.

'But don't we get penalised if one of our members gets caught and they're not with the rest of the team?' asks Tess.

'Yes, but don't forget if we all go, we'll increase the likelihood of us getting caught,' says Tim.

Who knew there would be so much to this escape and evasion? When I'd booked it, I'd naively thought the main struggle would be walking and carrying the backpack, but now we're trying to pretend like we're some kind of stealth force. If I didn't have this goddamn bridesmaid dress to get, I'd be loving it.

'OK, so who's going to go?' I say.

Everyone is turning to stare at me.

'Well, Penny. You *are* the smallest,' says Tim.

At five foot five, I'm hardly a short-arse, but I can see what they're saying.

'You've just got to do your commando crawling again.'

'Like the cougar,' I say.

'Leopard, Penny, you're not trying to pick up young men hanging out in the countryside,' says Tim.

I suddenly have an image of me dressed up in an animal-print dress prowling the countryside looking for young farm hands. I try and shake it away and concentrate on the job in hand.

'When you get there, go past the flag and get it from inside the tree line,' says Jack.

'Stuff the flag down your top,' says Martin.

'Sniff to make sure you can't smell any soap,' says Tim.

'What?' I say trying to cope with the information that my team are bombarding me with.

'If you smell soap, that indicates there's someone there. And who else would be hanging out by the flag other than a chaser,' says Tim.

'If in doubt, get out,' says Annie, before looking around. 'Sorry, it's just like the Crystal Maze for me. I can't bear the excitement.'

I can see now why, even though Annie is practically the same height as me, they have picked me and not her. In her over-excited state she might have got up and run, getting us all caught in the process.

I pass my pack down the line to Annie to guard, and I take a deep breath before assuming the position. The things I'm doing for the team.

If I thought crawling along the flat was bad, it's ten times worse crawling uphill. I shimmy myself along, ignoring the grass smell, and not thinking about what actually lives in the stinky grass. I don't want to have encounters with ants, beetles or anything larger than that. I do an involuntary shiver at the thought of meeting a snake in the grass and it propels me quickly forward.

I'm about three metres away from the flag and I'm lying still, trying to listen for noise. I do the sniff test and my bones go rigid in fear. I can smell the unmistakeable smell of cigarettes. And then I hear the words I've been dreading hearing.

'Caught you.'

I wait to be pulled up from my hiding place, but nothing happens. Instead what I hear is a commotion.

I carefully look up and I can just see another group the other side of the flag. They've been caught.

The chaser's got his back to me and I seize my opportunity.

Springing up, I grab the flag and stuff it down my chest quicker than I ever thought possible. My heart's beating furiously as I jump back down to the ground. I didn't miss the look on Gunther's face as he clocked me doing it. He winked and I guess that means he's going to keep silent.

I wouldn't say that my escape out of the area was very stealthy, but I managed to make it back to my team without being caught. My heart is hammering ten to the dozen and I feel like I'm practically taking a bath in my own sweat.

I get pats on the back and hugs from everyone, but we don't hang around for long, as we know that it won't be long before that chaser is back in operation.

'That was such a rush,' I say to Tim and Matt when everything has calmed down.

'It looked it,' says Matt.

'Look, there's the scout hut,' says Annie, as we come up behind it.

I don't know if it's because I am so close to the minibus that a plan has formed in my head, but I suddenly know how I'm going to have temporary leave from the escape and evasion and get to Brighton to get the dress.

'Guys, I've got an idea about how we could get more points,' I say. 'But it's a big risk, so you're going to have to trust me.'

chapter twenty-one

princess-on-a-shoestring top tips:
Get married in the winter

Winter weddings can be beautiful and you're just as likely to get a dry day in February as you are in August, thanks to the wonderfully unpredictable British weather. Getting married out of season is great because loads of venues do cheap wedding packages to get business. I've seen offers where you get venue, a three-course meal for sixty guests, hotel for the bride and groom for the night, welcome drinks and an in-house DJ for just under two thousand pounds. Just plump for a venue that looks pretty on the inside too in case it's a bit nippy for outdoor photos.

Tags: mid-week, out of season, winter, packages.

I can't believe my plan worked. As I put my foot down to floor the accelerator and pull out of the scout camp, I marvel at what just happened.

I convinced my team that we would get more flags if we split up. Working out the penalty points involved if we got caught apart versus how many points we would get if we got the extra flags, we decided it was worth a bit of a risk.

We decided to rendez-vous again in exactly an hour. Tim and Matt went off to get a flag slightly to the south, and I've gone off to get one to the west. Apparently. Only – shock horror – when I get to my one I will find it so heavily guarded by chasers that I won't bother.

I've clipped my Bluetooth headset to my ear and I think now's a good time to phone Henri, just to check that she's sticking to the ban and not calling the caterer. I also want to make sure that she hasn't started on the vicar. It would be just like her to have phoned him asking him to change the colour of his collar to match the bridesmaid dresses.

'Penny!'

'Hi, Henri, how's it going?'

'It's wonderful, we've got champagne and I've just had a mud wrap.'

How nice, we've both been caked in mud all morning. I know where I'd prefer to be.

'Great. So there's been no more, um, emergencies?'

'Nope, everything's been wonderful. I think we're there, Penny. We've done it. We've planned an amazing wedding and now we can relax.'

If only Henri, vision of tranquillity and calm, could see me now, dressed in a boiler suit, camouflage face paint, speeding along the Sussex countryside in a minibus; I must look anything but relaxed.

'Excellent. Well, let me know if you need me,' I say.

'Will do, see you tonight, Penny.'

I hang up the phone and I take a deep breath. When this dress is bought, then that will be it. I will be able to throw myself back into the team-building. Henri won't be phoning me with any more emergencies and I'll be able to concentrate on finishing the day. It's been going so well up until now. Surely I'm a shoe-in for this promotion?

All I've got to do is find the right street, which hopefully I will thanks to the Sat Nav. I have been to Brighton once before, but only on my sister's hen do. I arrived by train, which doesn't help in the recce stakes, and I only saw West Street and the Lanes. Although seeing West Street is a bit of an exaggeration as I don't really remember seeing any of it – I was that drunk. Although I think West Street saw a lot of me as I fell over and flashed my knickers before being sick.

322

I manage to make it to the city centre and find a side street where I leave the minibus and I just about remember that I'm probably going to get arrested if I walk into a shop like this. I look like a shoplifter, or someone on day release from an institution.

I do my best with a bit of spit and polish with an old snotty tissue and then I take my arms out of the boilersuit and tie it round my waist. Luckily, I'm wearing a vest top underneath. I reckon as this is Brighton, I might just be able to pull this look off.

I get out of the minibus and fill the parking meter with coins and I run to where I think TK Maxx is. There are a few distractions in the form of Bench and Superdry, and I have a feeling that I'm close to Peter Andre's coffee shop. I'm sure I recognise this street off the telly from when he was opening it. Luckily, the mortgage-like payment I had to make to the parking meter is keeping me focused on getting in and out as quick as I can.

I'm feeling slightly like Anneka Rice on *Treasure Hunt*, I've got my Bluetooth headset which though not as cool as the helicopter one she wore, is similar enough. And I might not have a skin-tight flying suit, but you have to admit that I do have a boiler suit on. I am so Anneka Rice.

Maybe I'm in the whole army frame of mind already as I'm

that mission focused that I head straight to the Customer Service desk and not to the Shoe Department.

I'm ignoring the strange look that fellow customers are giving me. I know my outfit is slightly weird but, hello, I thought anything went in Brighton.

'Hi, I believe my friend Henri Scott has got a dress on hold; I'm here to pick it up.'

'OK, I'll have a quick look out the back.'

I look at my watch and gasp at the time, it's been half an hour since I left the others. I keep my eyes straight ahead and avoid looking at any merchandise nearby. I've come so close to getting the dress, I can't be distracted by any other bargains.

'What did you say the name was?' asks the sales assistant as she comes back empty-handed.

'Henri Scott.' I repeat.

'I'm sorry, there's nothing back there by that name. Was it this Brighton branch that she reserved it at?'

'There's more than one?'

Oh my God. I didn't think to check. In all my haste I just typed in Brighton TK Maxx and took the postcode for the Sat Nav.

'There's another one a couple of streets across.'

I start to take deep breaths, as I'm starting to hyperventilate.

I can't be running around Brighton. I have got to get back to my team.

'What exactly was it?'

'It was a burnt-orange bridesmaid dress, in size fourteen.'

'Oh, we have that. Maybe it's being held under a different name?'

'Perhaps she put it in my name? Penny, Penny Robinson?'

'I'll go and have a look.'

I keep all my fingers and toes crossed that she's going to come back with the dress. Otherwise I'm going to have a whole lot of explaining to do to Henri.

The sales assistant comes back with the dress in her hand and if there wasn't a giant counter between us, I might have given her a hug.

'Here you go,' says the woman as she scans it in.

I breathe the biggest sigh of relief ever and pay for the dress.

One task down; one cover story to validate.

I'm trying to work out just how to get back to the minibus and whether I've got time to pick up a McDonalds when I bump straight into a person.

'Terribly sorry,' I say in my polite British accent, and that's when I realise who I've bumped into.

The guy mumbles a sorry, and I hope that I've got away with it, but just as I'm tip-toeing away the guy calls after me.

'Hey.'

If I didn't need to cross a busy road then, I might have made a run for it, but I don't want to add getting hit by a bus to my list of things that have gone wrong today. How would I explain that to everyone on the away-day? I'm not quite sure they'd accept that I got lost and ended up walking to the centre of Brighton.

'I thought you hadn't recognised me,' I said to the ex-Special Forces chaser.

'I don't think I could miss you, with your boiler suit and the camo paint smeared all over your face.'

I instinctively rub my face, and my hand is instantly covered in thick dark-green cream. No wonder everyone in the shops was looking at me.

I can't believe he's tracked me all the way to Brighton, I know he is supposed to be good, but I had no idea he was this good.

'So, doing a little bit of retail therapy, are you?' asks the chaser pointing at my plastic shopping bag.

'Um, it's not what it seems like,' I say feebly. I can't tell him what's really going on as it could get back to Giles or Gunther, and then they'd know that I'd deserted the team-building day.

'It never is. Look, I don't want people finding out I'm here, any more than you do, OK?'

I narrow my eyes at the chaser in confusion. And then it dawns on me; he's not been tracking me like some excellent hunter, he's here on his own accord and, he like me, has skipped the E&E day. I try and mentally weigh up who's got more to lose, me or him, and I decide to take a gamble.

'I'll tell you what, I won't tell anyone if you help me with a favour.'

Twenty-five minutes later, I've learnt to do a cheetah crawl thanks to the ex-Special Forces guy. We're currently hiding out by the flag I told my team that I'd get. The elite chaser is going to create a diversion for me, and I'm going to swoop in and get the flag.

He's true to his word, and after giving me some finger pointing at eyes which is obviously a highly sophisticated military hand signal, he crawls off at almost lightning speed. I take it as a sign to lay still until said diversion.

Sure enough, two minutes later I hear loud laughing between the chasers and I take this as my sign to rip the flag down and run. I've decided that Mr ex-SAS owes me at least a bit of a head start before I fall down and shimmy across the mud.

By the time I make it back to my group, I'm five minutes late and they're nowhere to be seen. I'm about to cry at the fact that they've been caught, when I hear a psst noise.

I look up and there, sitting in a tree, are my team. I'm suddenly ridiculously pleased to see them, and I give them a peak of the flag from under my fatigues.

'Penny,' they say as they jump down. They must have been doing the bonus task: set up camp in a tree.

'We were so worried, we thought you'd been caught,' says Annie.

'And we just saw your boss.'

My blood runs cold. Giles can't know that I wasn't with the group.

'Don't worry, we told him that you had a stomach upset.'

I could kiss Tim right now. Ten out of ten for initiative.

'Thank you, thank you.'

I glance at my watch. It's just after twelve, we've got three-and-a-half hours until we have to be at the rendez-vous point.

'I'm starving,' I say, realising I never did go in and get my sneaky McDonald's burger when I was in Brighton. Bumping into the chaser put pay to that.

'Well, when you were gone, Penny, we talked about it and decided that we don't want to cook our hot meals as we don't want to light our Hexi cookers,' says Tim. 'You know; the chasers might see the smoke.'

'Right,' I say, mourning the fact that I had beef meatballs in my ration pack, and in my head they were going to taste as good as IKEA meatballs. Not that I've eaten them since before the horse-meat scandal. But I'm sure that re-hydrated ration packs are all beef.

'Instead we just thought we'd have the crackers and pâté and biscuits.'

'Great,' I say digging out something called 'biscuit browns' from my pack. Not the most appetising of names. I take the little squeezy tube of pâté and spread it on as we walk along. The biscuit browns taste as bad as they sound, let me tell you.

We're walking up a hill covered in trees when, all of a sudden, I notice it's getting quite dark.

'Is this wood getting denser, or is it just getting darker?' I say, hoping my watch hasn't stopped and that it's not actually night-time. I'm tired enough for that to be the case.

'I think it's cloud,' says Martin.

And, just as he says it, the trees start to sound like they are moving. Only it isn't the sound of the trees, it's the sound of rain. Heavy, heavy rain.

'Oh, my God, I didn't bring my waterproof jacket,' I say as I realise that I didn't transfer it to the pack provided.

'Don't worry, you've got a poncho in your pack,' says Tim.

I look at him dumbfounded as he whips out a piece of plastic from his pack. I wrestle with my bag, and eventually pull mine out and shove it over my head. But not before I'm pretty much soaked.

'It wasn't forecast to rain this afternoon,' I say cursing the BBC website that I've been watching for weeks.

'It's probably just a light summer downpour,' says Annie, who I've discovered over the last day is an eternal optimist.

On this occasion, Annie was wrong. It was not a light summer shower. We're still cowering in a hedge two hours later. It seems that none of us are too keen to crawl like any type of big cat when it's raining. I did give it a go, but nearly choked myself with the poncho. So it seems I either lose the poncho or we stay where we are.

We opted to stay put for as long as we could, but we've only got just over an hour before we have to be back at the rendez-vous point. At least we've managed to escape evasion and to complete our shelter-building task, which we've taken a photo of. We did think our cover had been blown at one point when we heard footsteps, but after holding our breaths and clinging onto each other for dear life, the footsteps receded.

'We're going to have to go for it,' says Tim. 'I know it's not going to be very nice, but it's an hour, then we'll be climbing into a nice hot shower at the end of it and into nice dry clothes.'

I don't remember Baz saying anything about hot showers, but right now I know Tim is right. We've got to get moving. I wince before removing my poncho and I shove it into a side pocket of the backpack. Here goes nothing.

I give Annie a little smile of solidarity as she does the same and then I practically throw myself to the floor as if I'm diving into a freezing cold swimming pool.

If I thought it was bad crawling on the ground before, this is a billion times worse. Where once my elbows were banging across the rock-hard ground, they are now failing to get a grip on the muddy grass, which means it takes twice as much body power to move the same distance. Add to that the water hammering on my back, and the mud seeping through my boiler suit and it makes for a pretty miserable experience. Not even the smell of summer rain is making it any more palatable.

We manage to make it across the field and there's a hedge-row running along the side.

'Stay down, and stay close,' says Tim.

We do as he says and we follow the line of the hedge, bent at the knees, which ache, but it's so much more preferable to the crawling on our bellies, until we reach a river.

'Holy crap, what do we do now?' I say, sounding like I've appeared out of the *Batman and Robin* from the 1960s. 'Wasn't it on the map?'

'It was on the map,' says Matt, scratching his head. 'Only I thought it was more like a little stream.'

'Well, this rain isn't helping it,' says Martin.

We stare at the stream-slash-raging torrent of a river for a while before anyone speaks.

'We're going to have to cross it,' says Tim.

'But isn't it a little dangerous?' asks Annie.

'Yes, I think you're not supposed to go through rivers when it's raining. I'm sure I saw it on some programme,' I say.

'You're not supposed to go through fords in cars when it's raining heavily. But this is only a stream,' says Tim. 'Come on.'

I watch as he takes his backpack off and balances it on his head before wading across the river. He doesn't even flinch, despite the water being around his upper thighs.

'Come on,' he says when he makes it to the other side.

I look down at the water, which is probably about three metres wide. It looks like it's almost jumpable, but remembering my track record with the long jump from school was not good, I decide to walk it.

I hold my breath, and after placing my mobile in my backpack, I do exactly what Tim did, only I accompany my wading with a lot of 'weee' and 'squeee' noises. The water, despite it being mid-July, is freezing and my lovely waterproof boots, which were doing a surprisingly good job of keeping my feet dry are now sopping wet.

'Well, that wasn't so bad,' I say, lying, as I make it to the other side. I feel I have to lie to keep the team going. It's only going to make it worse if I tell people how bad it really was.

The other men are starting to wade, then Tess jumps in gung-ho, into the water, and soon everyone but Annie is safely on the bank.

'Come on, Annie,' we start to call at her, 'it's not as bad as it looks. Come on.' I hold my hand out to her and she closes her eyes for a second before stepping into the water. After a few steps across she grabs me, and the three of us pull her across.

'Well done, Annie, that was excellent,' I say.

'Yes, excellent,' says a voice. We turn around and there's the ex-Special Forces chaser. 'I always get everyone in the end,' he says, winking directly at me.

A sense of deflation sweeps across us, that we got so far through the day without being caught. I look at my watch, we only had thirty-six minutes until the chasers were called off.

'Is this the first time you've been caught today?' asks the chaser.

'It is,' I say despondently.

'Well, then, you should all be very proud of yourselves. You've obviously worked very well as a team.'

I can see his eyes burning into me as he says this, it's

almost like he's mocking me. But he has as much to lose as I do if anyone found out about our little jaunt to Brighton.

I've never felt as pleased to be clean as I did when I got back to the scout hut. Ice-cold shower aside, I managed between that and the wet wipes to get most of the mud off. But what's left is a whole lot of red patches which are going to make beautiful bruises right in time for tomorrow's wedding.

I now understand why they told us to wear loose-fitting clothing for the presentation. Every muscle in my body aches. We've just had the team presentations, and I was voted most inspirational leader in my team, from our secret ballots. I feel just a tad guilty that I got this, mainly because of my shopping jaunt. But, thank goodness, we didn't win the overall thing because of the points I got from when I cheated with the flag. Richard aka Mr-I-Don't-Believe-in-Armies' team won. They managed to escape evasion the whole time, steal a flag and do all their bonus tasks. I bet the ex-Special Forces man wishes he'd spent less time shopping and more time chasing.

'Penny, I just want to congratulate you on a brilliant trip,' says Gunther as he and Giles walk over to me.

'It was a great thirty-six hours, and I think we should give it the green light to do this bi-annually with different members of staff,' says Giles.

I'm trying to keep a smile on my face and not let my eyes pop out in horror as Giles has some unfortunate sunburn. I can only guess he went for Tony the Tiger stripes of camo cream on his face as those bits are white while the rest of his face is slightly pink.

'Great,' I say, wincing at how his daughter's wedding photos are going to come out tomorrow.

'Good job,' says Giles as he walks away towards the mini-buses.

'Oh, Giles, have a lovely time at your daughter's wedding.'

Let's hope she doesn't kill you for ruining the photos, I add in my head. Giles turns round and gives me a little wave and a big grin.

I can't quite believe I managed to organise a successful team away day. I didn't get lynched, and people are actually smiling. Now all I need to do is pull off this wedding tomorrow, and I'll be living the dream.

As I start to run to the minibus in the pouring rain, I do a silent prayer that this is just a little bit of localised summer rain, and the picturesque village of White Hartnell will be unaffected.

chapter twenty-two

princess-on-a-shoestring friend or foe:
Wedding Insurance

When you're planning a wedding, you don't want to think that your big day might not happen, but there's always a chance something might go wrong. I'm not talking doom and gloom that you and your HTB decide to part ways, but more that there might be a family disaster or the venue might go bust. Before taking out the insurance, look at your costs of your venue and suppliers, how much would you be liable for if you had to cancel and the time frames involved. Now, I've only ever known one person to cancel their wedding, but I'm sure it does happen. If it's only forty pounds, is it worth it in the long run? What do you reckon, friend or foe?

Tags: insurance, doom and gloom.

Not only was driving the hour and a half up the road in the minibus some of the most treacherous driving conditions I've ever endured, but it seems that the rain has got worse not better. I aquaplaned a couple of times which, when you're driving a minibus with fifteen people in, is a scary thing to do. I was almost in need of the extra pair of pants that I'd packed for emergencies.

After unloading my colleagues back at our office car park, and saying what felt like a surprisingly emotional goodbye to my team, I headed to Henri's mum's house. I didn't manage to get hold of Henri before the church rehearsal, but I'm hoping that they'll be almost finished.

I can only guess that her spa treatments have chilled out the bridezilla that she'd become, because I've not had any missed calls from her, no emails, no texts, no tweets. Ironic, considering that it's raining cats and dogs and it's the kind of thing that I would actually call an emergency the day before her wedding.

I just hope it clears up as quickly as it started. Or else the photos on the beautiful village green aren't going to be anywhere near as magical.

I pull up outside Henri's mum's house by the duck pond, only today it's difficult to see where the pond starts and finishes. I've been far too wet today to want to run out again in this rain. I'm trying to assess whether there is anyone home, but the longer I sit in the car the more it is fogging up. I count to ten and realise the rain isn't going to get any better, and I make a dash for the house. After six rings of the bell and a fierce knock, I try my luck at the cricket club instead.

When I'd had my close encounter with the cricket ball, I remember strolling across the nicely manicured lawn. Yet tonight I'm sinking into the mud and I feel like I'm ruining it with every step. I shiver in memory of my earlier commando crawling. I'm wondering if I'll ever look at mud in the same way again.

The clubhouse lights are on, and when I reach the doors, I see that Michelle, the captain's wife, is there with a mop in her hand. That doesn't do much to settle my nerves.

'Hi, Michelle,' I say, walking through the door.

'Ah, Penny, thank goodness you're here.'

'Is everything all right?' I ask trying to crack a smile as clearly it isn't.

I'm looking round, trying to see what the mop's for, but the floor looks nice and dry in here.

'No, I'm afraid it isn't. What's happened to your face?'

'My face?' I say instinctively reaching up to touch it.

Michelle walks up and looks at me closely.

'It looks like it's bruised.'

'Bloody face paint.' It's probably the only part of my body that isn't bruised. I hope that I manage to get it off by the wedding tomorrow. I don't think it's going to go too well with my dress.

'Oh, for a minute I thought something awful had happened. Anyway, there's a bit of a problem with the marquee.'

'What kind of a problem?' I ask, not wanting to know the answer. 'Is it leaking?'

'Yes and no, the water seems to be coming in from the sides.'

It hadn't occurred to me when I'd walked over the sodden ground that it could have got into the marquee. We'd made sure that we'd had the proper hard flooring and carpet put down rather than the cheap coconut matting, mainly as we thought that Henri's stilettos would get stuck in it. But still, the floor is supposed to be waterproof.

'I don't believe this,' I say, shaking my head.

'Max is in there at the moment trying to put sandbags round the edges. I'm afraid the carpet is pretty sodden in places.'

'Has Henri been down?'

'She came over earlier when it was pouring. At that point it had only been raining for twenty minutes and we thought it was a quick shower. But that was before the marquee started to flood. I don't think she'd cope too well with that.'

'No,' I say, 'she certainly won't. Michelle, I feel awful about you being here to sort this out.'

'Don't worry, we open on a Friday night as the team usually have a few drinks anyway, this gives us something to do.'

I was supposed to be coming along tonight to hang the bunting and give the venue a final once-over so that tomorrow I would only have to inflate the balloons and dress the tables. I always thought I'd get sucked into staying later to help Henri, but for some reason I assumed it would be for something totally mundane, like a broken nail, not that Henri would have thought it mundane.

'I guess I'm going to have to see it for myself.'

I walk down the now-flooded path to the marquee. I'm not even going to think about how many pairs of shoes it will ruin tomorrow. Not to mention how Henri's going to swish in her dress. I unzip and rezip the entrance at lightning speed when I get inside.

Poor Max is throwing piles of sandbags around the edges. It's the first time I've ever seen them inside a wedding venue before.

'Hi, Penny, I'm afraid we're doing our best.'

'Max, you're doing a fantastic job.'

'Before you come any further, take your shoes off,' says Max.

I look down at my shoes and realise I've bought inside most of the mud from the field outside. The carpet looks like it's in a bad enough state already, let alone without my stamping feet.

I walk over and start helping put the sandbags down. Michelle comes to join us, and soon the edges of the marquee are covered.

'Hopefully, that should work. I'm not too sure what we can do about the carpet though.'

I look at my watch and see that it's after seven, the likelihood of me getting anyone at the marquee company at this hour is pretty slim. I try anyway and leave an answer-phone message.

We go over and inspect the damage. The sandbags have done a good job of covering up the water marks. If only Henri was having a vintage wedding, we could have kitted it out like it was war-time. But, somehow, sandbags and princess weddings don't really go together.

I dig my phone out of my pocket; this calls for re-enforcements in the shape of my lovely husband. Mark is usually über-practical and he'll be able to sort us out. When it clicks through to answerphone, I do my usual swoon at his sexy voice and leave him a message:

'Hi, honey, it's just me. We've got a pretty big problem at the marquee, it's flooded. I could really do with your help. Any chance you could pop down, or give me a call back, that would be lovely, OK speak to you soon.'

I hang up the phone and wonder where my husband is tonight. I know that I said I'd be late home but still, doesn't he know he should be sat at home pining for me, looking at his phone, just in case I might have called. Hopefully he'll ring back soon, as I need someone to tell me what to do.

'Oh. My. God.'

I look up expecting to see Janice from *Friends* standing in front of me, but in fact it's Henri with her mother, and Nick.

'Henri, it's not as bad as it looks,' I say walking towards her with my hands out in a calming gesture as if I'm calming down an angry mob calling for blood.

'There are sandbags in my marquee,' she says in a wail.

'I know, I know. Calm down,' I say again. 'Take your shoes off and come have a look and you'll realise it isn't that bad.'

I'm lying, it's pretty bad. The edges of the tent have gone all mushy and there is a faint smell of mould permeating the room.

Henri walks towards me and I give her a little bit of encouragement like she's a wild horse unsure of her new surroundings.

'See, it's not that bad.'

Henri is pulling a face that says I'm deranged for thinking that.

'I've tried to phone the marquee company to sort out an additional carpet.'

'But we've spent the budget, and there's no money for another carpet.'

'Henri, darling, I'm sure I can pay for a carpet on the credit card, and we'll pay it off next month,' says Nick, walking over to put his arms around her.

Tears are rolling down Henri's face. We were so close to her dream wedding, and here it is unravelling before our very eyes. When I left here on Wednesday night, it looked beautiful and now it looks like a scout camp gone wrong.

'My beautiful, beautiful wedding,' says Henri. 'It's ruined. We might as well not bother. Why don't we call the whole thing off? It's not like anyone really cares anyway.'

She sits down at one of the tables and rests her head on her hands, the tears rolling down her face. I'm wondering if Nick's going to try and talk Henri into marrying him, but before he has a chance her mother goes and sits down beside her.

'Henri, don't say that. It's just a little bit of rain. A little bit of rain never hurt anyone.'

She's clearly a braver woman than I am, there's no way I

343

would have bought that up at this moment. And I'd hardly call three hours of torrential downpour a little rain.

'But what will Daddy say?' asks Henri, between sniffs.

'Your father can say what he likes, for all I care,' says her mother waving her hand dismissively.

'How did the rehearsal go?' I whisper to Nick. Henri's mother seems to be calming her daughter down and I'm sensing it perhaps didn't go to plan.

'It went well, except her dad didn't turn up. He said something came up at the last minute.'

'Oh,' I say.

'Yes, oh. And now this has happened. I don't know how much else she's going to be able to take.'

My phone rings and my first thought is that it's Mark. Yet, instead of being disappointed when it's not, I'm pleased when I see that it's the next best thing, it's the marquee company.

'Hello,' I say, breathing a sigh of relief.

'Hi, Penny, it's Frank from Visions Marquee Hire, I've just got your message.'

'Yes, thanks for phoning back. I was wondering if there was anything that we could do with the carpet, I mean whether we could get it replaced tomorrow? I know that it's supposed to be waterproof but it's still waterlogged.'

'I don't think there was anything you could have done, there's just been so much water.'

'We know that it'll cost us, but what are the chances of getting the carpet replaced tomorrow?'

'I'm sorry, love, but you've got no chance. All our marquees have flooded, and unfortunately we've got our biggest marquee out with one of our regular corporate clients and we've got to go first thing to sort out their carpet. I'm sorry, Penny, I've got to go where the money is. I did you a special deal as it was.'

He did do us a cracking deal in return for me doing an interview with him on my blog about how to keep the costs of a marquee wedding down.

'But we'd be willing to pay for the carpet,' I say in a last-ditch attempt.

'I'm sorry, Penny, we just don't have the manpower, we'd only be able to get to you after lunch.'

'But that's too late,' I say in a whisper.

'Sorry, Penny, looks like you'll have to have a bit of a damp carpet. Maybe it'll dry out by tomorrow.'

I hang up the phone and try not to scream. There's no point in upsetting Henri any more than she already is.

'I take it that was bad news,' says Henri, sighing.

'Well, it wasn't the news I'd hoped for,' I say, trying to make the best of a bad situation.

'Listen, darling, it's stopped raining,' says Nick enthusiastically.

It's true, the pat-pat-pat of the rain on the marquee roof has stopped. Henri looks up and I notice that she's momentarily stopped crying.

'Maybe that's the worst of it over,' says Nick.

'But the ground is still soaking. It's never going to dry,' says Henri. 'My dress is going to be ruined.'

'You'll just have to get your bridesmaids to hitch it up,' says Nick, winking at her. Bad time, Nick, my friend, to be winking, I think.

'But what about my shoes. They're IVORY,' shouts Henri. 'Not to mention that they'll probably get stuck in the mud.'

'Then wear wellies. Look, Henri. I'd marry you in anything. It doesn't matter to me.'

Henri's shaking her head. 'It's ruined, it's really ruined.'

'Actually, Henri, maybe it isn't,' I say, 'I've got a few ideas for some modifications which might just make it work.'

An hour later, and I've dispatched Henri on a trip home to pick up some essential accessories for her outfit tomorrow. I'm not going to pretend that she was thrilled about it, but she had at least stopped crying and agreed to let the wedding go ahead, so I'm taking that as a step in the right direction.

Nick, his best man Tom and I went on a speedy emergency

run to the local B&Q. It was like we were on *Supermarket Sweep* as we filled up the trolley with picnic rugs, toys windmills, empty sandbag sacks, some untreated wood and white paint.

We're now back at the marquee, which doesn't look any better than before. If anything, it looks worse. I'm suddenly starting to doubt that my plan to turn the marquee into a country chic wedding is going to work. But I guess if it all goes wrong, it would only cost us the princely sum of £148 and it probably can't look any shoddier that it does at the moment. I'm sure it would have cost a lot more if they'd had to call off the wedding.

'Right, where are we going to start?' asks Max.

I slip my phone back in my pocket, not that I'm checking it every few minutes. I'd expected Mark to phone me back by now.

'First things first, we've got to move the tables in. I think the guests are going to have to get a little cosier!'

'Well, at this rate they should be grateful that they're going to be dry,' says Nick.

'That's true,' I say, giggling.

'So, good news,' says Henri's mum, as she glides into the marquee. It appears that she is the only woman able to pull off wellies with an elegant summer dress.

I look up at her hopefully.

'The farmer has the hay bales and he'll bring them by tomorrow morning, just after eight. I hope that's not too early?'

'No, that's fine. I'm going to be here then anyway.'

'Good. Now I'm not going to tell you what this hay cost me.'

'Let me give you the money for it,' says Nick, getting out his wallet.

'I'm afraid money won't cut it, Nick. I agreed to go out to dinner with him.'

'Blimey, that's exciting.' I say. 'Right, then. If we could just move the tables in to allow for the hay, then I can dress them tomorrow.'

It doesn't take long with the four of us pitching in, and after that we get to work on the wooden signs. We paint a selection of phrases on the wood, 'Just Married', 'Henri and Nick 4ever', 'This way to the newlyweds' and we leave them to dry on the tables.

Taking the empty sandbags, we retire into the cricket clubhouse which is fairly abuzz with people now. It isn't long before I've coerced most of the cricket team to cut out sandbag triangles to be able to make bunting from it. I then start to secure it on the finest rough twine I could find at the DIY store, and you know what? It doesn't look half bad. The idea is that we'll put it behind the floral bunting that Henri made, just to set it off.

Nick and Tom are going to come and help me bright-eyed and bushy-tailed tomorrow, or at least I'll be bright-eyed and bushy-tailed. Tom has just bought a second round of shots for him and Nick to drink in ten minutes. It looks like it's going to be a rough night for them.

By the time I get back to our little terrace, I'm exhausted. It's only eleven, but I have been up since five a.m., and I can't say that I got much sleep last night. I think I must have been running on adrenaline today and it's finally all caught up with me.

It's dark in my house, except for the landing light which Mark's left on. He's obviously gone to bed already. After a quick brush of my teeth and a long scrub of my face to remove the residue of the face paint, I sneak into the bedroom and hear Mark snoring. Maybe he's had a tough day with his new manager status at work, and he went to bed super-early. As I climb into bed, I'm too tired to even worry about tomorrow's wedding, whatever will happen will happen, and there's nothing I can do about it now.

chapter twenty-three

princess on a shoestring:
Ask Penny!

Dear Penny,

I've always wanted a big swing band for my wedding. I've looked on all the hire websites and they're all out of my price range. Any tips?

Vintage Babe

Dear Vintage Babe,

I love swing bands! Try and see if you can find a local amateur swing band that play for fun. You'll still have to pay them but it won't be as much as a professional group. If you live in a university city or have a big sixth-form college, it's worth checking to see if they have their own band.

Pen x x

I glance at my watch and I feel all warm and fuzzy inside. At this very minute, a few hundred metres down the road, Henri and Nick are getting married. I was planning to be there, to make sure that it all went to plan, but one look at the marquee this morning told me that my skills were needed here instead.

In contrast to yesterday's frightful weather, it's fairly sunny today, if a little chilly, which means that although the pictures might be brighter, there isn't going to be any rapid drying of the marquee.

The hay bales arrived bright and early this morning, and I've clumped them over in the corner of the damp patch. I've thrown a rug over them and now they actually look like they're supposed to be there. I've also dressed all the tables, placing windmills in the vases of fairylights and hung the two sets of bunting and the wooden plaques. I'm convinced that we might have pulled off the theme and I'm keeping my fingers crossed that other people think we have too.

The only thing that's throwing a bit of a dampener on the

proceedings, excuse the pun, is the fact that the grass between the marquee and the cricket club looks like the morning after a particularly raucous festival. The farmer did say he'd drop down some loose straw to help mop up the mud, no doubt costing Henri's mum another one of her evenings, but I'm still worried that there will be shoe casualties.

Luckily for me, I won't be one of them. I'm wearing bright-red cowboy boots. I knew they were a great investment. Mark hasn't been convinced as I've only worn them once, but I bet he will be impressed when he sees them later on.

He was sleeping so soundly this morning when I got up at six that I didn't have the heart to wake him. After showering, I just threw on some jeans and a T-shirt and grabbed my dress for later. I did send him a text about half an hour ago to let him know that I wouldn't make it to the church, so at least he won't be looking for me.

I finish filling up the last of the helium balloons and all I need to do now is hide the canister in the clubhouse. We don't want guests thinking it's part of the evening entertainment. I even managed to resist the temptation of trying it myself. I guess it isn't quite as much fun breathing in helium without anyone to laugh with you. I tie the last of the balloons to the bunch and take them over to a corner of the marquee and slip the strings underneath one of the sandbags – they've come in handy after all.

I finally think the marquee is done, and all that we need now are the guests. In the next hour it will be brimming with people, I hope everyone gets the look we were going for. It might not be a classic princess wedding, but I hope that it has still managed to have a classy feel to it – even if it is a bit rustic.

Henri's not been too sure what her dad's going to make of it, and after hearing stories about him, I'm sure that he won't mince his words if he doesn't approve. I guess I'll find out one way or another pretty soon.

The cricket club also looks great. Michelle's done a great job sprucing it up this morning, making sure it doesn't smell of sweaty men like it did the night before. And with the sun streaming through the glass, it's also lovely and warm in here too. I know where I'll be when the evening starts to turn chilly. And, bonus, it's where the bar's located.

'Any changes to their ETA?' asks Brett as I poke my nose into the kitchen. I don't know how he knows I even walked in as he hasn't taken his eyes off whatever it is he's doing to the plates with a bottle of balsamic.

I've been impressed with how he's been able to transform the little kitchen into something a working chef could use. By all reports they were at Brett's house this morning preparing most of it, so essentially what they've got to do here is heat it and plate it up.

He's currently preparing the starter of Mediterranean vegetables and grilled halloumi on ciabatta. It looks amazing.

'No, I haven't had an update. They should be saying their vows around now. The best man told me that he'd let me know when the service was finished, once they'd left the church.'

'Great. Well, everything's ready to go here. We're all set for serving the welcome drinks and canapés in the marquee and then half an hour after that, we'll be ready for the food.'

I'm a little sad that we had to move the welcome drinks inside, seeing as it is so sunny, but visions of Glastonbury and people falling in the mud keep popping into my mind. Instead, hopefully, people can take photos dressing up in the cowboy hats and sitting on the hay bales.

My phone buzzes in my hand and I see that it's the best man, Tom; the service is over, which means allowing for photos, the guest should be descending on us in twenty minutes or so.

'OK, that's our twenty-minute warning,' I say to Brett.

He nods and continues to drizzle the vinegar. 'Beth, go in the marquee and find Sandra, she'll show you what to do with the drinks,' he says.

I walk out of the kitchen with Beth. She looks so different

dressed up in her black-and-white uniform, her hair neatly tied back.

'I'm so nervous, Penny. What if I spill stuff all down someone?' she says.

'You won't.'

'But what if I do? I can be so clumsy.'

'You'll be fine,' I say, rubbing her arm in encouragement. 'Yes,' I say to myself as she walks over to the drinks station. 'It's all going to be fine.'

I just about manage to get slipped into my lovely navy-blue dress as the guests start to arrive. Luckily it doesn't look too horrendous with the cowboy boots. They're not quite the nude Kurt Geiger heels that I had planned to wear, but at least there won't be tears later over mud ruining my shoes which would have inevitably happened.

I get my first proper look at Henri. I didn't think it would be possible for her to look better than she did when she first tried on the wedding dress, but somehow she does. As she comes into the marquee, she drops her dress down from where she was hitching it up to miss the mud, and I got a fleeting look at her gorgeous brown Judy Rothchild R Soles cowboy boots.

Henri's mum is dressed in a stunning aquamarine dress and a hat that looks like it could eclipse the sun. And then there's Nick, who's positively beaming with pride, which is lovely to see.

I spot my own husband, walking between the guests. I see him in a shirt and tie every day when he goes to work, yet I still find him irresistible when he's dressed in the suit he wears for weddings. It's navy-blue wool, probably a bit warm for a July wedding, but it makes his eyes sparkle. I bound over to him, perhaps a little too enthusiastically, but with everything that's happened to me in the last few days it feels like it's been a week since I last saw him.

'Hey, honey,' I say kissing him and throwing my arms round his neck.

'Hey,' he replies.

I notice that he's not hugging me back so I remove my arms, probably a bit much to be draped all over him anyway. He's obviously embarrassed as we're in a public place and he only knows Nick, Henri and me. Not the best place for public displays of affection.

'I'm sorry I couldn't make the church, but you would not believe what's been going on. The marquee flooded last night and it was just awful. I tried to phone you, to see if you could help.'

'Yeah, I had an early night.'

Considering that I've had pretty much the most testing

forty-eight hours of my life, he could seem a little bit more interested in what happened.

'Don't you want to know how my work thing went?'

Before Mark can reply, Henri walks over to us.

'Penny, this place looks amazing,' she says, leaning over to give me and Mark air kisses on both cheeks.

'Thanks, it didn't work out too badly in the end.'

'You look stunning, Henri. Please excuse me, I'm going to get a drink,' says Mark.

I follow Mark with my eyes and wonder if it was just me imagining it, or was he acting a little aloof with me? The last time I spoke to him was on the phone on Thursday night after the cook-out and there was no hint of a tone then. Maybe he's just pissed off that I left him on his own at the church, as he gets nervous around strangers. That's probably it; I should have been a bit more sensitive. I'll have to make a bit more of an effort to include him in the people I speak to this afternoon.

'So how does it feel to be Mrs Eves?' I ask.

'Amazing. Oh, Penny, I wish you could have been there, it was so beautiful. Even Nick cried.'

I don't doubt that for a second.

Henri's looking pretty cool at the moment, she's placed a large cowboy hat on her head, and it actually goes better with her dress than her tiara. Not that I'll tell her that. The tiara was ridiculously expensive, and a present from her father. Speaking of which.

'Was everything OK with your dad getting here this morning?'

I'm presuming if he'd still been MIA, Henri wouldn't be so perky.

'Oh, yes, apart from the fact he looks like he's got a starring role in *TOWIE*.'

I try and imagine just what this means when she leans in.

'He's been for a spray tan.'

'Oh,' I say giggling. I've got visions of my own dad standing in a cubicle in paper pants and it makes me shudder. There are definitely some things that are not meant for fathers.

'In fact, you should come over and meet him. I'm sure that he'd be pleased to meet you. He said this place looked amazing. I really think he likes it!'

'Good,' I say, smiling with relief that I've managed to impress her father.

'Let me see,' says Henri, scanning the room. I look round too, spying all the suitable candidates. He should be easy to spot, as he'll be in the same morning suit as the groom and the best man. 'Ah, there he is.'

I follow Henri's hand over, past the dance floor, and near the hay bale. But Henri's pointing to Giles. Giles my boss. But it can't be him as he's at his own daughter's posh wedding in the country.

'Let's go over,' says Henri.

'No,' I say, a little too abruptly. I'm frozen to the spot in horror. 'I've just realised that I've got to go and talk to Brett to double-check that everything's on schedule.'

'Oh, OK,' says Henri. 'Well, I'll have to introduce you two later. Oh, there's my Aunt Ginny.'

As Henri goes to disappear, I pull the cowboy hat off her head.

'Sorry, Henri, I just think that your tiara was so beautiful that you need to show it off some more.'

'Thanks, Pen.'

I slide the hat down, trying to shield my face. What the hell am I going to do? It's only half past three, I've got at least seven hours left of this wedding to go, how the hell am I going to avoid Giles for all that time?

And what is he doing here anyway? He's supposed to be at his daughter Harriet's wedding. Who the hell is Harriet? And if Giles is really Henri's dad, does that make me the top wedding planner that she'd hired? If it wasn't such a dire situation, I'd be laughing.

Think, Penny, think. What are my options? I could a) leave the wedding and therefore preserve my job, b) stay at the wedding and be out in the open and hope Henri doesn't refer to me as being the wedding planner. Or I could, c) avoid Giles all day.

I see Mark out of the corner of my eye but, as desperate as I am to confide in him with what's going on, he'd make me leave the wedding now. And I can't, not really. I'd feel like I was letting Henri down, as a wedding planner and as a friend. I'm just going to have to hope that I don't bump into Giles. After all, there are a hundred guests, and usually at weddings you don't speak to everyone. I'm sure I could get away with avoiding him.

'Penny,' I look round to see Nick standing behind me.

'Nick, congratulations,' I say, leaning up to give him a kiss.

'Thanks, Penny. It all looks fabulous.'

'Doesn't it? I couldn't have done it without yours and Tom's help this morning.' I say, nodding. I decide to take a risk and find out what's going on. 'Um, Nick, I'm just a bit confused – someone told me that the bride's name is Harriet.'

'That's right, but not many people call her that, mainly family, and her father. I think it confused a few people in the church when the vicar called her that.'

'But why Henri?' I ask as the dismal news sinks in that I'm not imagining that Giles is standing over there.

'I think it started when she was a kid, people used to call her Harry for short, and then somehow it got reversed from the whole Harry being short for Henry.'

'Oh.'

'Yes, I know, it's a bid odd when you think about it, but I rarely do as she's just Henri to me. Anyway, I think we're ready for everyone to sit down for dinner.'

'Great, I'm starving,' I say. Except for a couple of canapés, I haven't eaten since breakfast and my stomach has been growling at me for the last half an hour. I'm looking at Nick, and he's looking at me, and I'm wondering just why he's telling me, and then I realise: as the wedding planner I'm the one who's supposed to get everyone to sit down. It's my job to announce it's time to take their places. Only I can't as everyone will go quiet and Giles will know that I'm the wedding planner, and then the world, as I know it, will cease to exist.

'Um, Nick, I think it works best at weddings if you or your best man announces the call to sit down. It makes it much more informal, and in my experience it gets people moving more quickly as they listen to the bridegroom in a way that they wouldn't with little old me.'

I'm hoping that Nick buys that, as it does sounds plausible.

'OK, Penny.' He reaches over and picks up a knife from a nearby table. 'Right, everyone, can I have your attention.'

I wince and pull the cowboy hat further over my head so that it shields my face as much as possible. I hadn't meant for him to announce it when I was standing next to him. I might as well have done it myself. So much for me keeping a low profile.

'We're about to have the wedding breakfast served, so if you would like to take your seats.'

There are a lot of murmurings as everyone shuffles around, looking for where they're sitting. I know exactly where my seat is and, unfortunately, I've got a direct line of sight to the top table. And to Giles.

I watch Mark go and sit down and I see that from where he's sat, he's got half of his back to the top table.

'Mark, honey,' I say as I hover by his chair. 'Do you mind swapping seats with me so that I can see the entrance to the marquee?'

Mark sighs and gives me a stern look before he does what I've asked and he moves across. Anyone would have thought I'd asked him to give me a kidney rather than give up his seat. Perhaps I am underestimating the bond he had with the chair he'd been sat on for all of two minutes.

'Did you want to know how I got on with the team-building?' I ask, helping myself to a bread roll and buttering it.

'That depends. Are you going to tell me what happened, or your version of events?' he says, leaning in closely to me.

Where the hell did that come from? I'm momentarily stunned by Mark's tone and I can't answer him. By the time

I can feel movement coming back to my jaw, he's talking to the man sitting next to him.

'Are you the wedding planner?' asks the woman next to me.

'Yes, I am,' I say trying to put a fake smile on my face.

'Henri told me that she was going to put me on your table, although I didn't realise she was going to put me next to you. I'm planning my own wedding, you see.'

'Oh, really? Congratulations.'

Usually I'd listen with interest at anyone describing their wedding plans to me, but as the woman starts telling me about her wedding on a boat later in the summer, I'm barely paying attention. She could be telling me that she's getting married dressed in Lady Gaga's meat dress for all I know. Luckily for me, like most brides, she just wants to talk about her own wedding. As long as I nod my head every so often and smile, I'm sure she won't notice that I'm taking nothing in.

Eventually, the bride-to-be stops talking and says something to the man, presumably her fiancé beside her, and I turn to Mark.

'Is everything OK?'

'What do you think, Penny?'

'I don't know. That's why I'm asking,' I whisper.

We both sit back as Beth places our starters down in front

of us. I give her a little smile of encouragement before I lean forward again to talk to Mark.

'Now's not the time or the place to talk about this,' he says.

'Talk about what?' I whisper in frustration.

I can tell that the other couples on our table are starting to look at us. The talking's got quieter since the food was placed down, making it even more obvious that Mark and I are having a fight.

'We'll talk about it later,' he says. 'And take that stupid hat off when you're eating.'

I stare at Mark opened mouth. I've never, ever, heard him talk to me in such a way. And I'm so stunned that I remove the hat and put it down on the floor next to me.

Whatever I've done to Mark has seriously rattled his cage, and I've just got to rack my brains to try and work out exactly what it is.

chapter twenty-four

princess-on-a-shoestring top tip:
It's your wedding!

The golden rule to remember when you're planning is that your day is all about you and your HTB. It's not about what your mum or your mother-in-law think would be best, and it's not about having to make it grander or more spectacular than the last wedding you went to. At the end of the day, just do what makes you happy. If you'd rather have a candy-floss machine than an evening buffet - do it! If you don't want to have wedding favours or flowers or anything the mums think is controversial, then don't! You want to create YOUR perfect day and your vision will probably be different to everyone else's and that's OK. As long as you're pleased, that's all that matters.

Tags: calm bride, ignoring the parents.

By the time the Eton Mess arrives, I am fuming. Mark hasn't said a word to me throughout the whole meal. It's embarrassing. Here I am, the wedding planner, and I can't even have a civil conversation with my husband.

He's completely ruined the food for me; I wasn't able to enjoy it, and I actually left part of the main course as I'd lost my appetite. The only slight upside was that my appetite appeared again when the dessert was served.

With the food over, it seems that members of the wedding party are starting to drift around the tables, socialising. Henri's sitting on some man's lap and is posing for photos with friends, so I figure we've got a little while before the speeches.

'Mark, can you come outside a minute?' I say.

I can't take it any more. I can't sit here through the speeches, listening to Nick and Henri sickeningly in love, knowing that my husband is furious with me for reasons I can't fathom.

I look at Mark and I attempt to do Henri's puppy-dog eyes, I've been studying how she does them and I wonder if I can pull them off.

'Fine,' he says rather too loudly and throwing his napkin onto his dessert plate.

I'm too afraid to put the cowboy hat on to leave the

marquee and, instead, I pretend to be fiddling with my hair in order to block my face from the top table as I leave.

We walk out into the fresh air and Mark swears as he steps in the mud. At any other normal time I would have pointed out how great my cowboy boots are and how wrong he'd been about them being a whimsical purchase, as here they are being extremely practical. But I hardly think that is going to soften the mood. It feels like an iron curtain has descended on our marriage.

'What's going on, Mark?' I say as we reach the patio by the clubhouse.

'I'm disappointed in you, Penny.'

'Why. What have I done?' I spent the meal racking my brains and I couldn't think of anything that I've done that would have made him in this foul a mood.

'You know what you've done. You promised me before our wedding that you'd never keep secrets from me again. That was the deal. And here we are, one year on, and you're back to your old tricks.'

The only secret that I'm keeping at the moment is about Giles, but that can't be what he's talking about as it seems like his mood deteriorated at some point before the wedding. His uncharacteristic behaviour last night of ignoring my answerphone message perhaps being my first indicator that something was amiss.

'What secret am I supposed to be keeping from you?'

'Oh, you can't even admit it. Or is it that you're keeping more than one secret from me and you don't want to hedge your bets and guess which one I'm talking about.'

The heckles on the back of my neck go up in a defensive reaction and I blush furiously. No matter what he's talking about, I've still got the Giles secret that he doesn't know about.

'Blimey, Penny. I can read you like a flipping book. Right, I'm mad at you, as if you didn't know, because I've found out you've been gambling again.'

I look at him and my jaw drops, literally. I wonder if I've heard him correctly. Me gambling again? I don't think so. I've not been near a lottery ticket, and on a wet winter's day trip to the seaside with Mark I wouldn't even bet on the fake horse-racing machine at the pier.

'What are you talking about? I haven't gambled since last year and you know that.'

'No, Penny, I don't know that. I thought you were telling me the truth. I know alarm bells should have started ringing when you kept the fact that you knew Nick a secret. I should have wondered then if you could hide that, what else were you hiding.'

I can't believe I'm hearing this, I'm too stunned to reply.

'I feel like such an idiot. Do you know I've been going

round thinking to myself that I've got the best wife in the world. That you had this awful gambling problem and you'd solved it so quickly. And I was so bloody proud of you for giving it up and for becoming a mentor and then I find out that it's all a pack of lies.'

'It's not lies,' I say as a rogue tear rolls down my face. 'I haven't gambled since last year. I don't know how I can prove to you that I haven't.'

Mark laughs and runs his fingers through his hair which, at any other point in time, I'd probably find pretty sexy, but now I just want to slap his hands away and beat some sense in to him.

'It's funny that you should talk about proof, as I just happen to have some.'

Mark reaches into his trouser pocket and pulls out a folded piece of paper. I'm wondering what he could possibly have, when I see the little logo in the corner that tells me it's a credit card statement.

'Here you go, Penny. Here's the proof.'

He holds out the piece of paper and I snatch it from him. It's my credit card bill, my name on the letter and, as I scan down it, I notice a lot of transactions. In fact, the transactions exceed my credit limit, which surprise, surprise, seems to have been increased.

I feel sick to my stomach, much like I did when I saw my

weddings savings bank statements last year and there were all the payments listed for Carnivore Services – the company trading name for the bingo site I used to use. Only this time it's not Carnivore Services, it's Bill Hall, one of the biggest bookmakers in the country.

'But I don't understand,' I say in disbelief. 'I haven't been betting, Mark, I swear to God, I haven't been.'

'It's your credit card, Penny. Your name's at the top.'

'But I haven't done it. I swear.'

I try and think back to when I last used it, and then I remember that day in the camping shop when my card was declined. It wasn't the bank having an off day; it was the fact that I'd reached my limit.

'I just wish you'd be honest with me,' says Mark.

'I am. Mark, you've got to trust me. This wasn't me.'

'So some other gambler just stole your card and gambled away. What a coincidence!'

'Mark, look. I promised you last year that I would stop gambling and I did. I haven't been near as much as a raffle ticket. I didn't do this. You have to believe me.'

'Why do I? You lied to me for months last time, Penny, how is this time any different?'

'Because I promised you when we got married that I wouldn't keep secrets. And I haven't. Instead of trusting me and giving me the benefit of the doubt, you've jumped to conclusions. Well, thank you very much.'

Tears are burning behind my eyes, and only the anger I'm feeling towards him, for accusing me of lying, is keeping me from breaking down completely.

'Put yourself in my shoes. You kept Nick a secret, which makes me think that you're still keeping others. Who would you believe, the black-and-white facts, or someone who has lied to you in the past?'

I open my mouth and close it again. What can I say to that? My husband isn't ever going to trust anything I have to say.

'What's your explanation, Pen, if it wasn't you? Credit card fraud?' Mark laughs bitterly.

'I don't know; I've got to figure it out.'

'Ah, there you are,' says Tom the best man as he walks across the mess of straw towards us.

'That's right, figure out some lies, a cover story. Well let me know when you've got one,' whispers Mark as he storms off towards the village. I watch him go. What I really want to do is run after him, to scream and shake him. But what good's it going to do? He's obviously not going to take my word for it.

I'm still standing, watching Mark's wake, when Tom reaches me. I notice him freeze when he spots my face. I don't think he wants to come any closer for fear I'm having a womanly meltdown.

'Hi, Tom,' I say putting a fake smile on my face, which probably looks ridiculous seeing as I have tears rolling down my cheeks.

'Right, um,' he says, fidgeting nervously, 'Weddings, huh? They are always bring out the tears.'

I half-laugh and half-choke, mainly relieved that it hasn't sent me into a spiral of crying harder.

'Yeah, they bring the worst out in people,' I say as I tuck the credit card statement into the oversized pocket of the skirt on my dress. 'So, what can I do for you?'

'They're just about to start the speeches. And I needed to know what order they usually go in? And do I introduce the people?'

'Right, then,' I say, slipping back into autopilot wedding planner mode. 'So you start with the father of the bride, then the best man and then the groom. I know Henri has thank-you gifts planned for the mums, so she can do that at the start of the groom's speech. And yes, if you're willing to introduce everyone, then that would work best.'

'Great, thanks, Penny. Are you coming inside? My speech, is pretty funny. I'm sure you won't want to miss that.'

I smile at Tom, who's clearly trying to cheer me up. I look in the direction that Mark stormed off in and realise that I need to let him go. He has to calm down, and I have got to figure out what the hell's going on.

'Come on then,' I say, walking back into the reception with him. I wipe under my eyes and hope that my mascara is every bit as waterproof as it says on the tube.

Using Tom for shielding, I sneak back to my seat and pray that Giles doesn't clock me.

There's something surreal about being at a wedding and listening to the speeches without turning your head to watch them. I instead half-cocked my head and looked down at the table, so as not to catch Giles's eye. Without Mark there, I put the ridiculously big cowboy hat on my head, and luckily I don't look too silly as quite a few other guests have picked them up from around the venue. And I hope it's enough to hide me.

I had to get through Giles's speech first and it was awful. Not that the speech itself was awful, but it was more that I had to try and make sure that he didn't see me, when he was stood up and looking out into the crowd. I snuck a couple of looks at him and Henri wasn't lying when she said that he'd been on the spray tan. It seems as if he'd tried to cover his sunburnt tiger stripes. Only it backfired as now he looked like the Tango man with white go-faster stripes.

His speech was sentimental, about Henri's early childhood,

373

my favourite anecdote that he told was when they went to an ambassador's party and Henri went around asking all the waiters where the Ferrero Rocher were. But, as he talked about her getting older, there was less and less of the Henri that I could recognise.

Tom's speech was, as billed, pretty funny, and I'm glad that I didn't miss it. Nick looked suitably embarrassed and uncomfortable throughout and if Henri didn't know everything about the man that she was marrying before the speech, she certainly did afterwards.

Which just leaves Nick's speech, which is bound to be full of wonderful stories and is probably going to make me cry for the second time today. It is, as Brad Pitt would say, inevitable.

'I'd like to say, thank you so much for coming to witness one of the happiest days of my life,' says Nick. Henri complained at the word 'one of' and Nick corrected it to the happiest day.

'As I was saying,' says Nick, 'This wedding day would always have been special, but it's all the more special because all of you, our nearest and dearest, are here to share it with us. So thank you again.

'Whilst we're on the topic of thanks, I'd like to pass you over to my beautiful wife, Henri, who also wants to say a few words.'

Everyone claps as Henri stands up.

'I really just want to echo what Nick had to say about you all coming to be here with us. It means so much to us.'

I can hear Henri's voice wobble and I wonder if this is why traditionally the bride is not involved in the speeches. As Henri goes through thanking her mum, her new mother-in-law, and the bridesmaids, I can see her blinking back tears.

'And there's just one more person that I really want to thank. Without her this wedding wouldn't have happened, and also without her we'd probably sitting in a pool of water this morning.'

Oh no, my blood is starting to run cold. She can't be talking about me. I can't go up there. I close my eyes and pray that she's either referring to someone else or that she wants to thank me in words only. Either way, I don't want to get out of this chair; I don't want Giles to see me.

'Thank you, Penny. Where's Penny? Ah, there she is. We've got a little something for you.'

I am frozen to my seat and even if I wanted to get out of it, I can't as my legs have gone to jelly. I'm aware of everyone around me clapping and there's nothing else I can do but go up towards the top table. The only thing I can do now is hope that either Giles is steaming drunk and won't remember this on Monday or that the spray tan has affected his sight.

But as I get up from my seat, Henri discharges her niece

with a bouquet of flowers and a small bag. I bend down and take the flowers and shield my face from Giles and mouth a thank you to Henri.

I start looking at the flowers, and I'm about to wonder how much she'd paid for them, as they weren't in the budget, before I realise that a lot of the bright blooms look familiar. The bouquet is handtied with a little note that says 'grown with love in the Scott garden'. They came from Henri's mum's beautiful garden. What a clever idea, and what a wonderful money-saving tip. Henri learnt something from me after all!

I open the little bag, and it's a bracelet. A really gorgeous bracelet from Goldsmiths jewellers. That makes me smile as I know it means Henri's still been reading my blog as I did a post a few weeks ago that talked about how you could use your Tesco's Clubcard points there.

As Henri finished her tearful thank yous, she passes the microphone over to Nick. I couldn't tell you what he said in his speech about Henri as I was too busy staring at the bracelet. Lost in my own thoughts, trying to process everything that happened in the last hour.

Number one on my list was trying to work out where my new-found gambling habit had come from.

chapter twenty-five

princess-on-a-shoestring friend or foe:
Miniature guests

Deciding whether to invite kids to a wedding can be a very controversial topic. It's nice to see children running around on the day, but when all of your friends have kids it soon adds up and it can seem like you're almost having more children than adults at the wedding. At my wedding, I let close family bring their little ones and I asked friends to leave theirs behind. I think that most of the parents actually liked having a child-free day as they got to let their hair down without worrying that their child would somehow cause havoc in the service and/or wreck the reception venue. Do you think a wedding is a place for kids?

Tags: kids, controversial decisions.

As soon as the speeches are over, I head outside. I'm in desperate need of fresh air. I wonder briefly if I should find Mark, but I'm still cross at him for not listening to me and I'm no further forward in making sense of what happened.

I walk over the muddy green to the duck pond and I sit down on a bench not too far away from the infamous black-eye moment. I look over at the marquee and a wave of pride washes over me that I did that. Here are two people on the happiest day of their life, with the most wonderful wedding and I'm responsible. Only I know more than others how that happiness doesn't always last and the thoughts of Mark and the credit card statement soon come to the forefront of my mind.

I take out the credit card bill again and stare at it. It's all here in black and white, ten pounds here, twenty pounds there, running up to thousands. Only it hasn't just been happening this month, it appears that it's been used before that as I've been charged a late fee and interest.

I bring the Bill Hall website up on my phone. I don't even think I ever went on the site when I was in my bingo hey-day. They're a site more known for sports betting, so why is it on my credit card bill?

I scroll up and down the page. It's offering the latest bets on today's test match cricket, Rugby League games, and today's racing from Doncaster and Kempton Park. If Mark had even looked at the site, he would have realised that this wasn't me. And that's when I see the sparkling banner at the bottom of the site and I suddenly know exactly what's happened.

'Penny, are you all right?'

I find Beth sitting down behind the marquee on one of the spare hay bales, just where Brett said she'd be taking her break. She's still dressed in her black-and-white uniform, only now it's covered in a few food stains and strands of her hair are falling out of her ponytail. If I wasn't ready to kill her for stealing my credit card, I'd feel proud that she had the look of a hard day of work about her.

'Hi, Beth. No, not really.'

'What's wrong?'

She's clearly sensed that all isn't right with the world and she's stands up.

'Mark and I had a fight,' I say, trying to keep my anger at bay.

'Oh,' she looks confused. 'Do you do that often?'

'No. I guess we bicker, but I think that most couples do that. But we really fought. He's mad at me. He thinks I've been gambling.'

'Have you?'

379

'No, I haven't.'

'Then why does he think that you have been?'

'He opened my credit card bill and he saw lots of payments to Bill Hall.'

Beth is looking down at the floor. I had hoped that by telling her this much she would confess that she had used my card, but she's being eerily silent.

'Beth, is there anything you want to tell me?' I sound remarkably like my mother when she was trying to press confessions out of me when I was a teenager.

Beth's silent, but tears have started to roll down her cheeks.

If she's not going to confess properly, then I'm going to have to go all Miss Marple on her arse.

'You used my credit card, didn't you?' I say slowly. 'That's how you could afford to keep on gambling, because you stole my card details. After all I've done for you, Beth. I've tried my best to get you to stop gambling. I popped round to see you even though I'd been incredibly busy at work. I got you to meet with Mark's cousin to try and give you something to look forward to, and I got you this job.'

I'm aware that we're just behind the main marquee and that I need to be careful with how loudly I'm speaking, but I'm too mad to keep my voice under control.

'Why did you do it?' I say looking directly at Beth, but her eyes are fixed on her shoes.

'I couldn't help it.'

'When did you steal my card details?'

'When I came over to yours for cake that time.'

'That was months ago. All that time? All that time you've been attending meetings with me and you've been spending my money and getting me into debt. Do you know how much interest I've accumulated because the bills haven't been paid?'

'I'm sorry, Penny. I'm so sorry. You've been nothing but nice to me, and I've done this.'

'Were you ever going to tell me you'd done it?'

'I was going to. I mean I wanted to pay you back. I was going to pay you back with my winnings.'

I laugh out loud. God, gamblers sound so pathetic when they chase the win. I should know, I was pathetic once.

'You've nearly ruined my marriage. Mark thinks I lied to him.'

'I didn't mean for that to happen. I didn't mean for any of it to happen. I just was so angry when I met you as I didn't think I needed help. Then, at your house, you were trying to be all fake nice and give me cake, but behind your back I was laughing at you.'

This is great. This is just what I want to be told. Way to make me feel better, Beth.

'I took your credit card details and I thought I'd never see you again. I thought you'd give up like everyone else does with me.'

'But what did you think would happen when I found out?'

'To be honest, I thought you giving up the gambling all sounded a bit too easy, and I was sort of hoping that you were still doing it and then you wouldn't notice it.'

'I've heard enough of this,' I say as I walk off, dismissing Beth.

'Penny, wait,' says Beth as she comes after me. I have to admit I have no idea where I'm headed to, I just want to be anywhere but here.

'Penny, look. I stole your credit card before I knew you. Before you did all those nice things, and no one's ever done stuff like that for me. And you got me this job, and I was going to give you the money from this.'

'And how far was that going to get you? What are you getting paid for today, fifty quid? My credit card bill is over two-and-a-half *thousand* pounds. You're going to have to do a lot of shifts to make that up. Not to mention that you owe your mum five grand. Sooner or later, Beth, you're going to have to start taking responsibility for your actions because I don't think you understand exactly what you're doing. You're ruining people's lives.'

Beth's tears are coming thick and fast now and I'm

wondering if I'm taking out my anger with Mark on her. Maybe I am a little bit, but I've done everything I could to sort this girl out, and look what she's done for me in return. Hopefully this will shock her into stopping gambling, as it's going to get her into deep trouble.

'So you were going to tell me?' I ask.

'Eventually,' says Beth.

That's the Beth I know, the one that looks like a guilty liar.

I turn round to storm off again, only it's not so easy to storm off when you're wearing cowboy boots with little grip on the sole.

'I'm sorry, Penny,' she calls after me.

Sorry? What good's that? My marriage is in ruins and I'm thousands of pounds in debt. Suddenly the word sorry coming from a teenager doesn't sound sincere at all.

I'm storming round the front of the marquee and if I was cross before, I'm absolutely raging now. How did Beth ever think she was going to get away with what she did? And now, armed with the truth, I'm even crosser at Mark.

I'm so pre-occupied with the mental argument I'm having in my head with him that I fail to realise that I'm heading back to the entrance of the marquee.

'Penny.'

I freeze, as I know instantly the voice belongs to Giles.

'Penny Robinson, what are you doing here?'

I look up at Giles, and for the first time today I don't avoid eye contact. I look at him open-mouthed and wonder just what it is I'm supposed to say. I wonder if I should lie, saying that Nick and I go way back, which isn't exactly lying. Or I could learn from my mistakes and tell the truth.

But before I can do either, Henri struts up, armfuls of orange-tinted wedding dress in each hand and, before I know it, the cat's out of the bag.

'Daddy, I'm thrilled that you've met Penny, the wedding planner. Didn't she do the most fabulous job? We were so lucky to get her, she's that good she even writes for *Bridal Dreams*.'

'Is that so?' says Giles, looking at me.

If it wasn't bad enough being outed as a wedding planner, the declaration of me writing for *Bridal Dreams* just feels like the final nail in the coffin.

Despite my mute status, I'm still maintaining eye contact with Giles and I've managed to see his eyes widen in horror and recognition of what has gone on. I can only think of Indy and her cheese business and I know what will be coming next.

'Oh look, there's Aunt Rose, I must go and see her,' says Henri dashing off in her cowboy boots.

I look round wondering if there's some long-lost aunt I

can pretend to dash off and see but, alas, I've got nowhere to run to.

'So, Penny. You're the top wedding planner then? You're the planner that Henri's had on speed-dial twenty-four/seven. The one who snuck off from her work trip to get bridesmaid dresses.'

'Giles, it's not what you think,' I say. After all that's happened to me today it feels like this confrontation has knocked the stuffing out of me and I can barely put up a fight.

'Let's not go into it now. It's my daughter's wedding, that I have to admit you've done a wonderful job organising. But, Penny, you know my view on moonlighting. I expect to see you in my office at nine a.m. sharp on Monday.'

'Yes, Giles,' I say.

He heads over to join Henri and Aunt Rose. I'm left bashing my head against the side of the marquee. This time yesterday I thought that the promotion was in the bag after a great team-building trip. Now, far from getting the promotion, I probably won't have a job on Monday.

If ever there was a moment where you look at your life and wonder just how you've ended up in such a mess, this was it for me. I, Penny Robinson, have fucked everything up, royally.

chapter twenty-six

princess-on-a-shoestring cost cutters:
Feeding the Five Thousand

Chances are, your mum has told you that you need to have an evening buffet, but just think about your timings before you commit to one. If you're getting married mid-afternoon then you're probably not going to sit down for your wedding breakfast meal until around five p.m., which means by the time you've had your three courses you might not be finished until six or seven. It's definitely worth thinking about timings when it comes to an evening food option - will most of your guests do anything more than pick at the buffet if it hasn't been long since they've eaten? Things that work wonders are bacon sandwiches or cheese boards. Or you could go Marie-Antoinette style and just let them eat cake!

Tags: cheapskate, evening buffet.

I'm standing outside the marquee and, as I see it, I've got two choices. I could say my goodbyes to Henri – or I could stay and get drunk. And, like Bridget Jones, I choose vodka. After ordering myself two large vodka cranberries, I walk back into the marquee, just as Henri and Nick are just finishing their first dance to the band's rendition of 'It Had to Be You'. And remember how Henri found out about mine and Nick's secret meeting and Nick had to plan Henri a surprise? Well that's up next. I'm determined to get a good seat for that, so I position myself at the side of the dance floor.

The dance comes to an end and, much to Henri's embarrassment, Nick walks up to the stage.

'Now, my gorgeous bride over here wanted a wedding band and I thought that was a little safe. I know Henri and I know that she likes to throw memorable parties, so I hired something a little bit different. Henri, I hope you can forgive me. Take it away, boys.'

I look at Henri's bemused look and it just about brings a smile to my face until, that is, I see Giles standing at the front of the stage taking photos and it quickly falls away. Instead I bring the vodka to my lips.

I hold my breath as Nick launches into his rendition of 'Can't Take My Eyes Off You.' At least he can sing. I dread to think what the rest of the wedding guests will sound like when they get up to the microphone later. You see, Nick has kicked off this evening's first karaoke performance. I told him over and over again that karaoke at a wedding was going to be one of two things: legendary or a massive flop. It wasn't going to be anything in between. But watching Nick up there, with the band rocking it behind him, he may have just pulled it off. When I told him he needed to plan a surprise for Henri, this had been his first idea.

In the time it takes Henri to serenade Nick with a scarily seductive version of 'Don't Cha' by the Pussycat Dolls, which made me and Henri's grandma both blush, and for Henri's friends to sing the Spice Girls, I've downed my two vodkas.

I'm pleased that the karaoke seems to be a hit and they've got a steady stream of willing participants. I walk back towards the clubhouse in search of more vodka. I know that I'm going to regret all this booze tomorrow morning, but the mood I'm in, I don't care.

'Penny.'

I look up and see Mark standing in front of me, or at least it takes a moment for my eyes to focus and confirm that it's him. Talk about being a lightweight.

'I don't want to see you at the moment,' I say slightly slurring.

'Pen, Beth told me everything.'

'Well, that's just great. So now you know that I didn't gamble.'

'I know, and I'm sorry. I really am. I just saw the statement and I saw red and I—'

'And you what? Jumped to conclusions without giving me a proper chance to explain? Well, I'm sorry, Mark, but it hurts me that you wouldn't even listen to me. I mean we're supposed to have trust in our marriage, and we don't. You don't trust me.'

'Pen,' he says.

I don't want to hear it, I'm angry and I'm upset.

'Pen, how can I make it up to you?' he says.

'I don't know if you can,' I say, crying. Oh, yes, I know I'm being overly dramatic, and actually Mark's apologised to me. The logical part of my brain thinks I may have acted the same if the boot had been on the other foot, but the irrational, vodka-soaked part of my brain doesn't want to hear it.

I walk off back to the marquee. I sit down and listen to a woman murder 'Dancing Queen' and wonder what I'm going to do. For one thing I realise I shouldn't be sitting here, pretending my life isn't falling apart.

I spot Henri having a shimmy on the dance floor and I go up to say my goodbyes.

'But we haven't had a dance together yet,' says Henri

pouting at me. But not even her puppy-dog eyes are going to be able to persuade me. I've barely slept in the past three days, I'm exhausted, not to mention emotionally drained.

'I'm sure you'll have no shortage of people to dance with,' I say.

'But you can't go,' says Henri, grabbing my arm.

I wonder just how long this 'you can't, yes I can', Punch and Judy routine is going to go on.

'I can, and I am,' I say defiantly.

'But you can't when Mark is up doing karaoke,' she says, pointing up at the stage.

'Ha,' I say wearily, 'You've got someone mixed up with Mark. He would never in a million years do—' I trail off as I see Mark standing on the stage as bold as brass. If I wasn't so mad at him, I'd be drooling at the fact that he's looking pretty hot up there. His suit undone, his hair a little messy. He's holding onto the microphone stand with one hand and turning round to talk to the band. He looks like a rock star.

What an earth is he doing? In the eight years I've known Mark, the only time I've seen him on a stage is if he's delivering a deadly boring work-related presentation. And he has never, ever, done karaoke, despite us getting really drunk in Spain once and me trying to get him to duet with me on 'You're the One That I Want'. In the end I had to sing it with some balding, fat man from Glasgow. He was definitely *not* the one that I wanted, but it made Mark laugh for the rest of our holiday.

'I'd like to dedicate this to my wife Penny,' says Mark as he holds his hand up to block the lights, and he tries to search the dance floor for me. Henri makes his job pretty easy for him as she pushes me forward, right to the front. I get a few ahs and oohs from Henri's friends around me.

I'm standing here like a right lemon wondering what the hell he's going to sing. Everyone's convinced he's going to do a romantic serenade like Henri and Nick have done to each other, but top of my list of songs that he could possibly do are 'I Hate You So Much Right Now' or whatever that song is called. Actually, maybe that's top of the list of what song I'd sing to him.

The music starts up and I'm still none the wiser as to the song choice. And then I realise I have never heard Mark sing. I know that sounds ridiculous, but it's true. Aside from when we've been to Foo Fighters or the Killers gigs, when you all shout and can't hear anything, I've never heard a note come out of Mark's mouth. He doesn't sing in the shower, in the car, anywhere. He's definitely your silent-head-bobber-cum-finger-tapper.

As he sings the first lines of the song, I'm instantly confused. If I'm not mistaken, he's singing Journey's 'Don't Stop Believing'. Is that supposed to be a metaphor for our marriage? I'm looking at him in confusion, but he's staring so hard at the lyrics screen that he's oblivious.

I think there's a reason that I've never heard Mark sing before and that is because he's not blessed with a crooning voice like Nick. But, bless him, he's belting the song out with conviction. I look around the dance floor behind me, no one seems to notice the bum notes or the shaky speed of singing, everyone's just joining in and rocking along.

I turn back to Mark and smile at him to watch him, in this moment that I know will never in a million years be repeated. It must be killing him to be up there in front of all these people he doesn't know singing his heart out and asking for us to believe in our marriage. It warms the cockles of my heart. I have to close my eyes at a couple of the high notes, so I make up for it by whooping loudly at his impressive air guitar during the bass solo.

When the song finishes, Mark walks off stage. He grabs my waist and pulls me towards him before kissing me more passionately then I can remember for a long while. I don't know whether it was seeing him on stage, but I kiss him back like my life depended on it. I know in that moment that Mark and I will work things out.

'That was meant to be "Faithfully" by Journey,' Mark whispers in my ear, 'It's all about trust, but I guess the band didn't know how to play it.'

'That was much better,' I say. 'And don't worry, Mark, I won't stop believing in our marriage.'

I know there's a lot for us to sort through, but we're going to do it. And here, in Mark's arms, I feel a teeny bit happier that my life might not be such a big mess after all.

chapter twenty-seven

princess-on-a-shoestring real wedding:
Country Chic

Henri and Nick may have set out to have a classic princess wedding, but after a little hitch with the weather, we hastily transformed their wedding into a country chic affair. Henri rocked her TK Maxx dress which would have looked fab no matter what the theme. Ivory heels were replaced by beautiful brown cowboy boots from R Soles and the tiara gave way to a cowboy hat. Not only did Henri look great, but it was practical with the muddy marquee. The guests had a blast with the spare cowboy hats and hay bales, creating great photo opportunities. To get the look, you'll need: sandbags, hay bales, a few country props and some hand-painted wooden signs.

Tags: country chic, cowboy hats, Henri and Nick.

I wake up still in my blue dress, lying on top of my duvet. I've got my head buried in the crook of Mark's neck.

We didn't talk last night when we got back. If I'm honest I cried like a baby. I cried because I'd messed up my job, because I hadn't told Mark about Giles and because I was exhausted. But, most of all, I cried because I wasn't sure that Mark and I would ever have trust in our marriage.

'You awake?' asks Mark as he sits up.

'Yeah, I've been awake for ages.'

'So, where do we start?' asks Mark.

'I don't know.'

Mark rubs his hair briskly. If this was any other Sunday morning, with him looking all sleepy and sexy, we would have been trying for stage six of our life plan. But not today.

'I'll talk to Beth about a making a repayment plan for the credit card,' I say, knowing he'd be as concerned about the debt as I am. That's effectively wiped out the savings we've managed to accumulate since the wedding.

'You don't have to worry about that. When she told me all about it, she said she'd spoken to her dad and that he was going to pay it.'

'Her dad?'

'Yeah, apparently so. I don't know the details, but I'm sure you can phone her later on to see.'

I nod my head and hope that with Beth telling her dad what's going on, that she's starting to face up to her problems.

'That's one less thing to worry about then,' I say, sighing.

Only our marriage and my job to save now then.

'Why did you open my credit card bill?' I ask. 'Did you suspect I was up to something?'

'No, it was a complete accident. Both our statements arrived and I opened yours thinking it was mine. And then when I saw the Bill Hall payments, I just assumed—'

'But you were right to assume, Mark. I mean, it's logical assumption: I am a gambling addict, and I guess I always will be. I may not have gambled in a year, but I'm still a gambler.'

The words hang awkwardly in the air.

'What I don't know is whether you're ever going to be able to trust me again. I mean, maybe I broke our trust too much last year.'

'Penny, don't talk like that.'

'But it's true, Mark. I don't want you to always assume the worst of me when things go wrong.'

'I'm sorry, Pen, I really am. And I do trust you. I do.'

I feel Mark's arms pulling me into him.

'We've only been married a year, and we're already having awful arguments.'

'One argument, Pen, it's hardly the same thing.'

'But still, maybe we shouldn't have got married, maybe it was the wrong thing to do.'

'Well, therein lies the problem, Penny Robinson, I told you once that I don't believe in divorce, so I guess we're stuck with each other.'

I half laugh and half cry.

'Well, as long as you're stuck with me and you're not letting me go, then I guess I should tell you the one secret that I currently have from you.'

'So you were hiding a secret?'

'Well, yes and no. I found out at the wedding reception that Henri's dad was my boss, Giles.'

'Giles? Giles your new big boss?'

'Yep, Giles my new big boss who doesn't approve of moonlighting. He knows now about the wedding planning, about my magazine article . . . everything.'

Mark breathes out a whistling noise.

'When things go wrong in your life they really go wrong.'

'Aren't you mad? Aren't you going to tell me you told me so? You never wanted me to do the wedding planning.'

'I'm not going to lie, I wasn't thrilled about it, but it was pretty unlucky that Giles was Henri's father.'

'I know, what are the odds, right? What am I going to do?'

'I'm sure we'll think of something.'

'So you don't want to change your mind from what you said before, that you don't believe in divorce?'

'Nope, I still don't believe in it, Mrs Robinson. We'll figure this out together.'

I lay back into Mark's arms and whilst I am still not sure what is going to happen tomorrow, I know one thing for certain; that it feels a whole lot better facing it with Mark on my side.

Every part of my body is shaking by the time I get into work on Monday. I know what I have to do, I just don't know if I can actually go through with it.

Mark and I spent the whole day working out my options and talking through different scenarios.

Giles walks past me to go into his office, he doesn't even acknowledge that Shelly and I are sat at our desks, much to Shelly's disappointment. I see her look down like a hurt puppy as if she's wondering what she's done wrong.

'Penny,' shouts Giles, from his office.

I look at Shelly and give her a smile. In just a few minutes she's going to learn that she's got the promotion.

'Come in and shut the door,' says Giles as I barely get over the threshold.

'Giles—'

'Let me talk first, Penny, thank you,' he says coldly. 'I am extremely disappointed with you. I'd already decided that I was going to give you the promotion as I believe that you had the makings of a good manager.'

I know that sentence was past tense, but I can't help but be a little proud by his commendation.

'But then I find out that you've been lying and running your wedding planning business. After all that stuff with Indy; you know the risks involved in running a company on your own time without declaring it.'

'I know, I—'

'Don't interrupt. I spoke to Henri yesterday and she told me about how she'd begged you to plan her wedding and how it's going to be your last. Which leads me to believe your company is effectively wound up as of yesterday, am I right?'

I'm about to answer, but it seems that that was a rhetorical question anyway.

'Gunther couldn't sing your praises highly enough last week; he seemed quite taken with you. In fact, he suggested we put you on the company's fast-track management programme.'

I feel sick and I wonder if I'll ever tell Mark that. But then I know I will, after all, we're not having secrets, no matter how big or small.

'Taking that into consideration, I've decided that although

we can't promote you to supervisor, that I will take no further action and you can remain in your post.'

I open and shut my mouth.

'Thank you, Giles,' I say.

'Very well. Shut the door on your way out,' he says as he puts his glasses back on.

'I'm sorry, Giles, but I've got something to say. Thank you very much for being so understanding and for taking all that into consideration. And thank you for the kind things you've said about me making a good manager. It makes it slightly easier to do what I'm about to. You see, I'm resigning, I've got a letter here with one month's notice.'

I place the letter on the desk and push it towards Giles.

'Penny, there's really no need; I've said you can keep your job.'

'But that's just it, Giles. I've learnt a lot about myself over the last few months. I think, to be honest, I've been coasting here, and I've been coasting for a while. The chance of a promotion was a great thing to get me motivated and to invigorate me again. But do you know what? I don't want the promotion. What I've learnt is that I love wedding planning, and I'm good at it. I love the problem-solving, and I love the people. I know that a lot of the skills I've learnt in HR are relevant and it just feels like a good fit.'

Giles has taken off his glasses again, and I think there's a small smirk that's broken out across his lips.

'Henri and I wondered if you'd do that.'

'You did?'

'Yes. The wedding you organised yesterday was great, and Henri told me what kind of a budget you'd done it on. Anyone would have been able to see that you can't do that without having a passion for what you're doing.'

'So you don't think I'm crazy for giving up my job?'

'No, not crazy. I think you're brave. There are some people, like me, that will always be cogs in a corporate wheel, but then there are others who have a different type of drive and, Penny, I've seen that in you. I think Gunther saw that too.'

I breathe the biggest sigh of relief, I've been dreading handing in my notice ever since I made the decision. I know starting my own business is a risky strategy, but Mark's promotion will help us financially, and I can always get a part-time job – one without such a strict policy on moonlighting – whilst I get Princess-on-a-Shoestring properly off the ground.

'Thank you, Giles, for being so understanding.'

'Good luck, Penny. And if I ever find the next Mrs Bishop, I'll be giving you a call.'

I shudder at the thought of who would marry Giles.

'I'll be here until the nineteenth of August,' I say, standing up before he can dismiss me, for a change.

'Very well.'

I walk out of Giles's office while I still can. My legs have turned to jelly. I need a minute before I sit back at my desk, so I head outside to phone Mark and let him know that I did it. But my phone rings before I get a chance.

'Hello,' I say.

'Penny? It's Jane here, from *Bridal Dreams*. How are you?'

'Fine thanks,' I say with a sense of trepidation. I was counting on *Bridal Dreams* being instrumental in marketing Princess-on-a-Shoestring and now I bet she's phoning up to fire me after a month. This is just typical. The curse of Penny Robinson strikes again.

'Great stuff. Look, I just got a phone call from a literary agent I know. She wanted your contact details and I just wanted to check it was all right to pass them on?'

I'm too shocked to speak.

'Penny?'

'Yes, I'm still here. And yes, that's fine. Do you know what she wants to talk to me about?'

'She loves your blog and she thinks there's a market for a non-fiction title on budget weddings and that you should write it.'

'She what? Oh my God.'

'I know, that's why I thought I'd phone. I'll pass on your details. Speak soon.'

As Jane hangs up, I stare at the phone and wonder if I've dreamt this morning. Did that really just happen?

There's only one person that I want to tell.

'Mark, you're never going to guess what's just happened to me. Are you sitting down?'

As I tell Mark, I wonder what stage of life this Princess-on-a-Shoestring segment is going to be as it wasn't in our grand life plan. But maybe the last few months have taught me that you can't plan everything, and maybe that's why life's so exciting.

acknowledgements

Firstly, I should probably say thank you to those people whose wedding stories inspired elements in this book: AnnMarie, Christie and Simon, and my sister Jane, you know which bits!

Hannah Ferguson, and those at the Marsh Agency deserve a big thank you. It's been a great year – here's to many more.

To the team at Quercus – it's been lovely working with you on the book from start to finish. I'd like to thank my former editor Jo Dickinson, and Kathryn Taussig, for untangling the knots in the manuscript. Special thanks to Lauren Woosey, Caroline Butler, and Iain Millar for all your hard work on this and *Don't Tell the Groom*.

I've been overwhelmed by the support of my lovely friends and family. Thanks for not only buying my books but for also acting like personal PRs. My virtual friends in the shape of

Team Novelicious deserve a mention too for being fabulous cheerleaders.

As ever, I couldn't have written the book without the love of family. My husband Steve for being a great slave-driver and making sure I actually finish my books. My dog Rex for allowing me to take him for walks so I can iron out the crinkles of plots. My baby boy, Evan, we'll gloss over the fact that he made it tricky for me to write the first draft with the morning sickness, and instead focus on the fact that he slept so sweetly (often in my arms) whilst I edited.

Last – but not least – I want to thank the lovely readers, bloggers and tweeters that have enjoyed my books. On a bad writing day there is nothing nicer than a tweet telling you that your book made someone smile.

12 facts about anna bell

what's you comfort food?

It's got to be beans on toast. I lived in the US for a year and after a year without them I've never taken them for granted since

what's your favourite tipple?

If it's cold enough for a jumper, then it has to be Baileys. If it's not Bailey's weather, or it's a lively night out, then there's nothing like a nice chilled bottle of Prosecco to start the night off

dog or cat?

Always dog. I have a big soppy labrador that I adore

what keeps you sane?

Going for long walks with my husband and dog. I spend long periods of time shut away writing and my husband drags me out and forces me to get fresh air. Not only does it mean I actually leave the house, but I usually am so much more productive after

what would people be surprised to discover about you?

As a chick-lit writer, I think people would be surprised to know that I used to be a curator at a military museum. It means I have a vast knowledge on guns and military equipment. It was a fabulous job and meant I got to do all sorts of weird and wonderful things. I'm just hoping one day I have reason to call on this odd knowledge for a book!

town or country?

Having spent my teens living in a hamlet in the country, I always thought the answer would be town. Yet, my priorities have changed since becoming a full-time writer and now having the countryside on my doorstep for dog walks is far more important than being surrounded by hustle and bustle

what's your favourite holiday read?

I think holiday reading is all about indulging your guilty pleasures. I usually take two types of books to read on holiday: a cracking chick-lit read that you just know is going to be good, like a Sophie Kinsella, and a thriller by an author like Dan Brown or Sam Bourne

what scares you?

I have an irrational fear of fireworks. On Bonfire Night, you'll find me tucked up inside the house, away from windows, like one of the pets

sweet or savoury?

It really depends on my mood. I guess it would be sweet, as I'd never turn down a cake, although a good cheeseboard would come a close second

read the book or watch the film first?

If I'm going to be doing both, then it has to be the book first. I hate reading a book after seeing the film as I can only then see the actors. It takes away from my imagination, and there's always so much more plot to the book

night in our night out?

My younger self would have been horrified that I'm answering this as night in. Whether it's having friends over for dinner or slumming about in my PJs on the sofa, I'd much rather be at home now

what are you currently reading?

Freya North. Freya's debut novel *Polly* was my first introduction to chick-lit and the reason I started reading the genre. She's one of my go-to authors and I've read her entire back catalogue

hello again, penny here!

For more information about upcoming books, events and other fun stuff, you can go online:

www.annabellwrites.com

www.quercusbooks.co.uk

@AnnaBell_writes

@quercusbooks

lots of love,

penny x